Post-

Post-

short stories by

SHAWN BELL

JACKALOPE HILL

An imprint of Antelope Hill Publishing

Antelope Hill Publishing
www.antelopehillpublishing.com

Paperback ISBN-13: 978-1-956887-10-5
EPUB ISBN-13: 978-1-956887-11-2

~ Contents ~

~ Advent ~

The second he'd been awakened by the cessation of the somnolent jostling, he'd known that his miscalculation had been a grave one. Martial footsteps trod on gravel up and down the road of iron that had borne him there. There would be serious consequences were they to capture him. The men's voices spoke in an impenetrable dialect which he identified as being of a southeasterly nature. This too was cause for concern, for the southeasterly corner of his land (or God forbid, the westernmost region of the neighboring one) was a poor region, inhospitable to his particular trade. Yes, the miscalculation had been a grave one indeed.

Such considerations are luxuries, however, when one finds oneself on the cusp of a beating at the hands of mercenary goons, and the Sojourner snapped immediately into a state of full awareness. Though things had never before gone as sideways as this, he was by no means unaccustomed to finding himself in strange freight yards with hostile authorities closing in. The thing was to act, a truth applicable in domains far beyond train-hopping. There are no perfect opportunities, and even the worst-timed dash toward freedom provides a greater likelihood of success than freezing in place and waiting to be discovered. The Sojourner was never paralyzed. He assessed the gravity of his situation, took a breath to distance himself from the dismal results of that assessment, and proceeded to action.

Dogs barked, men yelled at him to stop. There was a pursuit—indeed, a much more dedicated one than the usual lax standard of a night-shift railyard crew—but a combination of desperation and luck had seen the Sojourner through. Thus it was that he disappeared into that sleepy, provincial town where he was to meet his destiny.

He found an all-night joint catering chiefly to truckers and vagrants. Only once he'd warmed his hands on a steaming mug of coffee with a shot of something foul in it did he begin to take a long view. The name of the city was a familiar one, located on the correct side of the border, thank God. A backwater though, poor indeed, with very limited panhandling prospects, which boded ill for his chances of obtaining a costly berth on the long train headed back to the capital, which is where he'd hoped to end up in the first place, having been all but sure that the freighter would make a stop at the by now familiar junction on the capital's southern fringe.

"Maybe you just slept through the stop," piped up a hopeful voice within his mind, but he squelched that thought with an irritated shake of his head. No time for such foolish hopes as that. He knew perfectly well after all these years that the instant the train came to a stop, he'd snap immediately into a state of horrid and ineluctable wakefulness.

By the time the next seventy-two hours had passed, he would be feeling the precious lucidity he'd only just regained beginning to slip away from him. Once he'd entered the madness, events would begin to unfold in ways he had very little control over. That was when bad things happened. Very little time remained for him to avert disaster. Still, the Sojourner remained at the counter, lingering over a cup of greasy soup and indulging in a bit of reverie, thinking back on the prosperity of years past, and his decline to abjection.

Once upon a time, he'd been quite comfortably able to indulge in what was then a mere habit, riding in first-class sleepers between the prosperous cities of the Eveningland. Even as circumstances changed, and such luxurious travel was no longer financially or legally feasible for him, there had been years of relative comfort back in his impoverished native land, as there had remained enough of a leisure class of Eveninglanders with sufficient resources to travel—tourists were the bread and butter of his particular line of work. Over the years of the slow decline, however, his once-glamorous lifestyle, financed by elaborate cons and schemes, had come more and more to resemble panhandling, as the decline of external economic circumstances had been accompanied by a steady upgrading of his habit into a compulsion, and eventually to an absolute necessity. Still, as long as there had been tourists, he had been able to sustain himself, and more or less avoid the madness which lurked around the seventy-second sleepless hour, a terrifying inevitability that he lived his life in desperate flight from.

He could pick out tourists with great accuracy without even understanding how he did it. Even when they weren't doing obvious things like snapping pictures, looking at maps, or smiling on Monday afternoons, he could always distinguish them. Maybe it was that tourists and children were the only people on the street who really noticed their surroundings. Maybe it was the lack of urgency in their movement. What-ever the subtle cue, he could spot them masterfully.

After spotting them, there was still some work to filter out the weaker prospects. Morninglanders were to be discarded, even though they tended to be flush with hard currency. Shy and retiring, they would become flustered upon being approached. What he needed was engagement, and with the Morninglanders, this was all too often a non-starter. Luckily, their distinctive looks made it quite simple to filter them out. Rather more subtle was the art of distinguishing local tourists from the surrounding lands, all quite poor, from their racial kin in the heart of the Eveninglands, a distinction that could not be made with a simple scan of facial features. Here it was the dress that distinguished his neighbors from the foreigners, as well as a certain wariness about the eyes; even those of his countrymen who were wealthy enough for the luxury of travel would have known deprivation and insecurity, for which reason they were much more averse to handing over their pockets' contents than were the decadents of the West. Once he'd picked out his target (or targets: couples were particularly easy pickings, as the men were desperate to avoid to be seen as cheap or heartless by the women), the approach would commence.

It was mere mentalism from there—a simple art to explain, but a daunting one to practice masterfully. He'd throw out a few countries, waiting for a little flicker in his target's face to tell him that he'd guessed correctly. And when the target would inevitably ask him, with no little surprise, how on Earth he'd known, he'd always come out with the same line—one Belgian (or whatever country) always recognizes another, my brother! From there he'd launch into a spiel about an uncle who'd built a business there, who'd always spoken about the kindness of the country's people, mixing in various facts he'd learned about the chief landmarks of the capital city, as well as little phrases of the language so as to make it seem more plausible that he had in fact once lived there (at his peak, he had had such facts on mental file for something like thirty countries, though he had lost some of the information as the economic decline had gradually strangled the consumption spending of the less prosperous of the thirty). He'd tell how he'd traveled there once himself to work construction one summer, planning at the time to stay forever until the factory accident which had left his father crippled and in need of constant assistance. The mention of his father's ailment (here there was a little room for improvisation, and the Sojourner rather enjoyed coming up with new, gruesome misfortunes to give him) provided a perfect transition into a tale of woe. All his family dead and buried but for his poor sickly papa and him. The problems in the country that had him sleeping on the street. The job offer he had, alas, in another city, and he without the money to buy a train ticket there. He always got a lusty little kick out of the change in expression that came over his targets' faces when they realized that what they'd taken for a friendly interaction had ended up being a panhandling shtick. They were trapped by their own politeness. Eveninglanders found it extremely difficult to rudely break off an interaction and walk away from a friendly conversant, and the Sojourner was a master of leveraging this politeness for his own ends. The longer he extended the interaction, the more uncomfortable they would become. Desperate to escape, they would become willing to let him name his price to set them free. He could make his pitch in five languages. Such a master was he that, in the salad days of tourism, he had been able to live almost lavishly, always able to afford the night's train ticket, never coming close to the madness of insomnia.

Only after the movement restrictions were instituted, and the long-dwindling tourism had been ceased overnight, did the madness become a constant threat, something he was constantly wavering on the edges of. He resorted to criminality at times, but with a week locked up being tantamount to a sentence of death by sleep deprivation, the risk outweighed the reward. Freight-hopping bore much the same risk, and he resorted to it only when the hallucinations were on the verge of taking over completely. Even on the nights when he came up short on cash, he'd walk down to the Glavni Vokzal nonetheless, to watch the gleaming train chug away from the station and dream of being on it, rocked to sleep beneath the stiff, sterile-smelling railway sheets, insensible to anything around him. And then he'd wile away the unprofitable nighttime hours, sometimes with the rest of the human refuse that lurks at train stations the world over, but mostly on his own, zombie-trudging the tree-topped promenades as the cheerful nighttime revelers swirled around him more and more thinly, peeling off and returning to their respective abodes to partake in the repose which he envied them so keenly.

In much the same manner, though with much less hope, did the Sojourner wander the streets of the sleepy, provincial city in the days after his arrival. Things were worse than he'd thought. The freight yard, and indeed the town itself, swarmed with military personnel, and when he'd inquired to some locals as to what the story behind the occupation was, they'd just looked at him with narrowed eyes, before lowering their heads and scurrying away. By the third day, he was no longer in any shape to ask anyone anything. In any case, the freight yard was completely inaccessible. It had been through the sheerest of dumb luck that he'd managed to avoid apprehension upon his arrival, and with every passing hour more personnel arrived, their encampments, including at the freight yard, growing ever more permanent and well equipped. His attempts at begging had proven universally unsuccessful. His vision began to darken and fragment. Before too long he'd make a mistake and wind up incarcerated, slowly expiring from exhaustion. His thoughts became scattered, and a horrible dread rose up within him. It was in this state that the Sojourner wandered down the sheer steps to the little municipal garden located halfway down the cliffs than overhung the stormy sea that battered the little city from the south.

The tinkling of a familiar melody cut through the rush of the waves upon the rocks, and through the fog of his exhaustion, and the Sojourner recognized a strain of an old song, well-known to all his people. As he approached the gazebo at center of the park, where the municipal authorities had positioned a ramshackle old piano for public use, the song became clearer and clearer, and a heaviness began to overtake first his limbs and then his eyelids. With an unnatural, charmed suddenness, sleep came upon him, and he was scarcely able to make it to one of the park's worn wooden benches before his consciousness left his body.

For an unknown period, he slept. It couldn't have been long, for the girl, though she devotedly visited the piano in the garden every afternoon after school, never stayed longer than an hour or so. Still, even that morsel of respite had been enough to clear away some of the gathering clouds of madness and restore him to precious lucidity. He watched in wonder as she rose from the bench—he'd snapped with the usual suddenness back to consciousness as soon as she'd lifted her fingers from the keys—and glided mysteriously away, a slim, mousy girl in an old coat, no more than fifteen or sixteen years old. It was the first moment of sleep he'd been able to snatch outside of a traveling train since his unusual malady had reached its acute state almost a decade before.

Not having all that much to do beyond fruitlessly attempting to lay hands to money, and waiting for the next brief period where the girl's afternoon ministrations would allow him a precious increment of slumber, the Sojourner had taken to following her around, learning her ways and tendencies, seeking to pin down something special about her that might explain the fact that she had managed to succeed where no drug, no therapist, no recording of soothing oceans sounds had been able to. What he'd discovered about her, however, was depressingly average.

Her home was not all that dysfunctional, relatively speaking, though her family had been subject to the same forces of degeneration which were in evidence the world over. It was a family of women, composed of the wisp of a girl; her cashier mother, a tart in her mid-thirties for whom the drama of the courtship ritual had become an end in itself; and her grandmother, a desiccated old woman of traditional morals whose congress with the outside world consisted of chain-smoking cigarettes in the plastic chair she'd set up by the muddy sidewalk in front of the house, and daily presence at the Divine Liturgy. The grandmother owned the house they lived in, and between the lack of rent payments and the little vegetable garden the dogged old woman kept, they were able to get by on the meager wage the mother earned scanning groceries at the little shop on the corner. Though raised voices were periodically audible from the street outside the house, the Sojourner noted that the girl's voice was never one of them. On those occasions where only one of the two voices was heard, the Sojourner assumed that the girl was playing the role of mute audience, her face as impassive as ever, and her inertia provoking ever higher dudgeon.

It was clear that the mother's and grandmother's respective irritations with the girl stemmed from their shared inability to dominate her, or indeed to influence her very much at all. Both older women were in complete agreement that the sullen teenager was in dire need of an attitude adjustment. As to the optimal nature of said adjustment, however, it was clear that the two couldn't have been at any greater odds. The grandmother wished for the girl to follow in her footsteps, living a simulacrum of the sort of traditional lifestyle based in faith, family, and rigidly-defined social practices of a bygone era—a simulacrum, that is, because this sort of lifestyle was no longer achievable beyond a superficial semblance, as anyone with more meaningful congress with the outside world than the deluded old woman would have immediately seen. The mother, meanwhile, had never moved beyond the coquetry and cattiness which had granted her such thoroughgoing social power through her sexual value as an adolescent— though she had squandered that power completely by producing offspring with a sneering punk who had of course abandoned her, rather than leveraging it into the sort of reasonable match which would have provided her with security, and indeed even opulence, so arresting had her beauty once been. Having once been a queen bee of her adolescent social hierarchy (and lacking the insight to fully appreciate the causal relationship between her sexually prolific, emotionally stunted youth and her current situation), it was only natural for the mother to wish the same for her daughter, and to become increasingly frustrated by the girl's morosity and refusal to engage in the sorts of activities the mother considered to be worthwhile.

The girl, meanwhile, seemed to want more than anything else simply to be left alone.

Indeed, the only thing that stuck out to the Sojourner as being in any way unusual about the girl was the inordinate amount of time she spent by herself. She was always among the first pupils to exit the secondary school where he waited every afternoon, following at a distance as she made her way down to the gazebo in the little garden, his heart always seized with terror that this would be the afternoon she was otherwise engaged, and he would be denied the salving relief of a few moments' sleep. She walked down to the garden alone, played him to sleep, and walked straight home where, although she was not strictly speaking alone, she may as well have been for all she interacted with her family members. When he'd peeked in her window, he'd sometimes seen her occupied with homework, but more often than not, she'd simply been lying in bed, atop the covers, awake but inert, staring opaquely up at the ceiling of her little closet of a room.

The music she played was bog standard. When he'd recorded one afternoon's performance to see whether the music's miraculous effect could be replicated away from a live setting (it couldn't), he'd listened through to the whole recording to see whether any musical genius shone through and, to be perfectly blunt, it hadn't. The girl played a medley of simplified classical tunes of the sort one would learn from an inter-mediate-level instructional piano book, along with some sentimental, contemporary pop songs and the occasional older folk tune. She did so with an unassuming amateurishness, with halting tempo and frequent false starts and missteps. And yet, it seemed as if he was not the only one who was entranced.

Over the weeks, the Sojourner noticed a definite uptick in the attendance at the girl's afternoon concerts. There were familiar faces among the devotees, though all made assiduously sure, out of some sort of strange shared intuition, to conceal the fact that they had come to the garden for any reason other than happenstance. Soon he began to spot them lurking in the shadows as he stalked the girl—they too were be-coming obsessed, surveilling her every step. It seemed, however, as though the girl remained as yet unaware of her power, for she continued her routine as ever, affording to the Sojourner just enough sleep to keep his wits about him as he planned his next move.

Perhaps he could find some little job, stay on in the city indefinitely. After all, it had been the need to purchase a berth in a sleeper car every night which had made an itinerant of him. And while the depressed local economy certainly had little to offer him, his experience in certain illicit lines of business would no doubt serve him well here; vice sells particularly well in gloomy places with unpromising futures. He even allowed himself to imagine hiring the girl to play for three, four hours per day, maybe on a piano that he'd purchase for his own house and place next to a king-sized bed with downy covers. He'd positively revel in the fantasy, though he never took any sort of action. For reasons unknown to him (and the rest of the secret acolytes of the unspectacular girl with the dark hair and dark eyes), the whole situation felt like a fragile, unstable equilibrium that could not, under any circumstances, be disturbed.

As it turned out, they had been correct in this hunch. As is the inevitably the case whenever a fragile equilibrium is allowed to persist for a period of time, a disturbance cropped up and blew it all to pieces. That is, one afternoon, one of the devotees, a young man whose infatuation had overwhelmed his terror of approaching the object of his adoration, had accosted the girl and gushed to her about the effect her playing had had on him. As he'd babbled on, she had begun to scan her surroundings with palpable apprehension. The Sojourner could see that, in a sudden, she'd realized that they were all there to see her, and he knew that never again would she return to play the piano in the park.

*

The girl had not, in fact, realized that she had admirers. Or to put it more precisely, though she had for a moment realized it, she had long since trained herself not to allow such realizations to solidify into persistent awareness. This was because such awareness gave rise to questions, and questions had answers that, more often than not, hurt.

One such question, for instance, might be, "why on Earth did I stop playing piano, when doing so had once brought me such joy?" So important had the piano become to her that, for some months previously, the girl had planned her days around the visit to the little garden. The thought of it had borne her through the constant indignities and impositions of interacting with the world, and when she'd played she'd felt relief. And now she no longer played. Answering this question would necessarily involve painful confrontations with aspects of herself she wished to avoid, the girl deftly avoided it entirely by almost completely forgetting that she'd ever played the piano at all, though if someone had asked her point blank about it, she'd have answered in her faraway way, without making eye contact, that yes, she'd played piano a bit as a kid, truly believing herself that this had all taken place in the distant past.

So it was with the Diggers as well. For a time, the girl had been an accepted junior member of the informal club of eccentric local men and boys whose favorite pastime it was to explore, map, and maintain the elaborate network of catacombs which spider-webbed beneath the city. During that period, she had found joy among the Diggers. And now, without once asking herself why, or even admitting to herself that the tunnels had once played an important part in her life, she had ceased to have any contact with them, and become cold and inscrutable to Gnome, the classmate who had first gotten her involved in the tunnel community.

This approach had worked wonders for the girl in terms of the avoidance of emotional discomfort. She thought she had perfected her defenses. Thus, it was particularly disconcerting when, after that run-in with the wild-eyed, foul-smelling vagrant who'd tried to snatch her off the street, all her work had come undone, and a lifetime's worth of questions had begun to arise unbidden.

It had been about a week after the conversation with that overawed young man had convinced her to walk away from the piano forever when the tramp had clasped her wrist in his leathery paw and begged her for deliverance, wrenching her arm in the direction of the municipal garden and forcing her to resist in the only way she knew how: passively. Through force of will, she anchored her slight frame to the ground and waited, unpanicked, for the other bystanders in the town square to free her. But though it had seemed to her at the time that even this physical attack had proven incapable of penetrating her impregnable defenses—none of her vital signs, which she kept constant mental tabs on, had appreciably increased beyond the level one would expect as a result of the physical exertion of her resistance—the ensuing days had proven otherwise. The bystanders had pulled her assailant away and carried him off to the authorities who had, in their turn, more than likely confined him to whatever space it was that they used for the warehousing of dangerous lunatics—but as they'd pulled him away, the glint of his yellow eyes had produced a sensation in her heart from which had ensued an outpouring.

Thus it was that the girl was confronted, among other things, by a number of nagging and unresolved questions regarding the meaning of her aforementioned time with the Diggers, and, seeing as these questions could not be made to dissipate by her usual methods, she had begrudgingly begun, for the first time, to sift through her memories of that time.

Her affiliation with the club had been the result of a group project in school. There is a certain type of kid who waits until all her class's students have paired off voluntarily, leaving herself to be assigned one of the undesirables still remaining. To the girl, this approach had numerous advantages. Through her passivity, she avoided the perilous vulnerability of seeking someone out, an attempt which entailed a risk of rejection, as well as, even more perilously, a risk of acceptance. Furthermore, by consigning herself to a partnership with one of the social rejects who, let's face it, are often such for legitimate reasons, the girl made it all the less likely that she'd end up endangering herself by forming a personal connection. Finally, seeing as the social rejects also tended to be academically marginal, both parties were generally perfectly content with a partnership which required no actual collaboration, as the girl would simply do the work herself. At first, the work she'd turned in had been exemplary, but upon finding that academic exceptionalism made her into an attractive partner, she'd scaled back her efforts so as to receive adequate but undistinguished marks.

Gnome, cursed by fate in several regards, had been a perennial reject from the very beginning, and as such, had been paired off with the girl on more than one occasion over the years. His receding jawline, stutter, and diminutive stature had been exacerbated by an ever-worsening skin condition as he entered adolescence, which was not helped by his lackadaisical approach to hygiene, as well as the fact that he could not keep from picking at the cysts until they bled. Socially, he had been cursed by a desperate craving for attention which expressed itself by a tendency to pester the less marginal kids, flooding them with attempts to impress, and degrading himself in the pursuit of some measure of acceptance, even if it were only as the target of everyone's derision.

His academic abilities were negligible, though this at least seemed not to cause him much consternation; the previous times they'd been paired off together, Gnome had been perfectly content to bite his nails and look out the window as the girl did all the work. Thus, when the pairing had been repeated, she'd been relieved. The assignment being to produce an original ethnography of a local community of one's choice, the girl could envision how the process would play out. She'd choose some safe topic, uncreative and deadly dull, and her defenses would remain intact. Thus it was that her stomach had dropped in trepidation when Gnome began, in a most uncharacteristic fashion, to excitedly chatter about a proposed topic which he was clearly firmly committed to: an ethnography of the local tunnel explorers, the Diggers, with whom he had become affiliated in recent months.

Twitching and sweating with the effort to get the words out, he told her all about the group of amateur enthusiasts, some of the most obsessive of whom had developed real expertise in the history of the local limestone industry which had produced the tunnels, being able to date the various shafts and contextualize them within local history by subtle indicators such as the dimensions or signs of the tools used for the excavation. Others had become more interested in the local flora and fauna, the rats and bats and tunnel-cats that had moved in as the labyrinth had been abandoned. There were rumors of criminal gangs having operated smuggling operations in the tunnels; of rebels and dissidents having used them as bases from which to launch their ambushes; of more or less permanent communities of down-and-outs; of ancient, hermetic religious orders; all of which rumors were hotly debated by the tunnel enthusiasts, as well as the old folks in the surrounding villages, who enjoyed scandal in all its forms. No doubt some of the rumors were true, while others were as fantastical as can be, but from an ethnographic perspective, of course, the facticity of such mythologies was not the issue, but rather the importance of the shared stories in creating a sense of community, of sub-culture, among the denizens of the catacombs.

The girl had to admit that it was a good idea—the sort of idea which, if well-executed, would be sure to attain them just the sort of outstanding marks she'd been trying to avoid. But the prospect of resisting Gnome, who was so invested in the idea that he had literally jumped out of his seat in his effort to explain, seemed like a grueling one. After his passionate pitch came to an abrupt and disorganized end, the girl had responded simply and flatly, "xorosho."

She hadn't fully realized that by giving in, she was agreeing to actually go down into the catacombs with him, and when she found herself standing, shivering, in a field of scrubby grass the following Saturday in gray, bitter November, she wished with all her heart she'd had the will to stand up to him, tell him his idea was stupid, and suggest a topic which could be researched from the warm recesses of the library. But when he'd pulled up on a bicycle rigged up with a sputtering benzene engine, disheveled, unshowered, but not more than ten minutes late, she'd had no more time for fantasies of a day spent alone in comforting tedium; after apologizing profusely for his lateness, Gnome had abruptly turned and walked off into the field.

"Well, come on," he'd called out over his shoulder as he walked on.

After five or so minutes they came upon a great fissure in the ground, and as Gnome scrambled down he explained that this entrance had been used as a garbage dump by some heedless locals and had been impassable until just a few months ago, when he and a couple of his compatriots had cleared it out. He'd passed her a flashlight, and without further ado set off.

Down below, Gnome's speech was as rapid-fire as ever, but somehow he seemed much more collected than he ever was on the surface. In his element, he spoke with an expert's confidence about the miners' graffiti, written in the elegant cursive of bygone days, but just as coarse in its content as the scrawlings in your average bathroom stall. Without pause, he gave a brief overview of the history of mining techniques and regulations, pointing out some scoring of the rock, describing which tools the scoring indicated had been used, and what that revealed about the period when their particular tunnel had been carved out. He shared the names of some of the more important sections of the catacombs as they walked through them, and decrypted the system of markings that the Diggers scratched into the walls to aid navigation. All of this was a simplified rehash of the things his more well-versed mentors had explained to him, but his confidence in telling it all was infectious. Though the girl had remained as outwardly silent and inscrutable as ever, she had been fascinated by the hidden world he had allowed her to access.

They squeezed through narrow passages on hands and knees, scattered swarms of rats with the beams of their flashlights, scaled heaps of debris, and splashed through the vile-smelling water which trickled through parts of the system. They went down and down, all of the girl's navigational volition entrusted to her new friend, passing through various interconnected sub-systems, all with their own names and stories. Periodically, Gnome would announce which local landmark they were standing beneath—there were hundreds of kilometers of ad hoc labyrinth under their city, though some of it had been rendered inaccessible by collapses or flooding. There was no telling how quickly time was passing, but it seemed to the girl that they had been down there for hours when they spotted the movements of another flashlight around the corner.

"Glück auf!" Gnome shouted, butchering the foreign words' pronunciation, though the girl was none the wiser, and, when the distinctive Digger's greeting was called back in return, Gnome had recognized the voice that called it. They'd come around the corner to find a spectral man with deep set eyes and a doleful expression, scrubbing away at the wall to remove a particularly filthy bit of graffiti.

"Oh, hi sir! Didn't expect to run into you here! Let me help you with that!" burbled Gnome, pushing the older man aside and taking over his lowly task. The man smiled wanly, a bit of irritation showing through, though he indulgently handed over his steel brush and stood aside. As he scrubbed, Gnome had stuttered through mutual introductions, referring to the older man as "The Mapmaker," evidently an honorific of no little significance among the Diggers. He'd proceeded to explain to the Mapmaker his idea for the school project they had been assigned, his tone implying that permission was being requested. The older man had been silent for quite a long interval after Gnome had finished speaking, but finally he replied:

"Yes, well, I suppose that's all right, provided you don't reveal any of the secrets. I know you, Gnome. You wish to impress people. But it's not worth giving away your place in the world. This place is special because it's ours."

His voice was reedy and hoarse, as doleful as his expression. He nodded briefly to the girl in acknowledgment of her presence before producing another steel brush from his bag and turning back to the wall. When she had picked up a third brush and begun to pitch in as well, neither of the two had looked up. In silent companionship, they scraped the wall clean, ate sandwiches, and performed a bit of maintenance on a support column the Diggers had built from scraps of stone to preempt the spreading of an ominous crack that had emerged in the roof of one of the most well-traveled branches. By the time they emerged once again into the superterranean world, the sun had begun to fade. In the sickly light, the Mapmaker had briefly explained to them, his eyes directed at his shoes, that some Diggers had planned an excavation for the next weekend, a relatively large-scale effort to safely clear away the caved in rock and soil that had blocked off what he had reason to believe to be one of the deepest and oldest sections of the labyrinthine network. He'd said they'd be welcome to come, shrugged, and shuffled off into the blustery evening.

Looking back on this saga, which she'd done her utmost to erase from her memory, the girl remembered, suddenly, that she'd walked home with a slight smile on her face that day, which had stayed in place until she'd caught a glimpse of her reflection and hastily wiped it away.

*

The next weekend, and indeed for several weeks following, the girl had taken part in weekly expeditions into various parts of the system of catacombs, always initiated with some specific and tangible purpose in mind. The Diggers collaborated with a remarkable lack of ego, all taking up shovels or brushes to pitch in where needed. They reinforced sections of ceiling identified by a retired engineer who, like the Mapmaker, had a particularly venerated status among the Diggers (though this status did not except him from performing the same hard, dirty labor as the rest of them); cleaned out trash from the various openings that the unappreciative savages on the surface decided, periodically, to use as dumping grounds; and sabotaged the sewage pipes that unscrupulous corner-cutting contractors would pipe directly from a house's toilet into the catacombs. There was always something to do and, absurd and pointless though the task of preserving and exploring the maze of tunnels seemed to be, doing so conferred a sense of purpose which the girl appreciated very much.

Best of all was the manner in which they left her alone. Hare-lipped and wall-eyed, rotten-toothed and socially maladjusted, the Diggers were a forlorn bunch. They took the hint from the beginning that the girl preferred to be invisible, and they treated her as such. Even Gnome, though he chattered away with his usual lack of awareness when the two of them were in transit to or from a Dig, had taken the cue. All there was, was the task, and the bare minimum of togetherness necessary to accomplish it.

Things were going as well as they could conceivably be expected to go. Irate as both grandmother and mother had become when they'd learned where she'd been spending her days, the girl would not be deterred. Without articulating the thought or naming the feeling, she felt accepted, and indeed joyful, albeit in her peculiarly restrained and unemotive way.

The weekend before the ethnography was to be presented to the class, the Diggers had made tremendous progress in one of the excavations the Engineer had been planning for some months previously. It had taken weeks of preparatory work, installing numerous supports and clearing away man-sized boulders from the collapsed passage. Everything had had gone precisely as planned until the moment when the girl's foot had broken through what they had previously taken to be solid ground, revealing a sheer drop traversed by a strikingly narrow and ancient bridge. It appeared to be a passage leading down to the storied fourth level, which had been much discussed by the unreliable tongues of the town's elders but never yet accessed, and it had been all the elder statesmen could do to resist the reckless exploratory urges of the younger members.

"A groundbreaking discovery, to be sure," the Mapmaker had agreed with them, peering at the girl who had inadvertently discovered it with discomfiting avidity, "but there are proper ways of going about things. We need to proceed with extreme caution. Without the proper equipment, as well as a good deal of careful testing and most likely restoration work, I cannot allow you in good conscience to cross that bridge." There had been grumbling, but ultimately the Mapmaker's authority had held sway, and the Diggers had agreed that there would be no harm in coming back next week with the proper gear for such an exploration, as well as having the new system fully explored by the most experienced members before allowing the younger, more reckless members to enter.

Gnome, who had been among those itching to participate in the introductory journey, had pouted their whole trip home, and, during the presentation to their class next week, made repeated reference to the discovery. He had spoken with the same poise and confidence, even in front of the judgmental eyes of his peers, as the girl had noticed during her introductory tour of the catacombs. The presentation had been a hit. Indeed, so successful was it that at lunch that same day, they had been approached (the girl and Gnome had taken to sitting together at lunch of late) by two older boys who occupied a much higher social stratum than either of them had ever dreamed of reaching. When they'd mentioned a party they were throwing, Gnome's eyes had gone wide. It was a moment he'd dreamed of. Explaining that they had grown bored with their usual subterranean haunts (pretty much every kid of the town would have spent a little time in the catacombs, though most stuck to an area in the immediate vicinity of the particular entrance through which they gained access), they wondered whether Gnome might guide the party-goers down to a more exciting region.

For the rest of the week, Gnome was aglow with anticipation, jabbering in the girl's ear about the various cool places he would show them, and studiously ignoring her uncharacteristic interjections. She urged him to remember what the Mapmaker had told him, wondered aloud about what it was that made him think those guys, Yuri and Valeri, were so cool in the first place, and flatly, repeatedly assured him that she, personally, had no interest in "partying" with the football hooligans (though she always caught herself mid-lecture, stopping short to remind Gnome, and herself, that he could do whatever he wanted—she didn't much care either way). That Friday afternoon was the last time she'd seen him, departing in a huff when it finally sank in that the girl really, truly had no intention to get drunk in a tunnel with a bunch of idiots. By Saturday morning, the news had made its rounds throughout the town, for Gnome, in his typically desperate and attention-seeking fashion, had continually upped the ante down in the tunnels, attempting more and more reckless feats after a couple of shots of samogon. He'd decided to take them down into them uncharted territory.

It had been the prudence of the other kids, who had nothing to prove, that had held them back on the Earthly side of the narrow bridge of stone— that and the chilling length of time that elapsed before a dropped rock was heard to make contact with whatever it was that was down at the bottom of the shaft. Gnome's stomach twisted as well, but the urge to show off won out. He called them pussies and enjoined them to wait while he checked out the new area for himself for a couple minutes.

There'd been a sound of feet scrabbling for purchase, a long, receding cry, and a decisive thud—all this according to the testimony of the ashen-faced teenagers, who had somehow wandered their way to an egress after their guide's unfortunate demise.

By the time the news reached the Mapmaker, quite the recluse, the police had long since closed off access to the fourth level in pursuance of their mission of recovering the boy's body. He had assumed the local authorities would approach the current situation in much the same way as the town's periodic tunnel deaths had been handled in the past: wall off the site of the accident with cement, perhaps maintain some surveillance over the next few months, and finally forget about it, leaving the Diggers with a layer of cement to chip away at, but no long-term barrier to their plans. Only when the flood of scientifically-credentialed foreigners had begun to arrive—buoying the flagging prospects of the local economy—did The Mapmaker begin to get an inkling that something odd was afoot. When the whispers first began to circulate—the preliminary reports to be leaked, and later confirmed, by world governments—he had finally understood that their situation was inconceivably direr than originally predicted.

This is not, for the record, to say that the Mapmaker was so singularly focused on his mission as to have been unmoved by the poor boy's death. Indeed, at the impromptu ceremony they'd held in a great hall in the depths, he'd spoken at length, through tears at times, about his sense of personal responsibility in the boy's death. Whereas other members had cited the boy's obvious lack of maturity as a grounds for denying him initiation to the club, the Mapmaker had vociferously prevailed upon them, insisting that, whatever his defects of character, the boy was a Digger born, a perfect candidate, who would in time and under proper supervision grow into an eminent role. This, the Mapmaker insisted in his eulogy, had indeed been the case. Gnome had been a Digger born—it had only been through inadequate guidance, chiefly the Mapmaker's own, that the boy had met his untimely end.

At the ceremony, it had been considered unseemly even to mention the potential implications of the boy's death *vis-a-vis* the club's *raison d'etree*. Nonetheless, certain whispers were heard, some more well-informed than others, as only the fully initiated could say for sure what the purpose of their club actually was. There were rumblings, indeed, of mutiny. The Mapmaker bided his time. In fact, the more events unfolded, the surer he became that the prophecy was in the process of being fulfilled, and that the Everyman would speak the resonant words that would shatter the Edifice of Lies. In the chaos that was to follow, it was prophesied that the Advent of the Anima would occur, putting an end to her period of exile and setting her once again in all-consuming spotlight. Only this time, she would be *truly* seen, according to the prophecy, and the goddess, who was to be identified as the one who breached a new realm (the first such breach in a thousand years) could take on fully human form. The age of culmination would be at an end, and only then would life take on its natural and ouroborean form, at which point the excavation could begin in earnest.

It was in the period after her friend's death that the girl had begun to make her daily pilgrimage to the piano in the municipal garden. With remarkable success, she had put the saga of the catacombs out of her mind. Until, that is, the madman had accosted her in the streets that day, bringing all the unanswered, and indeed unasked, questions roiling back to the surface of her usually placid mind.

*

The boy couldn't remember a time when his family room hadn't been reminiscent of a zoo enclosure, segregated with plexiglass with strangers looking in. The plexiglass demonstrated that the family room was a private area, for the use of the family, and not for the use of the flow of foreign backpackers (and penny-pinching domestic travelers) whom he grew up sharing his space with. The private sphere was a tiny, cordoned-off section of the apartment with a couch, a computer, and a television. The rest, apart from the bedroom he shared with his mother (his father slept on the couch behind the plexiglass), operated as an unregulated, cash-only hostel for adventurous, young-adult backpackers—or at least that had been the initial clientele. In point of fact, the boy could scarcely remember this retrospectively prosperous period of the hostel's operation, as economic and political circumstances had made leisure travel all but impossible when he was still fairly young.

As the story went, his parents, poor people, joined together only by their mutual irresponsibility in creating him, had decided to set up a number of bunks in what once would have been the apartment's master bedroom. They had somehow managed to hold onto the property, which was in itself a near miracle given their financial tendencies. It had belonged to his mother's grandmother, back in a very different time when a certain class of people had lived most ostentatiously. Such properties had been expropriated from the boy's mother's father during the period of the empire. After the empire's fall, there had been a lengthy process of adjudication, but finally, incredibly, the apartment had been signed over to the young couple, who had been struggling to keep a roof over their and their infant's heads. Only because it was signed over in the boy's mother's name was the windfall not squandered completely, as his father would have cashed it in for some doomed get-rich-quick scheme.

Faced with the constant barrage of recriminations from her husband who saw, in this case correctly, that the over-sized apartment amounted to a tremendous opportunity cost and a misallocation of resources, the wife had resolved upon a conservative, modest venture, and thus it was that the hostel was founded.

When the boy, as an adolescent, had gotten around to reading Metamorphosis, he had felt a certain kinship with poor Gregor Samsa, whose unfortunate condition had reduced his family to letting rooms to a trio of officious and demanding gentlemen. His parents, forced together only by the unfortunate fact of his having been created, no doubt saw him as something of a similar burden—or at least so the boy imagined. There is something deeply humiliating about watching your father bite his tongue as a horde of drunken, guffawing Englishmen disturb his sleeping family and make a mess of his kitchen after returning from a night out—something guilt-inducing about the knowledge that your very presence, as a non-contributing mouth to feed, had brought this situation about. This Samsan guilt had motivated the boy, from a very young age, to make as meaningful a contribution as he possibly could, picking up the *lingua franca* and interpreting for his parents, pushing a broom around, and greeting guests upon arrival with a cheerful smile and a well-rehearsed little monologue listing their city's principal attractions and pointing them out on a map, for all the world like a diminutive concierge.

This state of things, however, would not last, for as the tenor of the times underwent a noteworthy shift, the nature of the hostel's residents shifted as well.

Convergent global trends beyond the scope of this account conspired to reduce the numbers of (relatively) wealthy, leisure-pursuing foreigners intent on exploring such corners of the world as the boy's undistinguished little city. The combination of ever-increasing economic and political barriers to free movement had rendered travel a luxury attainable only by the sorts of travelers unlikely to wish to spend their nights in bunkbeds among strangers, as had once been the case with the Western students and young adults who had formed the core of the hostel's clientele. Thus it was that the hostel began to cater to a different demographic.

Undisturbed by political barriers that targeted only licit movement was the global class of roving, darkskin migrants seeking ingress to the wealthy Eveninglands—indeed, their movement was tacitly tolerated and even abetted by that very same political class. Being on the periphery of said Eveninglands, the boy and his family's impoverished land formed the perfect staging ground for the interlopers to bide their time before taking the plunge toward their final destination. Thus, the hostel became a sort of boarding house for Saracens and Abyssinians who filled the apartment with strange smells and sounds. This was the boy's early adolescence—a constant battle of norms and standards which the family was hard-pressed to successfully enforce, relenting on issue after issue; allowing the cost of a bunk, for example, to be split between two Afghans who used it on a rotating schedule, one sleeping while the other lurked with narrow, opaque eyes in the apartment's common spaces. The air became fetid, heavy with the scent of unwashed bodies, and the police, by no means eager to get involved, were summoned on a semi-regular basis, whether to deal with the belligerently drunken, or to quell the ethnic disputes which had been brought in from elsewhere.

Eventually the situation deteriorated such that even the migrants were no longer coming for lack of prospects. At this point, the family had had no choice but to cater to the very dregs of their own society, the druggies, drunks, and madmen still capable of scraping together enough kopeks for a night off the streets. Clearly the sort of man who has trouble managing the timing and manner in which his body fluids are excreted is not likely to be a practitioner of functional conflict management strategies, and as the boy entered adolescence, it was as though every evening brought with it a new shit-stain or bloody brawl. The boy's parents cursed the hostel, but the fact was that managing a flophouse was preferable to the alternative, and their relatively stable source of income placed them among a privileged few.

The boy grew strong and coarse—it was the only way of handling the situation. Still, he remained a good student, his motivation buoyed by the prospect of someday getting out, making it into the global technical-managerial class, and leaving behind his deprivation. Daily, he pleaded with the power above which he could not name. Little did he know that his deliverance would come in the form of the untimely death of a schoolmate of his, a younger kid he'd known by sight who, drunk on village samogon, had managed to fall down an abandoned mineshaft.

When the news stories had begun to trickle out over the coming weeks, reporting strange and wonderful discoveries unearthed in the process of the operation to recover the body, the boy hadn't paid much attention. Archaeology had never been a particular interest of his, and the more sensational reports had seemed to him to be worthy of a peremptory dismissal. More than likely, the "groundbreaking discovery" had simply been the subterranean lair of some addled monk who'd scribbled his inanities for the credulous public to find. For mysticism, the boy had nothing but contempt. He wanted to make things that worked, to justify his existence by the products of his labor, to become a cog within the machine which made everything run—a quite limited class of humanity indeed. Thus it was that for the pilgrims who began to trickle in to visit the site of The Discovery the boy felt a healthy contempt as well.

Pilgrims[1] they were indeed, dear reader, for The Discovery, silly as it seemed to the boy to be, had excited hearts and minds the world over, and in particular in the very core of the Eveninglands to which the boy so badly

---

[1] Note that the pilgrims would never have described themselves as such—this was the semi-derisive nickname which the locals had come up with for them. Indeed, the pilgrims were of the sort who claimed to have nothing but contempt for all "dogma."

wished to relocate—indeed, the bulk of the pilgrims were of the very class of technical-managerial Eveninglanders among whom the boy one day wished to number. To his parents, the flow of relatively well-heeled comers of any kind was as a blessing from on high, and they praised The Discovery to no end, with no interest whatsoever in its truth content. Indeed, the increased cost of overcoming the various barriers to travel and securing all relevant permissions for egress and ingress, as well as the monopoly prices charged for the compulsory periods of internment and observation which were to be served at nominally private facilities run, the world over, by government cronies, had resulted in a clientele even more well-heeled than the admittedly rather scruffy backpackers of yesteryear. Or perhaps it was simply the nature of their quest which distinguished them; having made the journey in the hopes of beholding sacred objects, it is perhaps no surprise that the pilgrims comported themselves in a much more dignified and respectful fashion than the backpackers of yore, boozers and sex tourists letting loose in countries where their currencies afforded them power.

For the boy, the experience of hosting the pilgrims had held a different significance entirely. The sight of the pilgrims who'd come to worship— their titties of fat that showed through t-shirts which displayed the subcultural identification of the wearer's choice, their jawlessness, the saccharine contentlessness of their mealy voices combined with the sanctimony with which they pronounced official truths—all of it repelled the boy, who was by now closer to manhood than anything. Yet as the boy conversed with them one by one, it emerged that to a man they numbered among the class of temple eunuchs to which he had so long hoped to belong—the programmers, data scientists, engineers, consultants, FIRE sector underlings, and junior academics who actually worked the levers of the great machine, in the core of which were ensconced the bloated, monstrous corpses of the true elites. The boy was not able to express what precisely it was that revolted him about the pilgrims. Still less was he aware of the role that their caste played in global affairs. All he knew, from his outsider's vantage point, was that it was they who were catered to in media, they who retained a modicum of the financial security that had once been promised to the many, and they, most importantly, whose labor seemed to him to be something more than drudgery. For the boy behind the plexiglass wall, such issues would remain unresolved until the drunken American spilled the beans all those years later. Still, the weeks of the pilgrims' arrival would form a critical turning point in his development.

*

The American didn't know the whole plan. He didn't even know whether it was strictly accurate to describe what was occurring as a plan, as such. He remained agnostic on the question of whether there was any sort of central authority through whom all the various aspects of the system of events flowed. Still more did he remain agnostic on the second and deeper question of whether said authority figures, assuming their existences, were correct in their belief that it was as a direct result of their string-pulling that phenomena unfolded as they did. To this question, there is both a Humean and a Tolstoyan layer, though this is an authorial insertion rather than a reflection of the American's thinking on the subject.

The American believed in the existence of conspiracy. He was himself, after all, a man in possession of secret knowledge, working as a part of a network of fellow initiates to manipulate events so as to produce a particular and illusory belief among the population. He was, that is, a conspirator. He also believed, however, in the existence of complex emergent phenomena proceeding according to internal logics whose intricacy give the impression of design when in fact, more often than not, the intricacy of such internal logics far exceeded the human mind's capability for scheming and machination.[2] He did not know which of these two paradigms was at play in the current instance. Nor did he much bother himself with the fact of his ignorance. These were questions for philosophy under-graduates. The American had transcended the sophomoric phase of futile wonderment and become a man who grimly acted. He took moderate, masculine pleasure in the fact that more often than not, the events he was attempting to influence went his way. A proud cog, he was reconciled to the fact that there were illusions which his masters chose not to dispel. He was satisfied with the fact that he was more conscious than most of the fact that there were innumerable unknown-unknowns which interacted with his life-path and world-interpretation in ways he could not imagine.

What he did know for a fact, however, was this: the extraterrestrial artifacts unearthed deep in the catacombs beneath the city of O were not genuine. He knew this because his role in the Plan (or Emergent

---

[2] I note, once again, that the highfalutin language of this passage is authorial, and not that of the American, who conceived of himself as a hard-boiled man of action, and thus had no truck with phrases such as "complex emergent phenomena" or "internal logics."

Phenomenon) required him to know it in order to move forward with the next step of the hoax—the Contact event which was to transpire.

All his time in the little city, apart from the hours he spent speaking wry, half-truths out of the corner of his mouth to the innkeeper's wide-eyed boy, were spent in the practice of his craft. The American found people. Given the most impoverished description, the profoundest imaginable paucity of information, he would without fail, like a loyal hunting dog, reappear from the underbrush with the struggling prey between his teeth. In this case, the description had been impoverished indeed. Those who had hired him seemed, in fact, to have no idea who it was they were looking for at all, and what's more their orders deliberately hindered him, prohibiting him ever coming into contact with his quarry directly, and instead relating to them what he could find from second-order sources. The explanation for this fetter was improbable—the American was a man who believed in the concrete reality that had always seemed manifest to him, in which any inexplicable phenomena could, with time, be winnowed down to material causes—but such was not for him to question.

It had taken him months of digging, of sideways questions that left the town's residents and the visiting pilgrims alike scratching their heads, of rifling through a vast array of documents which would likely have seemed to the untrained observer not at all related to the task at hand, and of pursuing false leads and wasting time, but at long last he had come across a curious incident in the town's police reports, which certain contacts of his had allowed him to obtain privileged access to—an attempted kidnapping committed in broad daylight by a vagrant against a schoolgirl. There was nothing about this event in itself which had seemed overtly related to the criteria his employer had forwarded to him, but certain details of the witness reports had struck the American as curious, namely the fact that a number of male passersby had come out of the woodwork to intervene on the girl's behalf, and that in their witness reports it appeared that said passersby knew a great deal more about this girl than strangers ought to have. It was as if there had existed a constant escort of silent men who lurked in the girl's presence, following her every move. These were just little details in the various interviews which less perspicacious observers than he had failed to collate. It was odd and subtle, but the American felt sure that there was something to it.

In his business, one trusted one's gut, and after a quick trip to the regional mental hospital to listen to the interned man's ranting, the American had been reassured that he was on the right track. Further details of the ravings, which had been ignored by the psychiatric authorities as being, well, ravings, had given him an idea of how best to proceed. A man of his type having certain connections, it was a matter of a few phone calls to set up what needed setting up.

*

"Sleep well?"

"Mmph. Suka blyat."

"Suka blyat indeed. You were pretty far gone there. Woulda stayed that way for quite a while if it weren't for yours truly."

"English. American." A pause—an involuntary movement in the American's face had given him all he needed. "Yes. American. I know from accent. Where from?"

"Cut the mentalist shit. You think I don't do my research?"

"… Where we are? Where, who, how long. All questions. Please."

"You were out for months, from what they told me in the loonie bin." A quizzical look. "Psychiatric hospital, I mean. Real primitive setup they've got there in O."

"O. That's right. I remember this. And now where?"

The American looked around and made a little gesture as though the answer ought to be obvious. "A train."

There was something slightly menacing about the way he pronounced the word "train," as though he knew. The Sojourner responded with a piercing glare as the American continued. "Listen, boss, you don't got to be going around asking questions. What you need to know, you'll know. Where you are is where I want you to be. Comprende? Ponyatna? Now, you want something to eat? Drink?"

"I want you tell me what is happening."

"The thing that is happening is Life. It is complex. Grand, even. Our parts within it are both miniscule and beyond our comprehension."

"You always speak like Hollywood character?"

"Always."

"Is not such good Hollywood character. B-movie."

A shrug.

"You want something. What?"

"Information."

"Information. About?"

"About you. Your record. Police report say you tried to rape a girl. Take her right off the street. About this, some information."

The Sojourner took a few moments to recover himself, after the revelation of the inevitable bad thing that had occurred, as he'd known it would, when his sanity had worn through and he was no longer himself. "Not the case."

"So tell me your side of it."

"Why I tell you anything? Who are you?"

"A man who understands your peculiar situation. Who can give you what you want." With a magician's attention to gestural drama, the American produced a plastic card, laying it on the plastic tabletop for the disheveled Sojourner to inspect. An international rail pass, valid for twelve months, valuable not only because of the considerable purchase price, but also because of the considerable degree of bureaucratic difficulty in being authorized for international movement. The two were seated in a first-class sleeper. Outside the window was a post-industrial wasteland. The train itself was an engine attached to a single car—theirs—a custom service which would have required considerable administrative clout to set up. The Sojourner took all this in at a glance. The American's suit was well-pressed for the occasion. He'd put significant effort into appearing every bit the international man of mystery. He'd seen to it as well that the Sojourner had been dressed in a paper-thin hospital gown, which he'd ordered sent from his homeland, such gowns being far more undignified and vulnerable than the institutional dress typically foisted upon the psychologically infirm of the Sojourner's native land.

"And who can take it away as well," the American interrupted his thoughts as he whisked the card away with a flourish, "and send you back to shit the bed and cry for the 'piano-girl' until they pump you full of sedatives. From where I'm sitting, it sounds like an easy enough choice, but you do you."

Shivering from withdrawals after months of narcotics and terrified that the feeling of mental fuzziness was perhaps a sign of permanent damage, the Sojourner had no reason not to spill his guts. But when he'd seen the interest piqued when he'd described the odd and inexplicable saga of the piano-girl, the mental fuzziness had not interfered with his fundamental character—when the American had eagerly begun to question him about the girl, he'd dragged his feet, buying time as he'd calculated exactly how much money he'd be able to demand in exchange for a mere name and address from a man who showed every sign of conducting his business with the loose purse strings of someone with a company card.

His instincts at least had not deserted him, and it was with great satisfaction that the Sojourner had patted the wad of bills in his pocket when he'd disembarked the American's custom train service back at the main station in O. Sick as he felt after the months of narcosis, he was sure that his fortunes were finally turning. Before he could bound away to the ticket counter to obtain passage on the longest journey he could find, the American had grasped him by the shoulder and grimly told him that if the information he'd given him departed in the slightest detail from the facts, he had the means to make him suffer. Then the two of them had parted, the Sojourner with a spring in his step, and the American with the purposeful stride of a man with his goal in sight. He'd find the girl, observe her from a distance, ascertain to the best of his ability the quality of his information, and report back. He had no way of knowing that, despite the perfect accuracy of the address given him by the Sojourner, the girl had been absent from her childhood home for long enough that the initial panic of the disappearance had faded to a sort of dull, aching acceptance among those few who cared about her.

*

In the preceding months she had come to feel more and more as though there was no escape from the bizarre and repetitious loop which had come to characterize her life, whereby whatever endeavor she embarked on resulted in the beaming of the hated spotlight and all eyes being turned upon her. No escape, that is, short of remaining motionless in a locked room and counting the seconds as they passed by. After the Diggers had prostrated themselves before her in recognition of her "Great Discovery"; after what she had thought were solitary and wholesome afternoons aimlessly noodling on the rickety, out-of-tune piano in the park had turned into yet another absurd tableau of worshipful adoration; and after that wild-eyed vagrant had raved at her about how she was his only deliverance and she had noticed in the eyes of the gathered crowd that they had agreed with him; she had thought that her sketchbook might afford her a refuge. But as ever, her work had drawn prying eyes, and within a few short weeks an admirer had gotten his hands on it when she'd left it behind in the school cafeteria for not more than ten minutes. The resulting photos of the sketchbook's contents had been shared far and wide, printed, posted, distributed, and lavished with unearned praise. What's more, it seemed to be getting worse. Just the previous day, an acolyte, an otherwise dignified older businessman, had fallen to his knees before her to praise the grace and dignity of her gait. A barista in a cafe had declared her manners to be queenly, seeming almost to have been brought to tears. Although she knew that to complain about such laudatory treatment could only be seen as ingratitude, in particular from those whose efforts won no such reaction, the fact of it all having been unearned made it rankle with her in a way which she could hardly explain to anyone else.

Yes, unearned, for the girl knew perfectly well that her efforts in all these fields had been amateurish at best, childish even; the result of no prolonged effort, no dedicated period of training. The praise was not for her, but for something else, some power she held latent, which she did not yet rightly understand. It was as though in place of her, all her many acolytes insisted upon seeing something perfect, worthy of worship, which had not the least thing to do with her, though she wore its face. It was maddening.

For all her dedicated effort to disengage from everything around her, to avoid attention and extraordinariness and even eye contact, the girl yearned no less than anyone else to be seen and understood. It was for well-justified fear that her efforts would be attributed to the godlike entity, feted beyond their merit, and thus denuded of the modest value they truly possessed, that she had embarked upon her ambitious program of total disengagement. Better to go unseen than to be wrongly seen.

One morning, when her panic had been particularly overwhelming, the girl had scraped together enough change to purchase a bus ticket to some nameless village in a nearby mountain range. The police (and later the American) had been able to ascertain this much, but no more. There was a period of obligatory mourning—a small town rent by two tragedies in one year!—but before too long, the girl was forgotten, and the American reported back to his masters that, as far as he could tell, the object of his pursuit had vanished without a trace. This outcome had been in full conformity with the desires of those masters—it saved them the risk and cost entailed by the operation they had originally conceived of setting into motion.

*

Times were good for the Sojourner. He never would have predicted that his fattest years would take place in his own once-impoverished homeland, let alone in that backwater town in the southeast whose name, for years after his period of narcotized internment, had caused his throat to tighten with distaste. When he'd cut his deal with that shadowy American (who was trying so hard to seem "shadowy" that he'd ended up verging on self-parody at times), he'd been sure that he'd be leaving that ugly place forever in his past, departing for the green pastures of the Eveninglands, where the money had flowed so freely, at least in the days of his youth. Then had come First Contact and the consequent *Große Ausgleichung*,[3] which had turned the Eveninglands into involuntary donors and the Krajina into the very Core of the new religion that had made Earthlings of them all, a center of gravity to which all the world's resources began to flow. Funny how things work out.

Still dependent as ever on the somnolent, rocking rattle of the country's newly modernized rolling stock, the Sojourner was as peripatetic as ever, but his center of gravity had shifted, along with that of the global community, to that very town which he'd sworn he'd left behind.

His bag of tricks bore many similarities to that of previous years. He still spent some days working his old angle, using basic mentalism to corner well-heeled tourists and press them for cash, but under the new circumstances, this approach had become a mere side dish of the Sojourner's bounteous meal, with the main course being composed of the street-corner harangues he'd deliver on the main drags of the various cities he visited. In sonorous, accented, grammatically-imprecise tones, he would spread the Bad News in the Eveninglandish language of a once-great empire, still known to the widest swath of his potential hearers:

"They create us, and what we do? How we treat this gift of the Galactic Committee? Disrespect! With evil actions we spend the precious life they give us. Yes, our Inventor, in Holy Grotto of City O, he make us, using powerful technic, beyond our foolish imagination, and he leave us here with all tools, all abilities, all character, to grow to moral goodness. And what we do in time that pass before return? Evil. Only Evil. We all hear this from Wise Ones, direct!

"What else they tell us? We are only planet that not use for good all what they give us. All other planets, they take also much time to develop, but when Committee returning, all exist in higher state. Unity. All became ready for come together, join galactic community, ascend higher level. But us, we are disappointment to our Creators. Only from mercy of galactic committee, they give us second chance, time to fix mistakes. Not in plan to have 'Second Contact.' Should have been prepared at 'First Contact,' but we make great failure.

"But even this mercy not enough! Even still, care more some people

---

[3] Great Equalization.

about keep self rich, even if bringing doom to all others, even self. And who it is doing this? Same. Same like always, rich Eveninglanders bringing problems to all Earthlings. We remember crusade. We remember colonial. Slave times. Also Nazi war against Jewish, Slav people. Now same people, Eveningland man, he take from us our only chance to be free, go to higher level.

"We see you coming here. We see you say, you commit to planetary solidarity. Say you true Earthling. But be Earthling, this not only faith. Also *to give* is requirement!

"Most important five year target, Committee say, this equality. This not meaning inside one country, for example. This not meaning even make equal all humans—human being, this only one kind Earthling. Be Earthling means, come tears when eating a fruit. Not necessary to commit suicide. But what is necessary, is sorrow. Sorrow, regret, knowledge that to live requiring take life. To be Earthling mean that Eveningland man accept, with peace of heart, that Abyssinian man, woman come take his life, just like he take life from eating apple. Better from eating apple, because apple not creating evil, only trees. Yes!

"Earthling man, he look like this," he would say, pulling up his shirt to reveal the horribly emaciated torso that the surgeon had given him, making him appear to be on the very edge of starvation. "And here we see man, look like this instead." Here he'd point out, derision in his eyes, the inevitable fat-tittied, reddit-dwelling pilgrim with a comic-book t-shirt. "This man come, think prove devotion with visit, before he take basic action for Earthling solidarity! He think he buy his virtue by take luxury trip! He think he become part of solution burning jet fuel, make even more poison! Only in flesh can your debt be paid, my Earthling brothers and sisters!"

After firing up the ire of the ravening mob with respect to his chosen totem of Eveninglandish decadence, the Sojourner would invariably, in a deft and jarring rhetorical turn, redirect the rage and disgust inward, with himself as the new totem for derision. For there was not one among them so deeply committed to Earthlingism as to stand in judgment of the sobbing, prostrate heap of flab besmirching his themed t-shirt as he writhed around in the mud, and even he, the visibly emaciated preacher[4] who had

---

[4] Note that the word "preacher" would never have been applied in such a setting as this for the same reason that a medieval priest would have gone absolutely bananas had you ventured to term him a "shaman," despite the fact that to an outside observer, the roles of priest and

filled them with such conviction, was imperfect in his commitment to the fulfillment of the conditions of Accession. And if such were the case, then the implied question remained: what were they, the lowly masses, taking a temporary break from their usual moral decadence for a short-term demonstration of faith, to think of themselves? They gibbered and rent their garments. They dove down into the mud beside their prostrate comrade and abased themselves at the feet of the shaman who had coaxed their passion to such a keening pitch. It was in this most lowly state that their eyes would light upon the misshapen figure of the Cripple hobbling past, an ugly boy, unfortunate in all particulars, unwashed, uncared for, and visibly of Gypsy blood besides. Now, he would be made the talisman of their fervor, the lightning rod through which the powerful, unbearable charge of thoroughgoing guilt might be discharged. Unprompted by the Sojourner, they would flock to the Cripple to shower him with currency and worshipful self-abasement—unprompted, this outpouring, but orchestrated nonetheless by the Sojourner's cynical and masterful design.

Yes, the Sojourner had lit upon this crucial detail of his performance upon discovering that, masterful as he had become at preaching the Bad News, the very nature of the message interdicted his attempts to cash in on the vulnerable state he'd put his audience in. Knowing that he had drawn near to a veritable gold mine, he continued to tinker with his message, practicing daily to perfect his ministry, and knowing that sooner or later the master stroke would occur to him. As it happened, it had been reality itself which, by coincidence, had provided him with his answer.

One afternoon, in the middle of his harangue, a nattily dressed Abyssinian had ambled by, on what business who knows. Unbidden, the whimpering, crawling masses had flocked to worship at the feet of the dumbly leering, yellow-eyed creature, which unashamedly took everything which was offered it. A partner, the Sojourner had realized, was the missing ingredient to complete his finest art.

The Cripple, a Gypsy boy whose ailments and deficiencies were too various to catalog, had not been difficult or expensive to obtain. As an ancillary benefit, their partnership provided the Sojourner with the sort of companionship most dear to him—as the two of them rode the rails at night, always sharing a single bunk, the Sojourner whispered in the Cripple's ear all those teachings which his mentor had once whispered unto him. The

---

shaman play strikingly similar roles in their respective communities. "Activist" would be the analogous neologism in the situation at hand.

Cripple would grow up to have the same sort of somniacal infirmity as his master, but so too would he inherit the parasitical trade which would provide him the living necessary to fulfill that unique need. "And you, one day, will have a boy of your own as well," he'd whisper tenderly to the Cripple in their first-class sleeper compartment.

As the new religion waxed in influence, as men were daily reborn into Earthlings, it seemed to the Sojourner as though there were no end in sight to these halcyon days.

So too did it seem to the boy, now a man, who, much like the Sojourner, had ridden the wave of global Revival into personal prosperity. When he looked out over the vast expanse of the gutted factory from the high narrow window from which the bosses had once looked down onto the floor, he would sometimes marvel at the residence pods stacked four high. As ever, he had nothing but contempt for the pilgrims who wandered the labyrinth of miniscule, high-price capsules, paying out what little cash they had to complete their Hajj. But when he looked out the window of his corner office, down at the newly-renovated square where the insufferable performance artist put on his thrice daily production, his old contempt for the cringing masses was mixed with a harsh and hateful feeling toward the manipulators, which feeling was rendered all the more complicated by the fact that it was, in part, directed inward. He too had profited from the quivering masses, leveraging a low-interest loan from a local oligarch into a massive expansion of the humble hostel in which the boy had grown to manhood.

By now, the business was unrecognizable, a corporate behemoth (albeit by modest local standards) housed in the five-story shell of a long-shuttered state-owned tractor manufacturer. His parents vegetated in retirement, gladly mouthing the catchphrases of the new religion though in truth they believed in nothing but their windfall of prosperity and the pleasures this afforded them. The boy, a man, mouthed these catch-phrases as well though, as stated, he found doing so a much more morally fraught endeavor than his parents ever had.

Even as the money flooded in, and his financial security became more and more a matter of certainty, he began to feel a growing dis-contentment. He hired subordinates, greedy but unambitious types who could be relied upon to embezzle from him only sustainable amounts that would leave the business intact. More and more, he spent his time outside the office, wandering the streets, and wondering about the meaning of his dissatisfaction. Wasn't this the deliverance from penury that he had appealed to the heavens for, all those years ago, behind the plexiglass wall in the half-living room of the humble little hostel?

It was with such questions in his heart that the boy, a man, had threaded his way through the heaving mob that thronged a gypsy boy on the promenade one afternoon, his disgust heightened to near-unbearable proportions.[5] It was at this moment that he was surprised by the sound of a distinctly familiar voice calling out a nickname which had once been his. The face of the man who'd called him had aged well beyond what one would have expected given the number of years which had elapsed, and the once-trim body had grown visibly saggy and distended. If it hadn't been for the distinctive, outdated attire of a mid-twentieth century spy flick, he'd never have recognized the American who'd stayed some six or so months in the miserable little apartment hostel after the initial discovery in the catacombs. They'd bonded back then over their mutual desire to master each other's languages, as well as their mockery of the true believers, who'd been of an especially whacky sort back then, in the days before the First Contact had caused the Earthlingist movement to go mainstream and before the public conversion of the sainted Barry O, who had since become something of a Constantinian figure among the faithful.

"Well, well, well…" drawled the American through a haze of cigarette smoke, his enunciation muffled by the cigarette which never left his mouth's corner. He looked like just as much of a spy-movie cliché as he always had, a fact which he consciously mitigated by being very self-aware and ironic about it. "Looks like little Billy's off the farm," he said before pausing for a long moment. The Hotelier's confused expression indicated to the American that he had expressed himself in a suitably vague manner, which pleased him. He went on. "From what I hear, you've really made something of yourself. Proud as hell of ya, kid! Sit down, I'll buy you a drink or something!"

The boy, a man, sat eagerly down and sipped expectantly at the minty

---

[5] Note that despite the detail in which I have described the Hotelier's disgust for the pilgrims and their fervor, none of those feelings found a clear means of expression, not even in his own head, for there existed no structure of interconnected concepts and beliefs, no worldview, no inherited lens through which his pre-beliefs and vaguely defined sentiments could be converted into convictions—at least not without venturing out into the treacherous waters of Denialism, which was the purview of the lowest of the low, and indoctrination into which required a point of access to information ecosystems which had been made nearly as inaccessible as such dissenting spheres would have been in the paper age, and perhaps even more so given the reemergence of mass illiteracy.

whiskey drink the waiter had brought him, knowing that, unless some significant change in the American's personality had occurred in the intervening years, he would soon be regaled by a flood of tall tales from the various peripheral locales where the American plied his mysterious trade. To prime the pump, the boy, a man, had gestured around at the square, the newly restored buildings, the throngs, and in particular at the heaving, raving Leviathan which the two-bit street performer across the street (whom the American, of course, had long since recognized, though he kept this knowledge to himself) had summoned into existence, and which would decompose back into its constituent atoms and be scattered to the winds as soon as its instigator released it from his rhetorical grasp.

"You believe this shit, man?" he asked the American.

"Believe this shit? Kid, I *made* this shit!" The American was more than a little bit sloshed, and the Hotelier had attempted to laugh off the comment, knowing that the American had always enjoyed pulling his leg, in response to which the older man, fat and florid, had cryptically shaken his head, murmuring, "Nah, nah, nah, seriously, kid. If you only knew."

"Yes, of course, I believe was you, all by yourself. But seriously, how are you doing, man? Where you been all these years?"

And the American had told him. The sun had gone progressively more gold, fading to orange and crimson as the two of them downed juleps and the American spoke in riddles about an operation he'd been involved in, down in the smoking hole that was all that remained of Persia. Though the specifics of his professional duties were kept deliberately vague, his time there had produced no shortage of amusing and grotesque anecdotes about one-armed whores and dignified old men stumbling around after their first tastes of American whiskey and the overflowing of gratitude which greeted him at every turn. Fanciful as it was—for the boy, a man, had his own private and critical perspective on the American's worldview, which he thought it purposeless to trot out—the tales were colorful and the company was welcome and diverting. Only after a lengthy monologue did it occur to the American to turn the tables.

"Say, what about your folks then? They must be living the high life, what with you being a hospitality tycoon and all."

"I guess. You know, life sort of beat them down to where all they ever thinking was 'I want rest.' And now they have it, sure. Father sleep all day, mother eating chocolate. I hear before, how after making retirement, many people dying very soon. Lack of purpose for life. Something to do, reason to go on. So this makes me little worry for them."

"I hear ya. That's why I'm never planning on getting out of this here game. Plus it's too damn fun!"

"So this is why you come back? For new round of game? Something professional?"

"Nah, nah. Sometimes you just want to come back and see the results of your work. See you made a difference. Like how a criminal'll come back to the scene of the crime," he smirked.

"This game. Always you calling it game, and always you not want explain to me. I know you are spy, you not have to tell me."

The American sighed patiently; it was a familiar topic of discussion. "You always did think I was being, like, deliberately vague or whatever, but like I've always told you, my work is pretty damn straightforward. Events don't just happen. And when they do, it's in the interest of my employer, or of his employer, to ensure that they unfold in such manner as is maximally beneficial to him. And they do this by sending certain vetted individuals, with particular sets of skills, into these situations were uncontrolled events are occurring. I perform particular tasks, nothing flashy, nothing illegal, and most critically, nothing providing me with very much of a vantage point from which I could clearly tell what the whole thing is 'about.' One presumes that all the individual threads weave together into some great tapestry, but there's no telling for sure.

"A spy, that's somebody who sneaks around in the shadows, rappels through skylights down into foreign embassies to plant bugs, photograph documents. I don't do none of that Hollywood shit. I'm just a guy with a boss, who gets a check from a legitimate, registered business for perfectly legal services rendered. Pay my taxes. No government agencies involved in the transaction. No gadgets. No guns. I'm a guy who can do research. Find things."

There's a pause. This oft-repeated conversation is familiar and thus comforting.

"And you still not tell me what you were trying to find? What you were looking, back those many years?"

"Well, hell. It's been a long time. I suppose I could give you a couple non-critical details, just to give you an idea." He says this like an uncle tempting a child with chocolate that both know he's going to fork over in the end. "Maybe it's these talking," he gestures at the empty glasses that litter the table, "but I was looking for a person. A girl. 'Bout your age, she would have been back then. Which is kind of why I latched onto you in the first place, back at the hostel, just on the off chance that you might have some connection to her—not that you weren't good company too, but, you know."

"A girl?"

"It was an odd one. Most times, I can piece together what my task has to do with, well, the grand scheme of things. Or get an idea, at least. But this, yeah, it was an odd one. A girl, real normal in every way. Didn't give me a name or a description or really anything at all, except for this idea that everyone who comes across her ends up convinced she's absolutely extraordinary. I don't remember the exact words, but that's the gist of it. All I had to go on. Oddest thing of all was they said I had to do all this research from a distance. Like if saw this magic girl in action, she'd have me under her spell, which I presume sounds just as ridiculous to you as it does to me. Plus, at the end of the work order, they said to 'trust my gut'—that intuition would be a guide. What that means, I don't have the faintest, though I suppose that when I did eventually find what I ended up finding, my intuition did play a not insignificant role. Odd, but then again, I've seen more odd than a Japanese game show host."

"I never know when to take you serious."

The American shrugged, seemingly pleased at the fact that he had left his interlocutor off-balance. They talked on into the night, both becoming progressively more inebriated, and it was only when the two were preparing to part that the boy, a man, had remembered the question he hadn't asked but had wished to.

"Wait, man, so you ever find this girl, or what?"

"Sure I did. You remember all those months I was there. Stacks of reports, all stacked up on your kitchen table. High school yearbooks, local papers, anything I could get my hands on. Well, what turned out being most useful was the police reports. Some freak tried to grab a girl off the street, which is unfortunate enough sure, but nothing too unusual in and of itself. But the witness reports raised an eyebrow. It was this long series of men, all talking about how, oh yeah, we recognize her, nice girl from the neighborhood, the most wonderful piano player you ever heard. Just a little over the top, how they said it. It's hard to explain. But it just felt odd. So like they told me, I followed my gut, and…" he slapped his hands together in a gesture that indicated that the task had been neatly concluded.

"But what this girl have to do with… well, I guess I always just assume you come here for something have to do with the Contact, no?"

"Ugh, the Contact, the Contact. You talk like one of them. But yeah, I mean, broadly speaking, it was something to do with… that whole series of events."

"So what she have to do with anything?"

"Look kid, I couldn't tell you even if I knew, which I don't. I feel like I've said it over and over—you never get the whole picture. Not at my pay grade, but I kind of suspect not at any pay grade, though that's just a hunch, which is more or less all anybody has to go on. All's I know is, the girl ended up doing the work for us. Vanished off the face of the Earth. I passed along what I found and, well, hate to say it like this cause it sounds real sinister, but who knows, maybe they made sure she stayed vanished. Gave her money, a visa, sent her out of the country, or... who the hell knows. All I know is this all worked out just the way it seems to me that they would've wanted. Though that's a hunch too."

"How it worked out. You mean the Contact?"

The American sighed, this time with real exasperation.

"Aw come on, kid. You ended up getting pulled over to the other side? They just repeated it often enough so's you couldn't resist believing it. Look," he said, looking over his shoulder in a conspiratorial manner, "I'ma tell you something. Only reason I can say it is cause it don't matter one bit who you tell about it. Ain't nobody gonna believe you, or me for that matter, don't matter what evidence you give, whatever. All this preamble is just to say that I don't mind one way or another if you think I'm bullshitting you, but this is God's honest truth, which doesn't mean that knowing it will change things one way or another. It's fake. The whole thing. From the discovery to the 'Contact.' We pulled it off and now it's over. And the thing is that, now that we got the weight of hundreds of millions of people all stampeding in the direction we wanted, ain't a thing on Earth can change that course. Not me, not you. But just for your own dignity as a man— goddamn I must be drunker than I thought, talking about dignity and truth... sheeit—I just want to give you the chance of not being made into... well whatever you want to call them folks out there crawling on their bellies. An 'Earthling.' So believe what you want, but just remember what I said. One gigantic hoax. The most tremendous, godawful spectacle of manipulation anybody's ever pulled off—that we know of—and one that I'm damn proud to have been a part of, cynical sumbitch though that might make me."

The American straightened up and slurred all this with his eyes locked on the Hotelier's. Then he shook his hand and departed, stumbling away down the promenade and whistling Dixie with surprising art for a man in his condition. And though the boy, a man, would always in the future shake his head in a gesture of jolly bemusement at having had the opportunity to get to know such an eccentric character as the American, the seed of doubt which had lurked somewhere within him, that had been the chief source of the contempt he'd always felt for the pilgrims, would begin, from the wee hours of that morning, to take root.

And all the while, the Mapmaker bided his time, knowing that the Everyman was out there, with the seeds of truth well sown. All was in alignment. He needed only to speak his piece.

~ Aspirational Negritude ~

C was one of those elementary school friends with whom I'd always expected to reconnect at some point in the future. We'd diverged in adolescence, as is so often the case, but as boys we had been so close. I had always been sure that, someday, we would get around to being close again. Certainly, it never crossed my mind that one day I'd be seated in his living room, sipping coffee with his street-wise cousins and making small-talk with his parents, the cordiality of the occasion an immaculate facade to mask the grief that loomed over us all on the morning after his death.

C and I had spent our elementary school years together running around as part of a multi-colored band of American boys—hyphenated-Americans with nothing but America to bridge the oceans between Honduras, Nigeria, and the Philippines. I'd been the only one of our little group who'd lost his hyphen, an American with no further explanation needed. I imagine that, to C's parents, seeing their youngest son with such a friend had felt like their dream's realization. They deeply desired for their son—or barring that, for *his* son—to partake in the same unhyphenated Americanness as me. As such, they had always been particularly kind to me, and keen to be on good terms with my family. Our fathers had coached our sixth grade basketball team together, our mothers had taken turns taking care of each other's children when one of them had an errand to run, and we'd made a tradition of getting together for Labor Day barbecues. They truly wanted to assimilate, bless their hearts, and they embraced whatever was American in their son, foreign though it often was to their working-class, Catholic, Central American sensibilities.

The Slipknot t-shirts C wore over hip-hop jeans, his wild, unkempt curls, and the way he'd said "nigga" with such confidence that the Blacks didn't mind it (though he was the kind of kid who'd throw a hard "r" on the end, just to rile them up, confident that his winning smile would get him out of any difficulties): all this was America, and thus, in his parents' minds, to be celebrated. In their ignorance, they had believed in the propaganda, believed in the American Dream, and as a result, their boy had found his way into that most quintessentially American situation: two cars full of mystery-meat brown-skin ethnics hollering back and forth about drugs or a girl or God knows what, all harmless macho posturing until a gun was drawn and cut him down. All hail the rainbow nation.

Regardless of the racially-conscious dissident I've become, there is still an ache I feel when I think back on that sweet, wild, charismatic Honduran kid I used to know who was gunned down like a dog at nineteen on the streets of my city.

I remember marveling at his parents' composure that afternoon. They had received the call only a few hours before I arrived to pay my respects. It was with great dignity that they had poured out coffee and made small talk about the rock band I'd been playing in and the various majors I was considering at the community college. It was as though they were well-accustomed to burying their sons. Perhaps it was a cultural norm they'd brought with them from the old country. Perhaps it was the constant flow of guests which held them together, simply because the injunction to exchange pleasantries and pour coffee acted as a sort of distraction. I can't imagine my parents reacting in this fashion, had it been me.

I sat there for about fifteen painful minutes before making my exit. I walked across the bridge, back to the east side of the river, where the neighborhood was White and growing more so with every passing year. When I was a boy, it had been a cusp of sorts. At that moment, C's body was cooling on a slab somewhere—the first of the gang to die (a song he'd liked, for the record; he had a bit of a penchant for emotional White boy music).

The more time passes, the more solidly ensconced I become in my own identity, and the more evident it seems to me that C was a walking identity crisis, an emo-punk-skater-hippie-gangster whose menagerie of subcultural identifications had swooped in to fill the gap that was left in him by his parents' choice to sacrifice Honduras in favor of the anti-culture of

America.

C and I had gone to different high schools, and his crowd during those years was rougher and browner. Thus, we didn't see too much of each other. I'll never know what happened in the years between our divergence and his death. Had he loved? Had he dreamed? Had there been anything on his mind but the next ruckus, the next party, the next blunt? For such questions, there are no answers. All I have are memories to piece together. The Boy Scout troop. The baseball field. The gymnasium where the parish events were held. The alleys we ran down in packs. One memory I dwell on quite a bit is the last time I saw him alive, which was about three years before he died, in the vacant lot across the street from my childhood home. A team of my schoolmates and I had faced off with some public school kids from the neighborhood in a brutal game of tackle football that had gone badly awry, devolving into a brawl between adolescent boys old enough to do serious damage to each other.

My last memory of C, who'd always been a gentle, goofy, class-clown type, is of his uncharacteristically rage-constricted face spewing spittle as he squared off with E, one of the neighborhood Arabs, their faces inches apart, snarling, speaking like hood Blacks: "Da fuck you lookin' at, nigga"; "Yo, fuck you, punk-ass mothafuckin' nigga." It has taken me some fifteen years to realize it, but there was a much deeper significance to this yapping than one might initially suppose. What they called each other, and what they called themselves, was what they were: niggers. These two sons of immigrants, despite their disparate backgrounds, had been thoroughly assimilated, brought down into the mire of equality. Whatever they had originally been, they had become aspirational niggers who listened to nigger music, dressed in nigger garb, and dreamed nigger dreams.

I'd known the Arabs since I was quite young as well; they lived down the street, and we had often found ourselves in the vacant lot together, playing pickup football, baseball, or just engaging in the sort of recreational violence that is so important for male development. Though I have no distinct memory of meeting them, it would have been one of those chance meetings between strangers that occur so naturally among children. More than likely, they'd simply seen my brothers and me tossing a ball around and casually walked over to see if they could play, too.

It was clear from the first that they weren't what anyone would call "nice" kids. The older brother, Y, was short, stout, and cruel, a powerful force at running back, and willing to throw fists at the slightest pro-vocation. The younger one, the aforementioned E, was friendlier, but in a sneaky and backhanded way; I quickly found that he would steal anything I didn't keep a careful eye on, which was a constant concern, as my brothers and I became known as the kid with "stuff," which meant that baseball would be played with my bat, street hockey with my family's sticks, and basketball on my family's hoop. Not only did I have "stuff," but I was also soft and sheltered. I was athletic, but having been raised in a household where the mildest profanity was forbidden, let alone fistfights, I found myself at a distinct disadvantage in conflict situations. Thus, they saw me as an easy mark, and the vacant lot became a place to be tested. Only once I'd proven that I wasn't the type to run home crying, that when hit I'd hit back, and that I was no slouch on the football field, either, did I win a measure of respect, first from the Arab brothers and their various relatives and co-ethnics, and later from the various other kids who hung around that lot: Mexicans, Filipinos, a few Blacks, and a certain number of lower-class Whites from broken homes.[6]

Looking back, it's not clear if my parents ever explicitly forbade or discouraged me from inviting the neighborhood kids into our house. They would have been justified in doing so, of course, but it also seems unlike something my progressive, yuppie parents would have done. Perhaps I had my own sense that, fun as they were to rough-house with, they were not the sort of people I wished to hang around with. For whatever reason, the neighborhood kids always remained at arm's length—acquaintances who might knock on my door on a summer afternoon when they had an odd number of players for whatever game was ongoing, but who were never truly friends. The only one who ever entered my house was E, the youngest of the Arabs, who, despite his negative qualities, was by far the nicest of the neighborhood band, as well as the closest to me in age. I'd invited him in one day for a closely-supervised glass of water after a long afternoon spent playing an improvised game he'd dubbed "jack-ass hockey," which was essentially a game of keep-away played on roller blades, with a tennis ball and hockey sticks (though the real fun of it had been occasionally slamming each other into parked cars). Somehow or other we'd ended up sitting on the couch for a while, shooting the breeze and waiting for the streetlights to come on and summon him home.

That's when he told me about Palestine. With a wistful tone, he told me about Ain ash-Shams, the village where his grandfather still lived. How he

---

[6] I was born in an era where the type of White kid I was—the children of intact professional families—were thoroughly domesticated. Kids like me didn't usually play unsupervised.

and the pack of village kids, most of them relatives in one way or another, would spend their days pelting through the rocky hills at a mad dash, freer by far than we were in the prison of concrete that was our neighborhood. How they ate what they grew on his granddad's farm. How Y, his older brother, had been judged old enough to slaughter his first goat—and how, despite the seemingly boundless cruelty he demonstrated in the vacant lot, he had been too soft for it, hurting but not killing the animal. How E had had a girlfriend there, a first cousin, whom it was more or less understood he would marry someday. When he told me that the fruit was sweeter, the water purer, and the landscape more heavenly in Palestine than anywhere else in the world, the statement was devoid of the usual pugnacious supremacism of the Arab Muslim. His love of home seemed pure to me, and his narrative carried me away with him to a land of olive oil and date palms which, as he told me, had been ripped away from him by the Jews.

C never, as I can recall, spoke to me about Honduras, but I remember that he used to visit in the summers when we were growing up. I imagine that his voice would take on a similarly rapturous quality were he alive to tell me about it today.

It would be another ten years until I walked the rocky hills of Palestine myself. On my first trip there, still enthralled by the normative progressivism of my upbringing, I was scarcely able to see the country itself, so dwarfed it was by the shadow of my towering, self-stroked virtue. By the time of my second trip, however, I had come to my senses, and was therefore capable of a much more unflinching and non-judgmental appraisal of an alien manner of being. My awakening to racial consciousness afforded me the ability to accept human difference, and thus to see Palestine and its people for what they are, in a manner which is relatively undistorted by the hegemonic liberalism of our day and age.

I freely admit to a visceral distaste for various aspects of their nature. From the dogmatic religiosity, to the tendency to remorselessly and Semitically scheme and cheat, to the penchant for animal cruelty, to the utterly unabashed lust for rape which proliferates even at relatively sophisticated levels of their society, I have no wish to live among Arabs, even though I've enjoyed my visits to their world. However, the particular appreciation of diversity which is the exclusive purview of the Dissident Rightist has also made me capable of appreciating their openhandedness, their unbreakable bonds of family, clan, and tribe, their uncompromising self-confidence in their culture and religion, and the glorious and impractical romanticism that spurs them to lash out at their Jewish oppressor in futile gestures that are all the more beautiful for their futility. They're brave and cruel, generous and untrustworthy, the descendants of camel-back conquerors and merchant schemers, Bedouin and Fellahin.

My appreciation for humanity's diversity is the reason I find it tragic that the fire of Palestine will one day be extinguished, suffocated by the relentlessly metastasizing cancer of Zionism.

Only after you've seen the hills of Palestine through awakened eyes will you truly understand the tragedy of what became of those Arab boys I played with, the degeneration that led to E's descent into negritude, the selfsame negritude that consumed C. How authentic, in comparison to the aspirational negritude of Brown America, is the organically deve- loped *Weltanschauung* of the Arab in his habitat, the holistic and all- encompassing expression of his being, foreign and indeed repulsive as it is to me in many regards! For the promise of material welfare, these boys' parents sacrificed their children's cultural patrimony and consigned their offspring to membership in an undifferentiated Brown Sludge which barks in unreasoning aggression, whines for the cameras in the hopes of extracting payouts from the White man, and spends its weekends in a THC- haze watching Netflix as hip-hop blares in the background.

I think about what this means for me, an American so long unhyphenated that the Something that my ancestors once were has been lost to living memory. This is what the non-Whites taught me: that I have lost something, and not just my country, but indeed my very Somethingness, for to be an American is to belong to the same entity as Alan Dershowitz, Ilhan Omar, Tariq Nasheed, and Desmond is Amazing. It is to be nothing at all.

Being a White American is of course a more meaningful identification than the creedless, colorless anti-culture which is now signified by the unmodified term "American." But Whiteness, too, is a mark of degeneracy. My people were neither Yankees nor Southrons, though they had long since settled the lands of the Northwest Territory by the time of the Civil War. Their story was even less reminiscent of those "poor and huddled masses" who arrived in the nation's cities with nothing, imported to inflate the numbers (and lower the wages) of the industrial proletariat. My people were Germans, humble *Hunsrücker* farmers who arrived with their pockets full of the modest proceeds of generations of hardscrabble tightwaddery. They came neither out of desperation, as the "poor and huddled masses" did, nor out of the Puritans' ideological fanaticism. My people came to own land, and to be left alone to work it. They came as Germans, and Germans they remained for generations in the foothills of Appalachia. Only after the first of the two great Brother Wars did the Great Satan come for them, grinding them down and producing "Whites," a group of which I cannot help but be a proud and self-identifying member, but a group whose very existence is a symbol of the losses my people incurred when we took the Devil's bargain and arrived upon these accursed shores. I too—like C, like E—am part of degenerate sludge. I, like the tragically negrified non-White friends and acquaintances of my youth, am an American.

Yes, to be an American, to be a "White," is tantamount to being a degenerate. The fact that this statement may rustle certain jimmies is an effect of imprecise language. Whereas the modern Dissident Rightist tends to make synonyms of degeneracy and decadence, the German term for degeneracy, *Entartung*, better preserves the sense of the term. *Art* is the German word for type, and the prefix *Ent-* is a negation, roughly similar to the English "un-" or "de-." Thus, *Entartung* can be very literally translated as de-type-ing, or detypifying. The loss of one's type, nature, or genus (de*genera*tion) is the definition of degeneracy (as opposed to moral degradation, which is better termed decadence), and this is the very essence of the American melting pot. Perhaps before my time, the myth was true: that the newly-arrived European agreed to undergo a process of degeneration in order to be regenerated into a new sort of American man. Whether or not this was once the case is beside the point, for it is certainly no longer true. For as long as I have walked the Earth, the only definition of "Americanness" has been that it has no definition.

To answer the question of why we fight, I will paraphrase the famous words of the French revolutionary, Emmanuel Joseph Sieyès:

What is the White man to America? Everything.
What has he been hitherto in the political order? Nothing.
What does he desire to become? Something.

Our task is as vague as it is enormous: to regenerate what remains of our people, to enact a new ethnogenesis, and to do so before occupied America has dragged the entirety of European civilization into a state of irreparable decay. Make no mistake: the substitution of tacos, hip-hop, and sodomy for culture has created a void, and this affords us an opportunity to form ourselves into something magnificent. Should we fail in this task, it is certain that we shall vanish from the Earth. What we shall become is, of course, in part determined by our underlying biological nature. To reference an old meme, we are bound to become what we are—but what we *are*, what any race *is*, is a range of possibilities. Thus, our task is to delineate an identity for ourselves from within the range that nature has allotted us. We must do this with stories, art, philosophy, and history before we are able to effect durable, radical political change; as greater men than I have repeatedly emphasized, our labor must be metapolitical. Only once we become Something with a coherent sense of ourselves and our place in the world will we have the strength to resist the corruption which is endemic in this age of protracted decline. Without thorough and compelling metapolitical work, all our efforts will be coopted and warped by the house of mirrors that is our enemies' ideology.

This is why I fight: for the honor of playing a minuscule part in defining the nature of the American nation, in carving out Something for us to become, an identity for us to inhabit. The risks are great and the odds are not in our favor, but by God, I am grateful for the enormity of our task, and for the momentous and righteous nature of our struggle. There is no more worthwhile labor that I can conceive of participating in.

- The Blue Mountain Trust -

The heavy, black fireman's helmet wasn't always a showpiece, tucked up on a high shelf away from where we kids could get at it. For quite a while, it had been a plaything. My dad, to whose grandfather the helmet had once belonged, was not a particularly sentimental sort and, besides, it wasn't as though there was much chance of us damaging it, great hunk of metal that it was. Things only changed after I found my great-grandfather's forgotten badge, tucked up in the sweet-smelling leather lining. My dad had been quite excited by the discovery, and so too had my grandfather when the two of them had spoken on the phone. As it happened, my grandfather would never get to lay hands on this precious keepsake of his own long-dead father. I had treated the badge with the same juvenile lack of care with which I'd been accustomed to treating the helmet, and one afternoon as I'd been walking down the sidewalk of our subdivision, tossing it to myself, it had slipped from my grasp and, as if guided by some malevolent Fate, slid between the grates of a storm drain, lost forever. Neither my father nor my grandfather were at all vindictive in their response to my crime against our patrimony—neither was sentimental, nor deeply attached to material objects—but after this incident, the helmet migrated to a high shelf and become a showpiece.

For the twenty-some years that elapsed before I told the story to John Haynes, the loss of the badge nagged at me intermittently. Every so often, I would close my eyes to relive my inadvertent betrayal, tracing the arc of the badge's descent in my mind, tracking the revolutions which, if they'd been off by a few degrees in either direction, would have resulted in the grate of the storm drain performing its intended function, and the badge having been saved. Every so often, I would reflect on the way my kindly grandfather had hidden his disappointment when my dad told him what I'd done. I suppose it's not altogether unusual that such a story would have some lasting emotional resonance, but the true extent of its significance would not be made clear until John Haynes introduced me to some of the idiosyncratic theories by which he lived his life, out in that remote cabin to which a more benevolent Fate than the aforementioned had guided me one winter afternoon.

I was a few months into my work as a snowshoe guide in the backcountry outside of Big Bend, Colorado, suffused with all of the unearned confidence that comes with a bit of experience, when a snow-storm had kicked up and I'd found myself completely turned around. I tried to play it off, play-acting unconcern and hoping that a landmark would eventually make itself known to me, but after an hour or so of wandering and doubling back, I think even the Denver frat boys I was guiding that day had picked up on the fact that things had gone sideways. When we spotted the cheery puffs of smoke emanating from the chimney of a ramshackle cabin, I'd nonchalantly suggested that we stop in to thaw and hope for a gap in the storm, secretly hoping that its occupant might point me in the right direction.

John Haynes earned my enduring gratitude that afternoon, beautifully hiding my navigational incompetence from the frat boys while giving me all the direction I needed in the form of seemingly idle conversation. As I recall, he'd asked me the name of the company I worked for, and upon hearing the name, followed up with something like, "ah, right on the south edge of Big Bend, right when you come out the eastern passage to the gorge yonder, no?", indicating the direction of the town with a seemingly casual gesture I'm confident none of the frat boys picked up on, so absorbed were they in the scarfing down the gooey grilled cheese sandwiches John had cooked up when we'd showed up on his doorstep. Eventually, I'd come to find that he'd worked as a guide himself many decades ago, back before the mountain had absorbed him. He had acted, I suppose, out of a sort of solidarity with a fellow practitioner of that thankless craft.

Other than the lifeline he threw me, I don't recall John Haynes saying much in the course of that first encounter, which would have been in perfect keeping with his taciturn character. For that reason, it struck me as a bit surprising when, just as he was about to close the door behind us, he'd tapped me on the shoulder with some embarrassment and spoken to me out of the corner of his mouth: "Say, this cow I got makes more cheese than I can eat so, if you and your company were interested in having a sort of rest stop on your tours where the folks could get some refreshments, I thought we could maybe transact some business. Everything fresh. Cheese, bread, butter, preserves. Could even put together some mulled wine." Having no knowledge at the time of John Haynes' considerable fortune, I'd figured that he, like everybody else, could use a couple bucks. In light of his tremendous wealth, however, I suppose the old man had just felt a need for social contact. In any case, as it happened, from that point on I made a habit of bringing any tourists I found sufficiently tolerable over to John Haynes' cabin for buttery grilled cheese sandwiches and well-spiced mulled wine. For many of them, I suspect that meeting John was the most memorable experience of the entire tour.

In contrast, I am quite certain that meeting me, or at least the man I was at that point in my life, was not a particularly significant or memorable experience at all. By that point I had become the very personification of squandered potential, a marvel of indistinctness, lacking any sort of purpose-vector by which to define myself. Not that I had ever been bound for genius or glory, but up until my mid-twenties I had at least displayed signs of being destined for the moderate prestige and comfort of middle management, with an earning potential in the low six figures. Then things had taken a turn somehow, as what my parents had taken for a post-graduation phase of directionlessness had gradually developed into a way of life, and I had become rather a liability in the merciless arms race of vicarious parental achievement.

"Last I heard, he was living in a yurt picking apples somewhere up in rural Canada."

"Oh he's bartending at the moment, but the plan is to save up for a climbing expedition, down in the Yucatan, I think."

"Well, since he's been living in his car, he's been more than a little difficult to keep track of."

Having to give such answers at gatherings of suburban fifty-somethings whose offspring had transitioned directly at the expected age of twenty-two onto the professional ladder must have been, on the one hand, rather embarrassing. On the other hand, I do think my parents were at least a little proud to give such answers to the inevitable inquiries of "well hey, how's little Johnny (or Billy) doing anyway?" They weren't total sticks in the mud, my parents, though they were very much the sort of moderately above-average people who had stayed firmly on the beaten path and thus fulfilled their potential according to the standards of their place and time: homeownership, ~2.5 children, reasonably successful careers, etc. I'm sure that, for all the concerns they expressed about the insecurity and dead-endedness of the path I'd chosen in life, they were proud on some level that at least one of their offspring had veered off in such an odd and unpredictable direction as I had, though I certainly can't say it turned out all that well for me in the end.

In any case, at the time that I met John Haynes, I was squatting in an abandoned hunting cabin on federal land that my former PhD advisor Paul Bruchweiler had told me about, most likely out of pity, after watching me growing increasingly demoralized, missing deadlines, going AWOL, and eventually squandering (there's that word again—a common one in my Lifelogic) my grant from the department, which could have been extended to support me for another two years if I'd simply done the bare minimum of showing up to meetings and doing a passable job of teaching the undergraduate seminars I was assigned. Paul had done a great deal for me. In addition to the tip on the hunting lodge, which was technically illegal but was tacitly accepted by the relevant authorities, he'd lobbied on my behalf to the department, normalizing my status with the university and leaving me in a semi-permanent limbo. I could submit my dissertation when and if I ever finished it, and, most importantly, I retained access to the university facilities (which I mostly used for the occasional hot shower). It was also good old Paul who'd put me in touch with Melody, a lapsed academic of his generation, who ran the wilderness guiding company I hired on with, which led in turn to my fateful connection with John Haynes.

As it turned out, Melody was familiar with John Haynes. He'd been one of the mountain bums of the generation before hers, and she'd been genuinely pleased that he'd been hanging around under the societal radar all those years. When she heard about John's offer to turn his cabin into an unofficial refreshment stop for our company, she had agreed wholeheartedly, and John's wonderful little cabin had become a place I frequented regularly.

It would be just as hard to sum up the wonderfulness of John Haynes' cabin as it would be to describe what made him such a fascinating character himself. The structure certainly displayed every sign of having been built by amateur hands. Its walls were visibly out of plumb and the floorboards, which he'd nailed in place before the wood had been properly seasoned, had shrunk, leaving finger-width gaps through which the insulation—sawdust and lime—escaped in clumps. And the place certainly wasn't kept in any discernible order, though he had few enough possessions in his three rooms to be able to keep track of everything nonetheless.

Perhaps what made the cabin so unforgettable was John Haynes' fanatical devotion to crafting every single bit of property on his homestead with his own hands, while those implements which he was not able to manufacture for himself were painstakingly chosen to be as close to permanent as possible. His hand-forged utensils and dull, uneven earthenware plates and cups were as roughly made as the cabin itself, but somehow everything on John Haynes' property seemed to come together into a coherent whole. There was something gained by the fact that the knife he'd forged sliced through the cheese he'd fermented from milk he'd squeezed from the cow he'd raised, that the knife sliced through to the cutting board he'd sanded which he'd laid on the concrete countertop he'd poured, that the cheese was laid on the bread he'd baked and the sandwich laid in the melted butter of the very same cow which sizzled and frothed in the painstakingly preserved old cast iron pan stamped "Flint, MI 1953" on the handle. Not that it made the simple sandwich taste perceptibly better. But one felt—or I did, and, as I found through a number of discussions with my customers, so did others—that the convergence of these various elements produced a sort of harmony or consonance, the quality of which would diminish were any one of the elements to be replaced by something not of John Haynes' hands, even if said replacement element were of objectively superior quality. When one gazed with well-filled belly upon the merry glow of the sloppy stove which he'd cobbled together in a one-off experiment in masonry, the stove filled with wood felled and split by the same hand that had built it, you knew you could be nowhere else but John Haynes' house. There was a story to the house, a progressive element, a noticeable uptick in the quality of the workmanship, which stood out when a repair was made in the direct vicinity of the original work. When the original window sill in the front room had rotted away and had to be replaced, the resulting contrast in quality between the new sill and the old frame testified that the house and homestead amounted to a life's work, rather than a ready-made consumer product.

The fascinating quality of the man himself, as I've said, was of a nature similarly baffling to that of the house. John Haynes was as gruff and taciturn as one would expect from a reclusive mountain man. When he did see fit to speak to us, his guests, the conversation would take the form of an interrogation, his searing blue eyes peering implacably out from their nests of white beard and pink skin. When he didn't like the answers he got, he'd make no attempt to conceal his utter contempt, snorting and turning away with an indiscernible mutter under his breath. And still, even those tourists who received this rough treatment were as impressed by John Haynes as I was. Maybe it was just a result of their relief at being able to duck out of the harsh weather and be refreshed by the restorative quality of the fresh, nutty cheese and salty butter, the spiciness of the mulled wine. Maybe it was the fact that everything the old man did could not help but broadcast its authenticity. He was a character, as a great many of the tourists and fellow guides who met him would resort to saying, for lack of any more penetrating insight. I am certain that not a few of the tourists who stopped in at John's for a sandwich, dropping a couple bucks in the coffee can by the door on the way out (John Haynes had an odd and unexplained aversion to monetary transactions), found him worthy of recalling for years to come.

As for John Haynes himself, I became sure over time that he was secretly overjoyed to hear human voices every once in a while. This was especially clear when it was a family I was guiding; every time kids were along, John would make a special effort to befriend them, showing them the cows, digging up something sweet and homemade from his secret stash, telling charming tales about the monsters and ghosts of the surrounding woods.

Things would most likely have stayed this way, with the two of us as parties to a mutually beneficial and ongoing business relationship, were it not for a camping trip I'd set off on by myself one spring afternoon. As I passed his property on my way up the mountain, John Haynes had been wrestling a great steaming metal cauldron of what I'd later find was a plum mash down the hillside to his still, and my quick intervention to help him with the precarious burden had earned me an invitation to dinner. Dinner had escalated into a "sampling" session, wherein the two of us had both "tasted" copious amounts of previous batches of brandy: plum, peach, grape, blackberry, wild blueberry. The night had ended with me sleeping it off on John Haynes' kitchen floor and, feeling I'd been repaid far out of proportion to the minor aid I'd rendered by helping him tote his mash, I resolved to do John Haynes a good turn the next time I got the opportunity. This, looking back, was the beginning of our real friendship, though we always shielded our mutual positive regard via the pretext of obligation to repay a previous debt incurred. Thus, after I'd helped him patch his roof a couple weeks later, he'd brought some chicken wire down to the little hunting lodge and given me a detailed crash course in keeping my birds healthy. As if by mutual, unspoken agreement, we both saw to it that the debt was never cleared, and the constant obligation to repay in one direction or the other always provided the excuse for further dealings, keeping us in frequent contact until he died. Spry as he was, there were some tasks that John Haynes, well into his seventies, was no longer up to. I was more than happy to lend him the physical vigor of my youth, while benefiting immensely in return from his instruction in the art of subsistence (as well as from the heaps of provisions he'd invariably send me home with). And of course, over the years that we traded favors, there was ample opportunity for me to learn the contours of his taciturnity, and master the art of coaxing him into conversation (an art best conducted under the influence of a couple jiggers of moonshine).

It was on one of those long brandy-soaked nights that the story of my great-grandfather's firefighter badge came up—the anecdote, dear reader, which I began this disorganized ramble with, though we've wandered so far afield that I certainly wouldn't blame you for having lost track of how this all started. With the sun long descended and the wind moaning bitterly, there was no question of me trying to make my way home that night—at the end of the night, I would be curling up by the stove on the pallet of dusty blankets where I'd found myself spending more and more of my nights as John's health had begun to decline. Somehow I'd thought to tell the story, and it had landed successfully. John, rather than huffing and snorting derisively, had closed his eyes, shutting off their usual formidable glare of icy blue, and nodding pensively as he pondered this new information. This was the highest compliment he would ever pay an interlocutor.

"That's it," he said after a long pause. "That's the story of your life." And when I'd pressed him on this enigmatic utterance he'd told me, for the first time, about his theory of Lifelogic, the idea that certain anecdotes were particularly pure illustrations of a central pattern, tendency, or conflict which permeated a person's existence—like a fractal, as he put it—every instant of one's life ineluctably imbued in some subtle way with this characteristic and indelible pattern. The "story of one's life" is just a particularly clear instance of this pervasive pattern. These unalloyed illustrations of one's Lifelogic occur, more often than not, quite early on in one's life, before the pattern has been complicated by one's desire to escape it. These attempts at escape obscure the underlying pattern, distort it, though even as one attempts to escape one's cycle, each attempt ends up, no matter how hard you try to avoid it, as another iteration of the very same accursed and inexorable Lifelogic—mine being an inability to refrain from squandering (that word again) my patrimony.

Now, John Haynes, just as one might expect of a woodland hermit, had developed a number of beliefs that seemed implausible and even wacky to me. More than likely, I hadn't taken the idea very seriously at all. Soon we had moved onto some other topic of conversation (or more likely lapsed into silence), and it wasn't until I received the news of John Haynes' death, some five years later, that I had occasion to consider his theory once again.

I was summoned to his lawyer's office, to the reading of his will, for I had unexpectedly been named a beneficiary, and as I listened to the last words I'd ever hear from my friend, he resurrected his odd theory of a life's intrinsic logic. Given the way things played out, I have no choice but to take my Lifelogic more seriously than I was initially inclined to, fanciful a notion as it may seem.

As I recall, what he had written was more or less as follows:

To my friend, Shawn Bell,

I leave all my land holdings on and around Blue Mountain, Big Bend, CO, the details of which are described later in this document. I only ask, in a non-legally binding fashion, that he commit to keep the property intact, to care for it, to live on it as I taught him, and under no circumstances to sell it.

Shawn, I forgive you for selling, as I know you will. It is, after all, the story of your life to let these things slip through your fingers. I just couldn't help teasing you one last time. In death as in life.

Your friend,
John

It was only after his death that I learned that John Haynes was phenomenally wealthy—and inter-generationally so. The tract of land that had come into my possession was beyond my wildest dreams; when the lawyer had first told me that I'd been named in the will, I'd dared to dream that John owned the entirety of the gorge where his cabin was located, but as it turned out, I had been made the owner of fully half of Blue Mountain, a holding that had been in the Haynes family since before Colorado had been a state. If it hadn't been for the request in the will (as well as the snarky manner in which he had impugned my honor), I'll gladly admit that I would have been tempted to sell a significant portion immediately. As a result of his posthumous provocation, however, I held firm, even as the representatives of the various natural resource extraction companies had begun to show up at my door.

The trickle became a flood, to invoke a cliché. It began to seem as though every time I opened my eyes, there would be some smooth-talking stereotype of a traveling salesman sitting on John's front porch, though in all the years I knew John, I'd never known such characters to bother him. He must have done something radical to convince them he was truly serious about holding onto the land, for no matter how nasty and ill-tempered I became, they insisted on taking me for an easy mark nonetheless. Without any sort of permission, they would show up with surveying equipment— on multiple occasions I found entire crews of men from various oil and gas companies brazenly making their way up the mountain. Obscenely lucrative offers soon followed.

I concluded that there must have been quite the subterranean treasure trove beneath Blue Mountain, for the companies expressing interest in the property were of all sorts. Having learned from the first round of offers and refusals that I was bound by sentimental ties via my "word of honor," they came back with all sorts of legalistic sleights of hand, offers to lease certain rights, etc., all intended to leave my title to the land, and thus my honor, technically intact. But I knew that accepting such a deal would be just as much of a violation of John's trust as selling outright. As the offers continued rolling in, from a wide variety of venerable old concerns, I held firm and learned to ignore them as best I could. The only thing that interested me was the fact that one of the recurring names among the bidders seemed to belong to a local, two-bit law firm—and what's more, the sums offered by this seemingly insignificant concern far outstripped the offers of the big boys who, by all accounts, should have had pockets deeper by an order of magnitude than the law firm of one Elizabeth Johnston of Big Bend, CO. Finally, one afternoon when I'd made one of my rare trips into town for flour, sugar, and a few odds and ends from the hardware store, my curiosity got the better of me. I smoothed out an envelope I'd left crumpled on the passenger seat and navigated to the address denoted in the letterhead.

It was a little storefront office on a side street just off the main drag of our mountain town, a small-town law firm that couldn't have had more than two or three employees in all. I parked my car and sat there for a few minutes, puzzled by the exorbitant sums being offered by this seemingly insignificant firm. Then I saw her, a commanding middle-aged woman who could not be anyone but the eponymous Elizabeth Johnston, and everything became clear in an instant: the cold, cutting glow of her blue-steel eyes was just as piercing as his had been, and there was no doubt in my mind that Elizabeth Johnston bore some blood relation to the late John Haynes.

Somehow, the issue of family had never crossed my mind. It had just seemed to *fit* somehow that John Haynes would be the last of his line, a singularity, giving away his fortune to me, a stranger, simply because I was all he had in his life. But the period after John's death had been one of repeated surprises, not least that of the fortune itself, and I suppose I oughtn't to have been as blindsided as I was. A bit of research sufficed to substantiate my hunch. Elizabeth Haynes Johnston was John's niece, the daughter of a still-living sister of his. What's more, a quick search of the sister's name had turned up land ownership records, revealing that the owner of the north face of Blue Mountain was none other than John's sister. I had no desire to be involved in any sort of family squabble. As overjoyed as I'd been upon first receiving the title to John's property, by now the whole thing was beginning to seem like a quagmire.

It was only a couple days after I'd driven by Elizabeth Haynes Johnston's office that she'd come up to the cabin herself. I'd been hacking away at the roots of some nasty weed that was threatening to choke out John Haynes' cherry tree when I'd seen her struggling gamely down the dirt road which led down into the gulch where he'd built his house. She picked her way down through the mud barefoot, sensible shoes in hand, with a lack of fastidious that was indubitably Haynesian. Before I could make out her features, I could sense the sharpness of her face, screwed up in its usual expression of determination as she trudged.

I'd spotted her a long way off, and the intervening minutes had afforded me plenty of time to dash madly about, putting on a kettle and hunting down the dented old laundry basin for her to wash her muddy feet in. By the time she'd made it to the steps of the porch, I'd gotten two of John Haynes' chairs positioned there (the older much wobblier than the more recently constructed one) with the kettle on a table between them (the table of my own even more rickety construction). She introduced herself, forcing a simulacrum of amiability to play unnaturally across her face, distorting her usual mahogany voice. We managed a few minutes of stilted banter over coffee. I'd shared a few memories of her uncle's last years, and she'd told me about visiting him in the shadows of the mountain as a girl, back when he was less thoroughly committed to his all-repudiating isolation. But her face, her blue-steel eyes and long straight nose were, like her uncle's, best suited for fearsome interrogation, and it would not be long before she reverted to her natural tendencies. When I'd offered her a grilled cheese sandwich for old times' sake, the cheese and bread produced according to John Haynes' standards, cut with his hand-forged knife on his hand-sanded cutting board atop his hand-poured countertop, she'd informed me that there was a more pressing agenda behind her visit than mere nostalgia (and that as a vegan, grilled cheese sandwiches were an impossibility in any case).

"Mr. Bell," she said with that oddly deep voice, "you'll have received our offers for the purchase of this property. Of this share of *my family's* land which my uncle, for reasons of his own, decided to cede to you. You'll have noticed that our offers far exceed the market valuations of the land's value. By a considerable margin, I might add. You won't get a better deal from any other party. What's more, if there's something in particular you're holding out for, you won't find more receptive ears than mine, right here, and right now. What needs to happen, for you to sign this contract?"

Resuming her usual mode of address, reentering the no-nonsense world of offers, counter-offers, and hard-cash, it seemed as though Elizabeth Haynes Johnston had returned to a state of ease that had been denied her in the brief period of chit-chat. She sat forward in her chair, her keen eyes searching mine. I'd responded the only way I could—with a flat refusal. I explained it as gently as I could, thinking she might be embarrassed or indeed outraged at the insinuation that, as it seemed to me, John Haynes had more than likely willed me the property because he considered me to be the most likely person to hold onto it, to refuse to sell under all circumstances, and, having been entrusted that task, I intended to live up to it. I'd assumed that she'd rejoin with a series of overwrought assurances that she would never, under any circumstances, sell her family's land, that she wished only to see the property, divided in some earlier generation, made into one again. Instead, Elizabeth Haynes Johnston made no bones about the fact that it was her unabashed intention to make the land available to the resource extractors and that the reason it was so crucial that I sell to her was the existence of prodigious deposits of certain rare minerals in the highest reaches of the mountain, precious substances previously undiscovered in the United States. It had been determined that, from an engineering perspective, it was simply not feasible to extract the minerals from one half of the Haynes property without disturbing the other half. It was for this reason that it was absolutely imperative that I sell as well. But when she'd asked me once again what it would take to make this deal happen, asked me what it was that I wanted, all I could tell her was that what I wanted was to live here, in the shadow of Blue Mountain, in the cabin that John Haynes built, though already in the few months I'd been living there, the work of my hands had begun to make it seem to be mine as well as his.

"Mr. Bell, the sum we're offering you could very easily afford you a considerable amount of mountain real estate for you to sit on and take up space."

"But that mountain wouldn't be this one. This mountain is mine. It's mine because of the years I've spent on it and the things I've built. And I love it because it's mine."

"Oh for goodness' sake. This hasn't been *your* mountain for more than a year and you're already talking like my uncle. If you've gotten so attached to this mountain within a year, you can go right ahead and get attached to the one you buy with the money we've so generously offered you. Silliness. I made some allowances for my uncle. Didn't press him too much to sell, as grotesque of a misallocation of resources as it was. The war was hard on him. The mountain was where he found peace. Et cetera. But you... you're some kid from a lily-White Midwestern suburb playing "mountain man." Isn't it more than a little bit silly to be so sentimental? Can't you play mountain man somewhere else? Get romantically attached to some other mountain?

"To be frank, Mr. Bell, you're a college dropout ski-bum who talked his way into a multi-million dollar payout by manipulating an old man no longer in full control of his faculties. If it weren't for the fact that I'd just as soon spare my mother that pain, I'd go after you in court. I heartily, sincerely suggest to you that you take very seriously the offer we are making you. Because we are not going to simply shrug our shoulders and walk away if you continue being intransigent."

I'm by no means a confident speaker. Certainly not as ready with the twenty-five-cent words as Ms. Johnston, Esq. But in a few more minutes I was able to make it clear that I would not be moved. She nodded, with the same pensive air as her uncle had used to evince, before rising decisively and departing without a word of farewell.

It couldn't have been more than a week before the rumbling began, imperceptibly at first, such that for some days I noticed only an odd numbness in the bottoms of my feet when I turned in for the night. But then had come a penetrating thud, like a titan-driven stake into the very heart of Earth, and after the sound came a shock which rattled the windows in their frames and cast two of the rough earthenware jugs John Haynes had made onto the floor. As I swept up the shards, there came another thud and then another, the rhythm like the strides of some infernal but impeccably drilled army on the march. I moved everything fragile down to the floor, padded the windows as best I could with balled up clothing and rags, and drove down and around to the other side of the mountain, though I well knew what I would find there.

As I looked up at Elizabeth Haynes Johnston's side of the mountain, the swarms of orange-vested contractors were visible at a number of different points on the slope, as I knew they would be. From the company name emblazoned on the machinery, I gathered that they were a natural gas concern. But I was sure already that they were only the first of many— within weeks, they would be joined by experts in coal and steel and limestone and petroleum and timber extraction, their simultaneous appearance calibrated not to maximize profits, but to maximize my suffering. I prepared, not for war, which would have required that I have some sort of offensive strategy, but for a siege.

Elizabeth Haynes Johnston made the skies of Big Bend, CO glow hellishly orange. The air became laden with ash and the stream went sour. All the day and all the night continued the infernal march of the machines, the thud of the great pneumatic rod which fucked the poor Earth in the most graphic and inhuman fashion.

The local crunchy-granola tree-hugger types came out in full force, with good old Melody at the helm of the ship of fools, and they even managed to turn the whole affair into a bit of a national spectacle. But as is always the case when a grassroots effort cannot be astroturfed into conformity with the preexisting desires of the Drahtzieher, their efforts had been utterly ineffective. The various legal challenges to the many obvious contraventions of environmental policy were tied up in the courts by so many reams of convoluted lawfare that no stop-work order could be issued, and the resource extraction companies worked around the clock to turn the whole thing into a *fait accompli* before an injunction could even be drafted. I suppose it's no great surprise that the authorities reacted as they did, given the geopolitical importance of the minerals Ms. Johnston had mentioned to me, but at the time I made no such rational calculations—it seemed to me as though the universe itself had reared up in a great typhoon of malevolence with no purpose beyond crashing down upon me and tossing me about beneath its swirling weight until my lungs grew heavy and my will weak. My fury grew great and formless. With Jobian ardor I cursed the skies, raved madly at the indifferent contractors as they defaced my land with barbed wire and portajohns, imprecated foully at John Haynes himself as the cause of my suffering, as well as upon that soulless money-hungry harpy that was of his blood.

Most of all I cursed the devious act of reverse psychology that had honorbound me to this suffering—and as the Mordorian fire rained down from the skies, I perseverated long upon John Haynes' eccentric theory of Lifelogic, and of its implication that I would inevitably squander (*that word*) this, my patrimony, in the end. The chickens died and the cow followed. The sleepless nights and sulfury air had done them in. The window panes had shattered despite my best efforts, and the nights became bitterly cold as autumn deepened. I developed a racking, intractable cough, and relied ever more on bags of groceries that long-time well-wishers—dear Paul Bruchweiler, dear Melody—would cart down into the gulch. But when they attempted to prevail upon me to spend a few months in one of their guest bedrooms, or even on a beach somewhere for God's sake, I reacted with bitter rage, shrieking that they too, like the rest of the world, were devoted to my failure, but that I would never give in to the unbending demands of my Lifelogic. And as I sat later that evening, fat flakes of sooty snow drifting in through the empty window frames, I resolved upon a course of action which would technically fulfill this commitment. No more would I allow myself to be made the passive object of such indignities. From under the warped and hand-planed floorboards I retrieved John Haynes' ancient Colt revolver and loaded it. To kill and then to die, I calculated, would not amount to an act of surrender.

The electricity which coursed through my body on the drive down was accompanied by an oceanic peace within my breast. My resolve was as a balm for my inflamed and unassuaged outrage, and the quiet of our mountain town's narrow streets was such a relief from the hellish clamor of the mountain that instead of proceeding directly to my destination, I elected to walk for twenty minutes or so, feeling the gun's weight on my hip and the weight in my heart of what I knew I had to do. Indeed, as I walked past the warm, bright houses, so cozily nestled together, I felt the rage loosen its grip upon my heart, and for a moment I seriously considered driving to Paul Bruchweiler's or Melody's or even to the university to pass a few hours on a couch in one of the innumerable campus lounges. But when my eyes passed involuntarily over the purple-orange haze that hung around Blue Mountain, a burning brand looming over the town, I knew that I had to go through with it. The thudding of the infernal machines was still audible, and as I stood in front of the door of my enemy's little storefront office, I closed my eyes to focus on the rhythm, reminding myself of the justice of my cause, and making my will as iron and my wrath as ice. Finally, I inhaled deeply, unholstered my weapon, and burst through Elizabeth Haynes Johnston's door, secure in the knowledge that my resolve was unshakable, and that my suffering had reached its endpoint.

I had miscalculated, however, the nature of my foe. That is, whereas I had gone over in my head the manner in which I would make myself invulnerable to her pleas as she begged for her life, not once had it occurred to me that when Elizabeth Haynes Johnston recognized me, and then my gun, and finally the nature of her situation, that she would react as she did: by leaning back in her chair with her arms crossed over her chest, peering at me through tired but still-keen eyes, for all the world as though it was she, and not the wild-eyed man with the gun, who held all the power. She regarded me with a thin smile as I stood there, pale, with my guts tied up in knots.

"Well? Go ahead." A long moment elapsed as my hands began to tremble, before I gradually lowered the gun, a wave of self-hatred breaking over me. She nodded, slowly. "I'm not going to mock you for not having the stomach for murder. It may well be one of your best qualities. How about a cup of tea?" And she pointedly stretched and yawned, before hobbling out of the room to start the kettle, stiff after a marathon of sedentary labor. Though I'd laid the gun on her desk, well within her reach, she hadn't even looked at it as she'd passed it.

When she returned to sit across from me, twin mugs of tea in hand, her expression seemed to be one of sympathy, or even pity. "You're not a killer, Mr. Bell. You're not even a mountain man or a pioneer or a survivalist or... anything really. For that matter, neither was my uncle. Ruggedness is something you play at, because at the end of the day you're just one more White man who isn't sure what he ought to be. Isn't sure *that* he ought to be. You were raised to believe you were destined for a certain role, when in fact that role has already been recast. All your life you were told you were a leading man, and it turns out your only role will be to exit stage right, make room for the new performers who've been kept out of the play entirely thus far, and to clap goddamn hard from the audience, even if you feel like it's tearing you apart. I can sympathize. I can see how that could cause a crisis. The problem is, you've chosen a damn inconvenient place to live out your crisis. I gave you the chance to go work through your issues somewhere else, but you just couldn't summon up the good sense to recognize a good deal when you saw it. But I suppose that's only natural. Systemic privilege isn't known for inculcating particularly good sense among its beneficiaries."

"You goddamn greedy bitch."

"Greedy? Bitch, I can see. God-damned… well, that's a matter of worldview, I suppose, and you're entitled to your opinion. But greedy? You think this is me wanting a big payday? Mr. Bell, you've got it all wrong. In fact, you're the only one here who could be construed as behaving greedily, I'm sorry to say." She made a little gesture to ask for my patience as she flipped through the printed slides on the easel behind her, set up as though she'd just been at a pitch meeting. She cleared her throat to repeat the spiel for me, the image behind her a fine glossy picture of my mountain—our mountain—and the slide entitled, "The Blue Mountain Trust."

"I'll give it to you very briefly, Mr. Bell. With a year's proceeds from the extraction operation, my trust—well, there are a number of donors, but it's my project and I'll be chairing the board, so I hope it's not too presumptuous to refer to it as *my* trust—but in any case, one year of lanthanide extractions would produce sufficient profits to feed untold millions of food-insecure people. Assuming volunteer labor, we could provide the materials to build tens of thousands of schools—and we could do this every year. We could pay in full the reparations due to hundreds of thousands of the descendants of enslaved people. We could save countless lives by digging wells or sending polio vaccines or any number of possible courses of action. And according to our surveyors, the reserves present in the core of Blue Mountain are sufficient to proceed at this rate for fifty to seventy years. Don't you think it's worth it for the White residents of this White state in this blood-soaked, stolen country to sacrifice a bit of the natural beauty they think is their 'right' in exchange for these outcomes? Don't you think that doing these things might be worth you shutting the fuck up, taking the money, and moving your ass to go be useless on another mountain somewhere? Haven't I offered you enough money for you to buy yourself a very nice new sandbox to play in? Haven't I?

"Let me tell you a little something about myself and my priorities, Mr. Bell. What I want more than anything on this Earth, what I want with, dare I say, a comparable intensity to the way you want to own hundreds of acres of land and play explorer, is to free myself of the moral burden of this inherited blood money my ancestors left me with. I doubt Uncle John ever told you about the money, seeing as he was busy playing the same game of pretend as you, but we're 'old money' WASPs. Do you know what that means? It means buying and selling people. It means dehumanizing people of color. It means colonialism, slavery, and genocide. And I don't care how goddamn inconvenient you find it; I'm going to pay my debt, and I will trample you into the dirt to do it. Doesn't feel good to be trampled, now does it? Well it's about time you got with the program. The rest of the planet, from women to Black and Brown people to animals, have known damn well, for damn long, what it feels like to be trampled on. And now you do to."

Her voice grew all the more dark and mellifluous as her ire intensified and her volume increased to a roar. From the flash of her eyes and the easy, infectious roll of her diction, I could tell that she was fully in her element, here in the realm of deepest ritual self-abasement.

"Now I'm going to offer one more time. I'm going to offer you a hell of a lot more than market value, not because you're *entitled* to it, but because even when White men are trampled, it's a very different sort of trampling than other people have to face. I'm going to make this offer because I, and all of life on Earth, am willing to pay a premium to be shut of you, now and forever.

"So what do you say, Mr. Bell," she said, quietly again, with just a hint of sugary, contemptuous mockery, "will you let me buy you a new sandbox?"

*

There's no use in dragging out the fact that I took the deal. So overwhelmed was I by the flood of lawyerly rhetoric, so inadequate did I feel my response would be, that it was right there, in Elizabeth Haynes Johnston's office, with my gun still lying on her desk, that I signed the paperwork. What could I have said? That I loved Blue Mountain, not because of the concrete qualities it possessed, but because it was mine? That the fact that Blue Mountain had come into my hands as part of a process that grew organically out of my life meant that it could never be replaced? These weak objections had evaporated as I stood there before her, staring shamefaced at my shoes like a chastised schoolboy, unable to formulate any sort of response, even though I knew on some level, even as she thundered down at me from on high, that Elizabeth Haynes Johnston's ideology, if rigorously applied, would justify confiscating the very shirt from off my back, and from off the back of those like me. Thus it was that I fulfilled the destiny that John Haynes had foreseen for me in my Lifelogic, and just as my great-grandfather's firefighter badge slipped away down the storm drain—just as the genetic inheritance which was my potential was squandered on shiftless, purposeless drifting—so too would this, my last and greatest patrimony, be squandered.

Yes, squandered, even by the definitions set out by Elizabeth Haynes Johnston and her ilk, for the bankers and corporate types from whom she had raised the money to fund the Blue Mountain Trust, and to buy me out of my land, had pulled off their usual shenanigans by legal sleight of hand, and seen to it that the exorbitant profits of the lanthanide mines were funneled into their already laden pockets. And they certainly weren't about to let some small-town shiksa chair their board. That's about the long and short of it, I suppose.

I never did get around to buying myself a new sandbox. For a decade now, that eight-figure sum has been sitting in my bank account, an indelible reminder and a burden I cannot shed. I suppose I might as well give it to Elizabeth Haynes Johnston's Africans, but for reasons I'm not quite sure of, I haven't done so. As for me, my circumstances forced me to finally start chipping away at the long dormant PhD dissertation. With yet more help from Paul Bruchweiler, as resilient an old bugger as there's ever been, still teaching in his eighties, I finally defended the damn thing. Since then, I've been able to piece together a living as an adjunct professor, picking up 100-level courses at a couple different local community colleges. It doesn't hurt that rents in Big Bend have fallen to next to nothing as the orange glow, noxious air, and incessant metallic racket have taken away all the charm of my little mountain town. During the day, I teach eighteen-year-olds that the price of a good is determined by the point at which the supply curve and the demand curve meet, which is the sort of bitter irony I can get a good laugh at these days, and in the evenings, I like to walk. Sometimes, when I'm strolling along what used to be the town's signature panoramic boardwalk, where White families would take pictures of themselves with kindly old Blue Mountain as the background, I'll see Elizabeth Haynes Johnston out and about as well. The years have turned her wan, with faded eyes. I look on her with a touch of sympathy. She doesn't look at me at all.

The only solace I can take these days, when I'm walking and the old ache of regret begins to grip me, is the knowledge that this is simply the sort of creature I am, a squanderer, doomed by inexorable Lifelogic to a fate that, no matter my resistance, was to unfold in just the way that John Haynes foretold it.

~ The Grand Tableau ~

The Wise Guardians who produced the New Entertainment won neither awards nor recognition for their efforts, as such things would shatter the central illusion, letting the spectators in on the fact that they were, in fact, viewers of an entertainment program. It was not only the audience that remained in the dark; more often than not, the stars themselves were unaware of the nature of things. Of course, a lack of recognition for the men behind the scenes is not a new phenomenon. Back in the days of the Old Entertainment, the glory allotted to the screenwriters, producers, and various other machers was always eclipsed by that allotted to the stars they puppeteered.

Still, when it came to the Old Entertainment, everyone knew, at least abstractly, that the actor was reciting lines he hadn't written, standing in the midst of a set he hadn't designed, caked in cosmetics he hadn't applied, and recorded by cameras he didn't operate; all in a situation that had been deliberately devised and was not, in fact, occurring. The first coup of the New Entertainment was to convince the viewers that the Grand Tableau was not an instance of artifice, as the action on the stage of the Old Entertainment had always been known to be. The main mechanism whereby this effect was achieved was the reclassification of the performers who crafted and presented the narrative at hand to the viewing public as mere transmitters of information about events which were occurring somewhere *out there*. A nigh fantastical state of affairs was achieved via centuries of conditioning whereby the viewers tended to look straight through the elaborate and well-funded apparatus that curated and transmitted the Entertainment, immersing themselves with a child's absorption, both uncritical and absolute, in the "events" that were "taking place," which they learned about through the various endpoint-devices of the transmission apparatus, which were stationed in their individual dwellings.

Most instances[7] of the New Entertainment vanished from the transmission apparatus after their "pilot episodes," so to speak. Others achieved tremendous staying power and the status of cultural icons. There were some entertainment properties of such narrative power that their viewers would die for them, lined up in the street in baying mobs whose precisely calibrated unruliness and chaos provided an illusion of spontaneity. Then the events which these mobs brought to bear would themselves be sliced-up, curated, and transmitted in precisely the same manner as the "events" which had occasioned the mob action in the first place. Mobs, being both responses to previous "instances" as well as the stuff of future instances, were one of the more colorful examples of this spooky tendency of the New Entertainment toward self-reference and involution, but the fact was that cultural phenomena of all kinds were scripted and managed according to the same general method, with the non-spontaneous reaction to the previous and likewise non-spontaneous triggering event being repackaged as a triggering event for future non-spontaneous reactions, the end result of which was that a viewer could view, through his endpoint-device, a program in which he'd played a bit part. Warholian, no?

The audience members each selected their favorites from the prefab sets of attitudes laid out in these manufactured dramas and interpreted the world according to them. They imagined this to constitute participation in life. And at the very center of their spiritual lives, above the various minor programs, tying together the cinematic universe as a whole, there was the Grand Tableau, an epic poem of centuries' vintage with repeated refrains that the audience knew by heart and a set of in-universe rules that rose to the level of mythology or even religion among the viewers. The Guardians

---

[7] Unlike literature, which came in books and stories, or drama which came in plays, there was no convenient name for the units in which the New Entertainment was packaged. This was, of course, by design, as it was necessary to preserve the illusion that the Entertainment was in fact reality itself.

watched impassively over this all, and it was stable, safe, and good.

Even many of those who worked within the transmission apparatus, as curators, crafters, packagers, or presenters, would lose track, with time, of the extent to which reality had been folded over onto itself. Though they thought of themselves as a cut above the typical viewer, they too would seek out their favorite programs after a long day's work, sinking into the comforting assurance of their own significance that emerges from beholding a hyperreal drama in which one is a bit player.

Sometimes when the Guardians beheld the absorption of their charges, they felt astonished by the degree to which the New Entertainment was believed in—even those who railed against its content proved only rarely capable of disbelieving in its reality. Instead, the dissidents would propose alternate interpretations of the Tableau, which had the sole effect of strengthening the illusion. There were those among the Guardians who foresaw the inevitable outcome they were app-roaching—that they, or those who would succeed them, would be subsumed by the Entertainment as well. With every passing year it seemed to grow more difficult for recruitment to keep up with attrition, as every Guardian eventually mixed up the number of folded layers of reality and was swept away, no longer useful to the maintenance of the Noble Lie. For most of them, though, such issues provoked little concern; they continued to believe, with the same hubris which had allowed their forebears to enact their agenda in the first place, that there would always be those who were able to see through and manage the illusion that they were tasked with perpetuating. Like fierce but loyal dogs, they'd protect their sheep from the wolves of the mountains, though they no longer remembered their shepherd with any sort of clarity. Would he come back to them before long? Had there ever been a shepherd in the first place? Was the shepherd not, perhaps, some type of patient, clever wolf playing a longer game? Such questions were asked, though the answers were lost to living memory.

*

Two Producers share a congratulatory night-cap. Low though they rank among the Guardians, they've had the honor of being involved in true entertainment history. Tasked with engineering one of the periodic reboots of the Grand Tableau, their team has pulled off one of those boundary-breaking, epoch-altering stunts that is never quite appreciated in its time. It had only managed a few seasons' run—precisely half that of the last, phenomenally successful reboot of the Tableau. But though the previous iteration had generated passionate love and hatred[8] among the viewership and had brought with it record ratings, conflict, drama, and intrigue, it had not been artistically ambitious in the manner their recently canceled version had been. Hope and Change, and a cult of personality centered around a redeemer figure. It had been so pre-ironic.

Meanwhile, their program, as avant as a garde can be, had excited unprecedented passion in the viewers without resorting to the shallow Bruckheimerian shock and awe that had long been the stock-in-trade of the Producing class. In fact, our audacious Producers had ginned up a veritable orgy of fear and hate and hero-worship without any sort of action at all. Their main character—as oblivious and immersed a stage-player as ever had existed—had fatly and bigly typed on his endpoint-device as enraged factions of viewer-participants had swirled around in a passionate, though artificial, simulacrum of social upheaval. A character-driven tragicomedy, whose very occasional moments of gravitas had been punctuated by fart jokes and absurdist meta-irony, the most ground-breaking aspect of their program had been the self-aware manner in which it acknowledged its own hyperreality—something which our two Producers had taken to calling "breaking the fifth wall."

Think of it this way. A character addressing his audience ruptures the self-contained world upon the stage, reminding the otherwise absorbed and invested spectator that the stage's goings-on are a contrivance, thus breaking the fourth wall. This device was initially employed in the hope that such a rupture would jar the spectator out of his immersion, alienating him from the artifice of the drama-world before him and placing him back into firm contact with reality ("reality?"). This was done, however, with the expectation, justified in the epoch of the Old Entertainment, that the viewer's suspension of belief was a contrivance on some level. For our two Producers, to temporarily rupture an artificial reality in which the viewer's belief was fully invested, in which the viewers had been made unwitting stageplayers, was a qualitatively different action, the breaking of the hidden fifth wall—an artistic master stroke, but one that needed to be managed with extreme care.

What the modernists hadn't realized was that breaking the fourth wall wasn't simply a slick meta-referential device; it was a tantalizing, nigh-

---

[8] In the theory of the New Entertainment, hatred is viewed as just as worthy a mode of identification with an entertainment property as any other emotion.

irresistible call to the audience. "If they can reach us out here," the audiences of the increasingly interactive, late-stage Old Entertainment increasingly thought to themselves, "why can we not reach them in there?" They'd come surging in to populate the world of artifice through the newfound portal, located where once they'd thought there existed an impregnable barrier, finding life to be much more compelling over there, in the dramas they'd once passively beheld. Even a life well-lived contains a great deal more of the quotidian than it does of the dramatic, so it's no surprise that an ingress to the Tableau proved an alluring possibility. Thus had the transition begun.

It had taken a few generations to complete the process of acclimatization, but in time, there had arisen a new kind of man, one who easily crossed the thresholds between the various interactive dramas, inhabiting artificial realities without even fully recognizing that he was doing so. As the fully-integrated population grew, both in absolute numbers and relative to the population as a whole—as it did in leaps and bounds with every generation after the installation of the first endpoint-devices in viewers' dwellings—it became easier to truly believe in it, the Grand Tableau. Soon, children were born directly into the stageplay, never imagining that "reality" could be other than it seemed to them.

Such developments had been very much in agreement with the inner logics of the artifice world, in keeping with its "desires," if we may so speak, for in the artifice world there was a vacuum; its "reality" was unpopulated but for a few players on screens. The artifice-world required more stageplayers, more texture, to become real, and everything wishes to become real—except for humans, whose defining characteristic is the Will to Artifice.

These developments "set the stage" for our Producers, who resolved to occasion a second-order rupture to no end but that of artistic exploration. In so doing, they were playing a dangerous game. Make the rupture too unsubtle, and the stageplayers would realize that they'd been viewer-participants in a scripted meta-production all along and, in all likelihood, a madness would ensue. The Tableau could not be enacted without players, and the collapse of the Tableau would occasion horror, for all order had come to depend on the Tableau. And so, instead of the jarring manner in which, for example, Allen's Alfie addresses the viewer, the Producers communicated their rupture with oblique semaphores. When viewer-players cottoned on to the Producers' signaling and threatened to defect, the Producers had seen to it that these participants received new parts that they'd written up to route any potential troublemakers back into harmony with their post-meta-absurdo-super-duper-irono-sadistic symphony; the script, as they'd drafted it, had ample use for cranks and loonies, as well as those who believed themselves to be "breaking the conditioning," but who instead directed their energy at some artificial faction within the grand, harmonic scheme. On the whole it had worked fantastically. With the most elegant of choreography, the robotic dance was carried through without its cogs knowing aught of what they were caught up in—though there had, of course, been those few unfortunates who had well and truly woken up, and had had to be destroyed.

Why go through all this effort, flirting with truly catastrophic danger, simply to break the fifth wall? This was a question that the disapproving factions of the Guardians had incessantly asked, and it seemed as though they'd won in the end; the newest iteration of the Grand Tableau would be a stale reboot of the previous, pre-ironic incarnation. The rival faction would try its utmost to override the story arc of our Producers' artistic *tour de force*, scrub it from the canon, and reconverge with the tried and true themes which had carried them through the previous decades. The Producers' divergence from this tradition would, in the view of the rival faction, be seen as an abortive failure, a barren spur which shot off from the main body of the tree without producing fruit. Our Producers, half-sloshed, think differently. These audacious transgressors, who in earlier epochs would have conquered sea and land, had done what they'd set out to do. Somewhat unsteady and voluble, they assure each other that it was a seminal event in art history, albeit one which no one would ever know about outside the industry (which itself was rapidly dying off as increasing numbers of Producers and Guardians were swept away by the irresistible pull of the vacuum to become characters, stage-players, participants in the Tableau they'd once orchestrated). Even though it was all for naught, they slur to one another, it had been worth doing for its own sake. There, in the Hyatt ballroom just off the 495, they clink their glasses and go their separate ways into the Beltway night.

- The Last Rhodesian -
(Or, Thumos Calling)

"Screw your optics, I'm going in."
Bowers

His dream, his favorite fantasy, oft-revisited, is to casually cast down his life in a demonstration of steely resolve. *To throw his body on the gears*, as that shitbag commie put it back at Berkeley in the sixties. For only once you have given up everything can you be said to have been truly dedicated to a cause. Even to risk it all and survive, to blithely roll the dice and hit his number—such would suffice for the young man's purposes. What's most precious of all is the knowledge of the truth or falsity of one's deepest commitment, a knowledge that cannot be attained other than by being so tested.

To face his fate with the stoicism of McVeigh. To carry out the Act with Tarrant's brutal joviality. To select his target with Breivik's farsighted precision. To leave behind an immortal compendium of his thought, a manifesto on the order of Kaczynski's. These are his innermost desires.

The young man knows on some level that what he's doing is decadent and self-indulgent, not least because of the failures of previous terrorist endeavors to awaken any sort of nascent popular solidarity. He knows only too well that his heroes are heroes only to a particular sect of alienated outsiders who, before the dawn of the internet, would likely have had no contact with anyone else who thought the way they did. He knows it will be ineffectual, his Act, and that it will be ultimately inconsequential or even counterproductive. The only thing the Act will achieve will be the satiation of his otherwise unquenchable inner thirst. That old cliché, "it's easier to die for a cause than to live for one," seems to be posted more and more often on those little-known corners of the internet where the young man makes his spiritual home, for he and others like him are lurching closer to the brink with every passing day. The siren call of violence seems ever more irresistible, though for the moment he defies its lure.

It's true, incidentally. The cliché, that is. A life spent in the pursuit of any lofty goal is a hard and humble slog. Often it offers no payoff at all. How many forgotten lives are spent in the service of forgotten causes? How many days of donkey's drudgery in a life of humble striving? How drab such a life sometimes seems in comparison with the allure of a blaze of glory. Glory! However often the young man upbraids himself for the irrational nature of his lust for glory, it remains nevertheless a constant temptation.

Over and over, innumerable times per day, he tries to persuade himself of the fundamental illogic, the counter-productivity, the pig-headed stupidity of what he's got planned. The problem is that the feeling that drives him operates in an arational realm in which such arguments have no currency. Sooner or later he knows he'll find himself down in his basement once again, stacking and restacking his stockpiled ammunition, assembling, disassembling, reassembling his rifle. He'll peer intently at the bags of fertilizer stacked on a pallet in the corner, calculating and recalculating to reassure himself that It will be powerful enough (*It will*). And all the while, a feeling will grow in his gut, something like the queasiness of unsatiated lust. He *needs* it, this Act, and rationality be damned.

It is in Plato that he finally finds a name by which to call this ravening animal within him which will not be sated by reason. It is Thumos calling out to him, that irrational craver of honor and glory that translators have typically and utterly inadequately termed "the spirited faculty." The knowledge of an action's impracticality or even counter-productivity, appealing as it does to Logos, the rational faculty, does nothing to counter this siren song. Revenge is the only satisfaction for the man who is transgressed against, don't let no one tell you any different. And while the hegemonic ideologies of contemporary 'Murica and her satellites in Western Europe may have abstracted Thumos out of existence and put Logos in chains as a tool in the service of Eros, know that he still lives, our Thumos, though he's grown emaciated through his centuries chained in the intellectual dungeon.

To demonstrate the inadequacy of our approved political philosophies' attempts to explain the young man's rage via reference to material well-being (i.e. "socio-economic status" or, *shudder*, "utility"), know that he is by no means badly off, financially, this particular young man. Whereas insufficiently penetrating analyses of the current pathology of relatively widespread White male alienation tend to emphasize the deterioration of professional opportunity as a result of post-industrial America's ever-increasing wealth concentration, in conjunction with simultaneous in- and out-sourcing producing downward pressure on wages, the fact remains that a significant contingent of these newly dispossessed hold other motivations closer to their hearts.

Being a degree-holding homeowner with a well-above-average income, the young man's concerns cannot be effectively addressed by the accepted folk wisdom of his milieu—that all social strife is ultimately reducible to the exalted "socio-economic factors." Well aware though he is of the historically unparalleled luxury of his material conditions, he continues, helplessly, to stockpile munitions, striving all the while to leverage the other two faculties of his tripartite soul to restrain him from carrying out that Act, irreversible and brutal, which the beast-god of awakened Thumos demands of him as a sacred offering. He sates Logos with deep and varied reading, though the content of that reading often serves only to further rationalize the call of Thumos. He sates Eros with cheap wine and Tinder whores, but in the grips of wine's amplification of passion, beset by disgust with his own sexual profligacy and the ubiquitous degeneracy of the crumbling unsociety that is nominally his, the call of Thumos only becomes more irresistible.

There are, of course, a number of purported solutions to the combustible and endemic alienation of this young man's unsociety. In particularly intractable cases, one is encouraged to rationalize away the storms of one's passion, one's Achillean wrath, by "talking things out" with a "trained professional," and by medicalizing what is in fact an organic and righteous dissatisfaction with the manner in which Life has been nerfed and restructured into something that may suffice for rabbits or women, but not and never for a man. "Imagine a society that subjects people to conditions that make them terribly unhappy, then gives them drugs to take away their unhappiness." And when medicalization and psychologization, inevitably fail, never fear: a steady diet of Netflix and craft IPAs will do the trick. Heroin is preternaturally effective as well.

Feed Eros. This is the essence of the Modern strategy: make Eros mighty, that he may lay Thumos low. His power grows with every further step down into the warm and pungent mire of bodily fluids and psychoactive chemicals that the Moderns have ruthlessly battled to normalize. And as the tumor that is Eros metastasizes, his emaciated brother, Thumos, enchained, slowly wastes away. Logos, King of Kings, is made a servant, a mere means to further pleasure and consumption.

For many of the young man's contemporaries, this strategy seems to work just fine. At the digital marketing start-up in the sprawling megalopolis where the young man works, corralling data as his ancestors once corralled cattle, he is frequently astounded by the seeming contentment of the gleaming young scions at the desks around him. They are bright, cheery, and unfailingly pleasant. Most of them genuinely care about their job performance as a worthwhile good in itself, and not as something imposed upon them by Kapital. They have interesting hobbies to pursue in their free time, home-brewing beer, performing original indie-folk music, or collecting graphic novels. They despise the inanity of the slightly-more-mass-produced culture of Main Street: indeed, their contempt for Walmart and Fox News flag-wavers and gun-toters is equaled in intensity only by the reverence in which they hold NPR, the *Atlantic*, and the various progressive hashtags by which they define their worldviews (despite which reverence they nevertheless hold in positive regard the critiques of their more radical acquaintances, who castigate the aforementioned "progressive" milieu as mere neo-liberal apologism. This type of critique carries a certain cultural cache that the young man's contemporaries perceive and perpetuate, though they don't deeply understand it).

It is to be noted that the young man's feeling of alienation from his coworkers does not translate into perceptibly strained relations. Though he is seen as somewhat reserved or aloof, he is generally thought to be pleasant, competent, and, indeed, something of a "character." There was, of course, the matter of the office Christmas Party, during which the young man, after having had rather a lot to drink, had proceeded to rant to anyone who would listen about the evils of democracy and sexual degeneracy. But his polemic vitriol had had a self-aware, tongue-in-cheek undertone to it, and none of the office colleagues had taken it amiss. In fact, the incident seemed to have affected his reputation positively, solidifying his colleagues' impression of him as an intriguingly eccentric fellow. Among his coworkers, the young man has a certain number of people with whom to discuss shared interests over after-work beers, and on the whole, despite his alienation, he does not find the social environment overwhelmingly unpleasant. The work itself is neither dull nor stressful; he works at a moderate pace in a climate-controlled office, drawing a more-than-adequate salary in exchange for solving curious technical puzzles. In the standard utilitarian calculus, there is no accounting for his discontent.

And yet the Call of Thumos abides, and the young man's desperation only intensifies with time.

*

Only on certain Sunday evenings does the young man feel himself delivered, for a moment, from his own soul's turbulent siren song, when his oldest buddy, a dude he's known since grade school twenty-odd years ago, is able to chisel free a few hours usually taken up by his various duties. Once upon a time, during the summer vacations of their youth, they'd spent weeks on end in each other's company, but as is typically the case, life had interceded and grown more complicated, in particular for the buddy, a working-class hero with a mortgage and a young family. The scarcity of their meetings makes them all the more precious.

In summer they strap the buddy's cheap plastic canoe to the top of his mid-range family SUV and drive down to the stinking, toxic river, stopping off at a corner store for a cheap, domestic sixer. They park the car, unload the canoe, and struggle down the steep, muddy river bank. They plop the boat down into the languid water and are never able to alight without plunging a foot into the fetid muck at the bottom of the water. Once they've gotten their bearings and begun gliding along against the current, a peace descends. The city's traffic rushes over the river's bridges. Under the bridges are parallel civilizations of down-and-outs, some of whom call out as the friends pass by. Most of the calls are friendly, and even the profanity doesn't seem to be particularly threatening in this most peaceful of environments. Indeed, sometimes the young man and his buddy stop to chat with them for a moment.

Perhaps it is the case that the buddy's constant struggle to keep his head above the proverbial water, bearing stoically the weight of debt and paternal duty, distracts him from the calling of Thumos. Perhaps it is the innate balance of his soul which predisposes him to phlegmatic practicality. But for whatever reason, despite the fact that he listens patiently when his friend begins furiously monologuing, he remains more or less unmoved by political concerns. And even in those rare cases in which the two are of a mind, the young man's evident bloodlust draws only gentle disapproval from his friend. This disapproval casts a shadow of discomfort over their rare and precious outings, and so the friends have come to a tacit agreement to avoid the subject.

Instead they chew over the same ambitious plans they've been discussing for years without ever following through. A multi-stage bike trip through the paths of the county forest preserves—the buddy has even mapped out a route from up near the Wisconsin border, south through the western suburbs, curling all the way around the city through the south suburbs over the Indiana border, and ending up at the dunes. A weekend in Wisconsin or Michigan, camping, with fishing poles borrowed from the buddy's curmudgeonly father and a plentiful supply of booze. The West, with its broad skies and natural splendor.

As they reach the midpoint of their journey, turning around to allow the current to gently bear them from whence they came, they each crack a beer and become more voluble, their plans becoming increasingly unfeasible. Oktoberfest in Bavaria, or a jeep trek through the Australian outback. A Europe which is so far away as to be more or less undifferentiated, in the minds of these provincial Midwest Amerikaners.

When the future is exhausted, they revert to their shared past, recounting old adventures antagonizing mall security or picking fights with other packs of loitering adolescent teenage males. Sneaking into movies, straw-buying booze, smoking blunts under bridges. Long-gone buddies who've since moved on to better (or sometimes worse) things. Teachers who hated them. Teachers who found their mischief endearing. All the times they'd ended up dirty, sweaty, bloody, or soaked are fair game. In their friendship, only the present is neglected.

Eventually they wash back up where they'd cast off. Once again, they splash clumsily around, cursing, as they climb out of the boat and haul the plastic frame back up the muddy slope. It's always a chore to fasten the great unwieldy boat back to the roof of the car, with some crucial strap or bungie cord having somehow gone missing in the course of their brief trip. And it's dark and buggy, and each time they bitch and moan about how it's just not worth the effort to go for a little paddle, especially in such a sewer as their local river, though of course they'll be back in a few weeks. Only once they get back into the car for the five minute trip back to the buddy's house do they touch briefly on the present.

The buddy's blue collar job is under constant threat. His girlfriend's too. Their two kids are increasingly expensive. One is learning disabled. Their house is simultaneously run-down and expensive. The property taxes keep ratcheting steadily up. The young man commiserates. As a part of the commiseration, he alludes to the fact that there is much to be envied about his buddy's lot in life—he finds that this is fairly effective as a commiseration tool. And then the buddy will ask about the progress of the young man's fruitless Love Quest, about his general alienation from the people around him, his sense that his life is utterly lacking in compelling purpose. They make reference to the conundrum of the relativity of grass's greenness with respect to fence location. It's a brief conversation, with a good deal of silence interspersed. They shrug and sigh and grumble, and in five minutes they're back outside, bitching, as they detach the canoe and hang it up in the buddy's garage.

On these occasions, Thumos quiets, and for the moment, the young man is no longer a terrorist.

~ *Lies and Traps* ~

However much Tyler, in retrospect, would think of his friendship with Nick as having been a tyranny, and their eventual drifting-apart as having been a "getting-out-from-under-the-thumb-of," it's worth noting that Nick had never seen things that way. It's true that Nick was wont to sulk, berate, or even take violent revenge when his best friend sat in an uncustomary location in the lunchroom, or picked a different classmate as a partner on a project, or basically defied him in any way, be it something as simple as the movie they watched during a sleepover or the game they loaded up on the PlayStation. As unpleasant as this behavior had been for Tyler throughout their seven years of friendship, the fact was that it all sprang from the font of love and the attendant and all-too-common fear that love might stray. From fear of losing love sprang the tyranny of Nicky Morris, and though we might not excuse it, there's nary a one of us who hasn't acted on similar motivations in one way or another.

Whatever the unpleasant elements of their friendship, there is no denying the closeness of their bond. Since kindergarten, the two had been inseparable, and over the years they had gone through an awful lot together. While it's true that the power imbalance in the relationship was glaring, it's also true that Nicky had played the central role in getting his buddy, who had arrived in kindergarten unwilling even to make eye contact with his peers, to come out of his shell. He'd taught Tyler to brave the disapproval of teachers and parents, forced him to learn to stand up for himself, and even initiated him, via cable television (which Tyler's parents were dead set against), into a youth culture that provided him with a set of common references that allowed him to interact more smoothly with other kids their age.

Now though, as they entered adolescence, the power dynamic had shifted. Tyler had begun to resent his subordinate role, and the bond between them had begun to loosen. Having developed his social fluency and assertiveness, Tyler had even begun to exceed his best friend in popularity, and in recent months had been spending more and more time with Cedric and the skateboard kids, a group which tolerated Nick only begrudgingly, and that on Tyler's surety.

Nick had had to change tacks. No more was he able to tyrannize with impunity. In fact he increasingly found himself in a supplicatory role, attempting to lure Tyler back into his orbit with the gift of a spare handheld gaming console and an invitation up to his family's lake house in Michigan where they'd shoot guns and drive ATVs. He even begged his parents for a skateboard so he could attempt to hold Tyler close by adopting his friend's new hobby, though he lacked the nimbleness to get the board airborne, as well as the indifference to pain which allowed the skateboard kids to hurl themselves down ramps and off staircases. No matter what he tried, he could feel the friendship slipping away.

Still, despite the undeniable loosening of their bond in recent years, there was still a great deal holding them together. From the force of habit, to the convenience of walking down the street to each other's houses, to the genuine bonds of friendship that still did exist between them, the two boys continued to spend a good deal of time together, and it was no surprise to anyone that when the field trip was announced, Nick had called "dibs" on Tyler as his assigned buddy.

This was, of course, exactly the sort of controlling behavior that had begun to wear on Tyler in recent months, but within a few minutes of bouncing around in the back row of the yellow school bus, making faces at motorists and tossing whatever objects they could find at the backs of their classmates' heads, his momentary irritation at having been imperiously "laid claim to" had faded away, and they'd ended up having a lovely day at the Planetarium, learning precisely nothing and bringing the rest of the class's day to a screeching halt when they wandered away from the group to disrupt a presentation on constellations with their laser pointers. Tired and still somewhat giggly, it was on the ride back to school that the Lie entered Nick's mind, and presently exited his mouth.

It was the sort of easily investigable lie that could only have been told in a moment of pure dunderheadedness, such as when you're tired after spending a great day with a guy who once again feels like your best buddy, and all you want to do is keep the high going by sharing a secret, the content of which might inflate your depreciating worth in his eyes, and the act of sharing might succeed in fortifying your mutual sense of closeness, if only for a time. And so it was that Nick had implied, in a manner he'd thought was subtle at the time though it had no doubt been just as clumsy as the lie itself, that he'd engaged in certain quasi-sexual activities at a mutual friend's annual pool party with a female of unspecified identity. He'd proffered this information within the context of an oath to strict secrecy, but on some level he'd imagined or even hoped that the information would come out one way of another, as such things so often do, which would have boosted his reputation while affording him plausible deniability as to the source of the rumor. What he hadn't accounted for was the fact that the number of girls at the party could be counted, if not on one's fingers, then certainly on one's fingers and toes. Furthermore, the entire party had consisted entirely of mutual acquaintances, schoolmates who had known each other, in most cases, since kindergarten—there was none of the buffer of anonymity that an adolescent boy would typically make use of in such situations (e.g. "I met her at summer camp and she lives in Canada, so you don't know her, and her parents are really strict so that's why she can't call on the phone or otherwise prove her existence"). Almost as soon as it had left his mouth and his friend had responded with the sort of probing questions and teasing which are obligatory in such a situation, he knew he had made a grievous error.

Tyler, meanwhile, had known from the first that what his friend was insinuating was utter horse-hockey. There were a few kids in their seventh grade class who'd engaged in some sort of preliminary fooling around, but Nicky was not one of them. Unlike the few oversexed, unselfconscious, prematurely bearded individuals with respect to whom a rumor of sexual activity might have seemed at least plausible, Nick's voice had started to break, like, yesterday, and he had yet to move beyond the most utterly juvenile methods of interacting with the objects of his attraction (i.e. hair-pulling, backpack-stealing, or eating strange objects to get attention). The idea that he had seduced one of their female classmates and coaxed her up to their mutual friend's attic for a bit of over-the-clothes rubbing, even as the pool party was going on around them, was preposterous to say the least. Smelling bullshit, Tyler had reacted most craftily. Instead of immediately calling out the lie and proceeding to publicly roast his friend, he'd pretended to be taken in.

It was with an odd, instinctual guile that Tyler had gone back and forth with his friend, enticing him into making ever more concrete statements about the alleged events of that afternoon. Nick, though trying to remain elusive, was unable to overcome the urge to tantalize—there is a power that comes with ownership of a secret, and he hadn't the inner strength to abjure the rapt attention he was receiving as he gradually made his revelation. With every additional detail, Nicky staked himself ever more to what both boys knew was an absolute untruth, committing to specifics even though the whole foolish exercise hinged on his keeping everything vague enough to be able to maintain, half-truthfully, that he'd never said anything of the kind, if and when the rumor spread and eventually led to blowback in his direction. Thus did Nicky seal his fate.

It's worth noting once again that both the initial Lie and the subsequent Trap were undertaken with a profound lack of consideration. Neither boy quite knew what he was doing, much less why. Neither possessed, as yet, the wisdom to head off the social catastrophe they were building towards, even as both began to understand the inexorable logic of the situation and the unfortunate consequences it would inevitably lead to.

The very same instinctual guile which had led Tyler to outwardly accept his friend's lie had led him to a master stroke at lunch the next day. The two of them having sat down next to a well-known blabbermouth, it entered his mind to allude, in a private conversation that would be "accidentally overheard," to "that thing we talked about yesterday, you know, from the pool party." Nicky had responded in such a suspicious and guarded manner that the eavesdropper could not help but butt in and begin to press him—a situation in which Tyler could not be implicated as having done anything overtly malicious. The more defensive and cagey Nick became, the more he revealed that he did indeed have something important to hide and the more insistently the gossipmonger pressed him, the spectacle drawing the attention of other kids around the table, most of whom had themselves attended the pool party, which was one of the premier annual social occasions of their particular little Catholic elementary school. If something scandalous had occurred there, it was of interest to all and sundry, even to those unfortunates who hadn't received an invitation.

Tyler's vicious cunning revealed itself once again in the artful manner in which he broadcast to the table that his friend's secret was of a sexual nature, "letting slip" the pronoun "she" and then stopping short to demonstrate that this had been an inadvertent revelation. With this, it became a mere matter of time until the rumor reached the girls, at which point things would become all the more combustible. Nick could see the consequences coming, though he couldn't figure out how to change course; he would be known as a slanderer, a creep, and in these, the days of an ever more fraught sexual politics, even a borderline criminal. It was the sort of thing which could result in parents being contacted, in public humiliation rituals, and of course in irreversible damage to one's reputation. Watching his friend sweat, it began to dawn on Tyler as well; the potential enormity of this thing he'd set in motion for motives unclear. But he too was too young and too foolish to figure out an exit strategy.

Nick's evident discomfort made it impossible for him to claim that Tyler had fabricated the rumor from whole-cloth—everyone could tell just from looking at him that there was a *there* there. It never occurred to him to play it off as a joke he'd pulled on Tyler (the old "I was just screwing with you, and you actually believed it!" defense—never convincing, but conveniently unfalsifiable). Too young was he to know the face-saving power of simply owning up to one's lie, shrugging it off, and making it clear that you aren't going to provide the sorts of volcanic reactions which make prolonged teasing such irresistible fun. Instead, he just sat and sweated, responding with a combination of shame and defensiveness that only made the sharks swarm all the thicker.

Just as little as Nick could articulate the complex web of motivations that had prompted him to tell the lie—to increase his social prestige, sure, but there was a painful complex of emotions and desires with respect to his dying friendship which had been involved as well—so little too could Tyler articulate his motivations in playing such a nasty trick on a longtime buddy. There was the fermenting resentment he'd accumulated during the years of his friend's tyranny, and the alluring possibility of revenge. There had been a certain measure of that wanton, all-too-human cruelty which leads to ants crisped under magnifying glasses and tin cans tied to cat tails. But now, with the situation utterly beyond his control, and his friend bearing the onslaught with reddening face and tear-filled eyes, he felt utterly rotten inside.

The flames needed no more stoking. The mob did what mobs do, and it would not be sated without the sacrifice of a victim. Things played themselves out in the way they were bound to, and the friendship between the two boys never recovered.

- Of Mothers and Witches -

Danny's dad was a straight-laced type. Not entirely by his own choice, mind you, but nonetheless the sort of man for whom a six-pack of domestic beer, a Blue Jackets game, and a night of solitude in the darkened basement represented a rare surrender to hedonism. On such occasions, it was known to his three sons that certain of their father's exacting standards of behavior were liable to be moderately relaxed, as a result of which fun had been observed, on occasion, to ensue. The father tended, when in his cups, to become so engaged in his own monologues as to relate what one might characterize as somewhat age-inappropriate stories to his sons. They were not particularly seamy, these stories, for Danny's father simply didn't have any particularly debauched tales to tell. It was more that these often ordinary stories were colored by an underlying shade of jaded adulthood that the father, when sober, felt it important to protect his sons from prematurely experiencing. It was like a bit of the fatherly authority fell away and you'd feel like he was talking to you as an equal, even though he was also sort of talking past you at the same time. For these reasons, Danny rather liked his father's drinking.

It being a Thursday, the clink of bottles was rendered all the more unusual to the boy's ears, Danny's imposing mother having made an exception to her usual stringent proscription of weekday alcohol consumption.[9]

---

[9] Danny's was the sort of home in which it was not unheard of for the father to invent tasks

This particular weeknight, the father had returned from a particularly unpleasant day of work, during which he had been forced, due to a round of layoffs at the hotel, to act as the bearer of terrible news to an employee of his, the sort of thing which any decent manager takes real hard. He'd slept badly the past several nights out of dread and that night had come home glowering to find that his wife had purchased an exotic (by his standards) six-pack of *imported* English ale, a pizza with sausage and peppers, and a mid-sized stogie which she would never otherwise have suffered to enter her house except under such circumstances as Danny's father's current emotional upheaval.

She'd conducted him to the basement and parked him in front of the TV. She'd set the pizza and beer on the coffee table, kissed him on the forehead with seeming hesitation (they were the sort of parents who deliberately hid their physical affection in the presence of the children), and made herself scarce, glaring at Danny, who'd been minding his own business in a corner, in a way that meant "if you bug him now, I swear to God…." Then she'd gone off to grade social studies tests, later on leaving the house to retrieve Danny's older brothers from whatever extracurricular activities they'd been engaged in that evening.

And so it'd come to be that Danny and his dad shared the evening together, alone in total silence but for the television, the *psst* of opening beer bottles, and the occasional bursts of muttered invective—complaints of "that's shoulder on shoulder, these goddamn refs," or "you call that fucking hooking?!?" and so on, the expletives shocking in their novelty since the parents were assiduously attentive to the sort of language used in their home, cracking down even on such mild curses as "dang" or "crap" with threats of confiscated allowance. In times of drunkenness or home repair, however, Danny's dad had been known to grant himself exemptions.[10]

By the second intermission, four beers deep (Danny's father was the type to divide things evenly—two beers per period), the father had become rather more enlivened and verbally expansive. He gestured at the pizza.

---

for himself which required him to spend a weeknight hour or so in the garage, at which point the distinctive *psst* of a can of Coors would be heard to emanate therefrom, the imposing mother rolling her eyes at the man's ineffectual sneaking but not bringing it up afterwards— the fact that he snuck was tantamount to a submission to her authority, and his bungling ineptitude ensured that he'd never be able to put anything over on her, and she could store up these transgressions as ammunition for use in future marital conflicts.

[10] The mother, on the other hand, granted herself exemptions only in cases of particular idiocy on the part of automobile operators.

"Arentcha gonna eat?"

"I already did."

"You could pick off the peppers and give 'em to me,"—this being another exemption from everyday household rules, as gastronomical pickiness was typically heartily discouraged in Danny's house. The boy took a piece.

"Can't stand these idiots," the dad had muttered at the sports channel's intermission game analysis crew, a half-circle of suit-wearing former hockey stars reading off cue cards and pretending to be the best of buddies as they commented on the previous period's highlights. He'd started idly flipping through channels.

"Boy, I'll tell ya, life gets tough real damn fast." His voice is gravelly and Great Lakes-accented. He's short with pale eyes and thinning hair, the sort of middle-aged man who tucks his t-shirts into his jeans. Danny, eight, sits rapt in a way that is neither conscious nor constructed, the sort of attention only a child can give, where the body language is not tainted by the purposeful attitudes which adults learn to use to signal their active engagement. "You heard what I had to do today, huh?" Danny nods—the information had somehow filtered down to him via the older brothers. The father sighs. "Dmitri was with us three years. Good worker. Someone you hate to lose, you know?"

"So why'd he get fired?" asks Danny, hesitantly, not having quite pinned down the exact meaning of "lay-off."

Another sigh. "A business has gotta make money. It's been a bad year. Not enough guests to pay expenses. You've gotta pay employees, insurance, maintenance and upkeep—they had to shell out about a hundred grand, *one hundred thousand fucking dollars Danny*, fixing up the plumbing this year cause it's an old building—a hundred grand they don't have. Utilities. Stock for the restaurant. Linen for the rooms. A million little things that all add up. And Christ the lawyers—in this country you gotta spend on legal cause people sue at the drop of a hat. You have no idea. So they look over the balance sheets, figure out what costs to cut, what they can afford to lose. Always the same answer. Personnel. Lay-offs, every time."

"So they fired Dmitri?"

"Well… really they just tell me my payroll is eating up too much cash. They just say 'fix it,' and leave it at that."

"So you fired Dmitri?"

"I mean… well, yeah, basically. But not *fired*. Fired means he did a bad job. Means he deserved it. Which he didn't."

"I like him."

"That's right. You met him. At the company picnic." A pained expression crosses the father's face. "Jesus. Yeah, he was great. I never knew he knew all that outdoorsy stuff. You still do that blade of grass whistle thing, huh? God. By the end of the day all you kids were crazy about him…"

"But why Dmitri, Dad?" Danny's voice quavers a bit. He's remembering taking turns with the children of the hotel's employees being thrown by the big, bald, foreign-accented man off the dock and into the cold, choppy waters of Lake Erie.

"Well… it comes down to money, Dan. It's not a friendship kind of decision. I had to think about who we could do without. Where we could be short a man and still run the restaurant. Can't lose a waiter. We're swamped as it is. We're already paying Manny cash under the table to wash dishes which, yeah it's illegal, but what're you gonna do, gotta cut costs. But so you're not gonna find anyone cheaper and more reliable than Manny—and plus even if you cut him, he gets so little it's not gonna make that much of a difference. So I had to look at kitchen staff. And, well, Dmitri does a great job as a line cook but he didn't seem like he was going to be moving ahead in the organization. Plus he's older. More experience, so he gets more pay. Like it or not, the job is basically entry level. We can find someone right out of culinary school, someone who just needs the experience, pay him a fraction of what we were paying Dmitiri, and then potentially we have some young talent we can move into a higher-responsibility role when Felix or Iliana move on in a couple years." It's like he's trying to convince himself of the rectitude of his reasoning. When he looks over, he can see from Danny's face that the boy isn't satisfied. "It's horseshit, okay! It's shit for me; it's shit for Dmitri. But if we don't make the cuts, there's no hotel. If I don't do this, there's no work for eighty people, instead of one. That's what I'm saying. Life gets tough. You gotta learn to see two bullshit options and pick the one that's slightly less shitty. That's being a man." A silence.

"What did Dmitri say? When you fi—laid him off."

"…Well. He wasn't happy. He, well, he sort of let me have it. Not that I blame him. He's fifty-seven, fifty-eight… to be looking for work at that age is just… he's gonna have a hell of a time."

The intermission is over and for the moment they turn back to the game. The Jackets are up one on the Preds. It's been a dramatic game, the go-ahead goal having been a short-handed breakaway wrister that'd gone off the crossbar and in, in reaction to which Danny's dad had howled like a wolf. As the third period ensues, the father cracks his fifth beer and, regarding the bottle for a long moment, turns to Danny and says, "You might not see it yourself yet, but just know that it's a hell of a thoughtful thing your mom's done here." He gestures himself, simultaneously indicating the beer, pizza, and hockey. "Like, I've got buddies, old friends from high school who, when their wives try to do something nice it seems like they just make it worse somehow. I tell you all a man needs is quiet, beer, and mindless entertainment. Well, I suppose there's guys who read Proooost and drink, like, a vintage Bordeaux with a plate of charcuterie, more power to 'em. There's all types. But speaking for myself, there's nothing like an extended period of isolation and mind-numbing entertainment in a dark hole such as this very basement. Keep it in mind." He suppresses a burp as Danny sits awkwardly by, unused to being party to discussions touching upon his parents' relationship. "I wish I was so perceptive. Boy do I. In all these years, I have yet to figure out what to do when that lady's having problems. *Would that it were so simple as isolation and intoxicating beverages,*" he gestures dramatically in accompaniment to his uncharacteristic and semi-ironic use of the subjunctive. "It's something with talking, I've gathered. And listening. But not just listening—listening accompanied by a very specific sort of supportive talking that I frankly do not understand. I just outsource it. Take you kids out somewhere and leave her to commune with a woman friend. I'm sure it's not enough, but I'm trying, you gather?"

The Jackets set up a wicked deflection play from the blue line, a real pretty goal, but it's immediately put up for review, the officials suspecting goalie interference. For a minute or two, father and son watch, rapt, as multi-angle, super-slow-motion replays play over and over. "No way," says the father. "No way," echoes the son. The hometown announcers chime in their agreement. The officials do not agree, however, and the goal is overturned, the father bursting into bitter invective. Danny hazards a "damn," which sounds lame and hollow, as it always does when one curses unconfidently. The father notices and raises an eyebrow as Danny shrinks a little.

"Now, it'd be hypocritical of me to give you some lecture about bad language after the display I just put on, huh?" Danny nods very hesitantly. "You know why me and your mom are so strict about cursing?" Danny shakes his head. "Give it a guess. Think about it."

"Cause it's rude?" Danny responds in a pale voice. His dad clicks his tongue in irritation with the uninspired answer.

"Use your head, Dan." He would do this semi-regularly, drunk or not—demand an answer and put the boy on the spot.

"Um… cause people will get mad at you? Maybe they'll think you're mean?"

"I mean, you're getting there, approximately. Like, it's not so much they'll think you're mean exactly. Grown-ups say bad words all the time. I'm sure you've heard it, like, at a ball game or something, huh? Just joking around like. So it's not like people'll be offended exactly. It's just, there's people their parents never taught them don't swear, so they can't get through a sentence without bad language. They never got in the habit. And lots of them are, well, sort of lower class. Just makes you sound uneducated, dumb. So I'm not saying never say 'damn.' But what I'm really getting at is that you oughta be in control of exactly what's coming out of your mouth. Which, maybe I oughta take my own advice though, huh?"

"Well I don't mind if you swear sometimes," Danny replies, to which the dad chuckles through his nose.

The game enters into one of those weird lulls you see in hockey where no one can keep possession of the puck and nothing much of interest is going on—at least to the untrained observer. The puck'll sort of bounce around along the boards behind the net, where the defense picks it up and finds an outlet to the wingers who carry it up through the neutral zone and chip it deep into the opposite zone where it bounces along the boards behind the net, at which point the process repeats itself in the other direction.

Throughout the night, the boy's attention has been about equally divided between the game and his father—it's as if children have a greater total amount of attention to give, such that they can be engaged in two directions simultaneously in a way that is lost to adults. It's often hard to capture or channel this surplus of attention—thus the childish tendency to be reverently engaged in a pursuit in one moment and in the next to be swept away into a chaos of undirectedness, or perhaps a multi-directedness that only appears chaotic to the adult onlooker. But here in the dark, damp-smelling basement, with nothing to draw him back into the disorder of the idle spirit, Danny raptly observes both the events of the hockey game and the expressions which play across his father's profile, flickeringly lit by the television. The father speaks to Danny out of the corner of his mouth.

"What the hell was I talking about? Before the goal?" They both ponder for a moment. "That's right, your mom, and… God, I dunno. Just that men and women are different. I feel like people don't say it enough. Like, you're not supposed to say it. But if you go through your life thinking there's no difference then, well, you might end up getting surprised, so it's important you know about it, although for God's sake don't tell your mother, she'll... look, did I ever tell you about the Ferettis?"

Danny's dad had proceeded to tell his son a story to illustrate his point about gender differences in communication strategies, which story Danny'd related to me some years later.[11]

*

There had been a couple at Danny's father's high school, both parties of which Danny's dad had known since the early years of grade school. *Thoroughly mediocre* was more or less the extent of what you could say about them, he'd said. Boy's daddy was a mechanic, mom stayed home. Girl's daddy drove a truck, mom worked part time at the Kroger in Hudson, the one that's a Target now. Both families'd had a whole crowd of kids. They were children of parents who were themselves children of folks born and raised in northeastern Ohio, all of which was normal back then—the functional, intact working-class families with crowds of children, dwelling inter-generationally in one basic region. Both had grown up in big houses in the inner ring of Cleveland suburbs, houses which had been feasible for such families to purchase at the time. The boy and girl had been middle children who'd worn nothing but hand-me-downs until they'd found independent sources of income, starting with the cash-in-hand odd jobs that you'd get in your early teens (e.g. babysitting, lawn mowing, paint scraping, weed pulling) and followed by the low-wage service jobs which were abundant and accessible to high school students in those days. Such jobs also used to be flexible regarding school schedules and after-school activities in a way that such unskilled jobs are no longer required to be, what with the illegal Mexicans waiting in the wings to snap up your position as soon as you tell your boss at the Dairy Queen you've got, like, basketball practice after school or whatever, all willing to work forty-plus hours for minimum wage or below—so who's gonna hire a sixteen-year-old to work ten, fifteen hours a week? (This last bit of editorializing added in by a young-

---

[11] The adult version of Danny had paused to explain to me that his mother, as an initiate of the cult of Education, tended to view gender differences as relics of patriarchal social structures and thus would not have taken kindly to the father's "essentialist" tendencies—this being the reason for the whole "don't tell your mother" thing.

adult, marginally employed Danny, whose politics had veered towards
something more hardline than the merely nativist during the Obama years.)

But so they'd taken the meager earnings of those entry-level jobs, this
mediocre girl and boy, and gone to the movies, took the train into Cleveland
to sneak into concerts, and adorned their physical persons in the
unfortunate fashion of the mid-seventies. They'd acquired cases of beer
through straw purchasers and consumed them in the woods with friends,
Danny's dad among them, always in a sort of fun and experimental rather
than addictive and unhealthy way. Summer of junior year, they'd lied to
their respective parents (the boy claiming he was visiting a grade-school
friend who'd moved to Michigan, the girl saying she was spending the
weekend at a friend's summer cottage) and conducted an ill-fated though
fondly remembered tryst, which had been discovered almost immediately
by their respective parents and punished by several weeks of grounding.

The mediocrity of these two youths manifested itself in the academic
realm as well. Each had received grades throughout the entirety of their
respective academic tenures that indicated unambiguously that neither was
destined for post-secondary education, nor for the ranks of the professions.
The parents had shrugged at the steady Cs or perhaps gently admonished
their not particularly high-achieving offspring. But the fact was that these
kids were not prone to truancy. They were seen to complete their
homework with a respectable degree of diligence, occupying the kitchen
table in the evening hours and squinting studiously at thick tomes of, like,
trigonometry or whatever; classes their parents had never even taken, let
alone aced. They weren't on drugs. They weren't criminal, disobedient, or
insolent beyond the expected and tolerated degree of adolescence. They
were just average, which was okay in those days, at least in Danny's dad's
part of town.

And so, post high school, the average boy had gotten a job in sales at
some place or other; Danny's dad had recollected that it had been a
company that repaved driveways, or something of that sort. It was the sort
of gig where a high school diploma and a winning smile got you hired,
which in turn gave you a shot at an upwardly mobile lifestyle, at least in
comparison with, say, the guys who did the actual repaving, who were
drafted from the ranks of the diploma-less and non-charming. Meanwhile,
the girl had taken a touch-typing class and found a position of a secretarial
nature which required her to dress up and take the train into the city. They
were betrothed by this point, or perhaps shortly afterward. Both sets of
parents had been sufficiently approving of the match as to allow the young

adults to remain at their respective homes after graduation, so as to give the couple time to amass funds for a down payment on a house.

Then the wedding, of course, which Danny's dad had not attended but had heard about. A run-of-the-mill Catholic ceremony, followed by an open bar and a mulleted band at a suburban banquet hall. According to one of the father's friends who had been in attendance, the reception had featured a laser show and a synthesizer, which tells us all a little something about the peculiar era that was the late seventies. Thence followed the inevitable house purchase, a little further out into the boonies than where they'd grown up. This, incidentally, had been the pattern followed by the past several generations of Danny's family as well, his grandparents having grown up in the city of Cleveland itself, his parents raised in the inner ring suburbs, and Danny himself having been born far enough out as to have had school fellows who wore trucker caps and listened to country music, which pattern had occurred as a result of the Africanization[12] of the city proper and the fact that the inner ring of suburbs had become prohibitively expensive, everything having been bought up by the increasingly long-lived older folks. The new house, the one purchased by the young couple, had been a split level of moderate size, conveniently located near the highway, with ample land for playing children and backyard barbecues.

The obvious and mediocre next step was then initiated: namely, the begetting of children. Thus, within a year of marriage, the secretarial job was abandoned; an unformed, squalling, pink blob brought forth; and an entirely new phase of life begun for the young couple. The husband, supercharged with motivation for the first time in his life, sold driveways like a man possessed and was therefore rewarded with a promotion, becoming the immediate supervisor of the diploma-bearing, winning-smiled, average White youths who were hired to fill his place on the front lines of door-to-door sales. This new position afforded the young man significant time in the company office, where he would network with the "big-wigs" of the twenty-person office staff: the accountant with his CPA license and old-fashioned hat; the recruiting and personnel people with their university degrees; the heir, some five to seven years the young man's senior, fresh out of business school, irritatingly sleek and confident; and the old man himself, who'd built the whole thing up from scratch after a stint on a road construction crew had provided him the capital and know-how

---

[12] A term inserted by Danny in his retelling, which would certainly not have been used in the father's original version.

necessary to procure and deploy the used paving equipment he'd hauled around with him as he made his door to door rounds, doing it all by himself until he'd gotten enough momentum to hire paving contractors, salesmen, accountants, et al., at which point he'd devoted himself exclusively to cigars and automobiles, meting out the occasional rambling tongue-lashing he seemed to think necessary to the functioning of an efficient workplace.

In other words, the young man had stumbled, despite his thorough-going mediocrity, upon the makings of what amounted, almost, to a white-collar career. In the meantime, the woman had very much taken to motherhood. She had mastered the entirety of her own mother's Midwest-American, salt-and-pepper, meat-and-potatoes culinary repertoire and had begun to subtly push her new mother-in-law towards the eventual revelation of her husband's family's culinary secrets.[13] She was enchanted with her son and reverent toward the budding personhood that seemed more evident within him with every passing day, in the as yet non-verbal sounds he made, in the ever-more efficacious movements of his body and in the ever-more expressive workings of his face. She savored the extent to which her husband had come to rely on her to serve as the curator of a distinct and protected space that was his, hers, and theirs.

Did they suffer? Sure. On many occasions, the woman felt cheated of the excitement and bustle of her secretarial job; missed the crush of commuters alighting from the Rapid at Terminal Tower, the barges on the noxious Cuyahoga, and the eminence of Cleveland's provincial approximation of a major US city's skyline. She missed the fellowship of the tough, independent middle-aged women who were her secretarial comrades; the overbearing and condescending but on the whole enter-taining young college-educated men; and the even more condescending and peremptory (and occasionally lascivious) older men who ran the place. She had, it's true, reimagined this phase of her life into something more glamorous and exciting than it had in fact been,[14] but the constructed

---

[13] For the record, the mother-in-law's *oeuvre* had been largely similar to that of the girl's mother's, but for a smattering of vestigial Italianisms, the events of this story having occurred subsequent to the White American ethnogenesis, at a point where the cultural standardization of the post-War era remained in force. Thus the two mothers were trained in a style of unpretentious Midwest American cookery that was largely homogeneous. The young woman however had wished to avail herself of the aforementioned smattering of vestigial Old World ethnic culinary vocabulary, being particularly covetous of the mother-in-law's confidence with such exotic ingredients as garlic, eggplant, and basil.

[14] The woman, much older, had nodded with recognition when HBO's *Mad Men* had first

memory nonetheless fed the flame of her occasional dissatisfaction. Meanwhile, the young husband had found himself afflicted, occasionally, by waves of envy and resentment for the unshackled and sexually exploratory youths he was tasked with training, and by pulses of bitter jealousy towards the sleek and confident heir, who had begun his climb up the professional dominance hierarchy from the advantageous perch allotted to heirs and degree-holders, who remained, as yet, free to climb even higher; his potentiality relatively unbounded, unburdened as he was by concerns of home and family. So yes, as is the case with all emotionally normal humans, the young couple occasionally resented each other, their employers, themselves, their birth families, their circumstances, life generally, and even—and this is a hard pill to swallow for those with an overly optimistic understanding of humanity—even their baby itself, now approaching two years old, beginning to become truly ambulatory and verbal. On the whole though, the members of the young family felt themselves to be loved and mutually supported, purposeful and forward-moving—that is, they felt themselves to be very lucky indeed.

*

I interject to make clear that the preceding has in fact been nothing more than set-up for the story which Danny's father told him that night, halfway through beer six, the closing seconds of the Jackets game draining away unobserved as father and son became utterly engaged in speaking and listening respectively. The preceding set-up had been necessary in Danny's retelling of the story to me, unacquainted as I was with the various recurring characters who'd formed the cast of Danny's childhood neighborhood. However, for eight-year-old Danny, much of this background would have been more or less unnecessary—the basics of the Ferettis' marriage, for instance, having been long known to Danny due to Mrs. Feretti's status as the sort of neighborhood fixture who attracts the whispers of children: the kind of broken, isolated woman your mom tells you to be nice to but also somehow, without ever quite saying so, discourages you from seeking out; the prematurely aged woman around whom accretes a spooky mythology in the shared consciousness of the neighborhood kids—and because of this

---

come out, to give you an idea of the degree of her idealization; one can be sure that the mid-sized, late-seventies Cleveland-area property management firm, post workplace sexual harassment reforms no less, had been rather less than Draperesque in reality.

status as local curiosity, also the sort of person one asks one's parents prying questions about, as a result of which questioning eight year old Danny had already been fairly familiar with much of the backstory related above.

The meat of Danny's father's story had been the following: the young father, driving along one early 1980s afternoon with the boy in the back seat, had failed to effectively monitor the activities of the newly ambulatory child. To do so would have been unfeasible for any human being of two eyes and two arms, the father's attention having been engaged with the expressway before him. All of this had occurred in an era before the installation of child safety locks was industry standard, as well as before the advent of contemporary attitudes towards the mandatory use of car-seats for young children. The newly ambulatory child had inquisitively grasped at the car door's brilliantly shining interior handle and had tumbled out onto the middle lane of I-271. Danny's father, in his cups, had illustrated the impact with a graphic, onomatopoetic squishing sound. The father, rather than face his wife, had seen fit to dispatch himself in the closet of the police precinct to which they'd brought him, making use of his belt, a chair, and a closet rod, an event which Danny's father had likewise related to his son in an uncharacteristically graphic fashion.

At this point, the horn had sounded, signaling that the hockey game had come to an end and distracting the father from his monologue. He'd cursed himself for having missed the end of the game, finished his beer, and watched a bit of the post-game show to catch any replays of the last few minutes that they might show. Then he'd gone out to the porch to smoke his cigar, having forgotten to explain to his son the lesson which he had gleaned from this unfortunate story.

*

Danny had told me all this as the sun dipped below the scraggly trees, the two of us sitting with beers in the lawn chairs he kept in his garage for the express purpose of sitting in the driveway and drinking beer.[15] It couldn't have been identical to the way his dad had told him the story fifteen or so years back. All the broader social subtexts which had inflected Danny's retelling—the digressions into reactionary politics (largely excised from my retelling of the retelling), the idealization of the bygone era of the

---

[15] He'd previously kept the lawn chairs outside in the driveway, but they'd gone missing (for reasons to be explained imminently), after which he'd taken to storing them in the garage.

Boomers—must have been shaded in after the fact by a Danny who was bitterer than I remembered him. I was not quite sure at first what to make of this embitterment. I'd come to visit him, my cousin, during a period of personal dysfunction. Something had drawn me back to the place that was, for better or worse, all I had for an ancestral homeland, a drab section of northeastern Ohio where generations of my antecedents had spent their days, though I myself had never lived there. Danny was the only one left.

I'd driven all day to get there, having been released from a harrowing two weeks in the psych ward at Chicago Lakeshore Hospital the afternoon before. As I'd exited the Ohio Turnpike, the last glimmers of daylight had flickered chaotically through the unevenly clad branches of the trees which framed that asphalt line, seemingly Euclidean, perfectly straight and infinite. I'd wondered again why exactly I'd decided to come, what exactly it was I expected to find. It had been one of those pale, fitful autumn days, cloudless but somehow still gray. I had begun the day driving into the sun with squinted eyes, but by the time of my leaving the Turnpike, the shadows had begun to stretch out into the East, the sun behind me, the gray of the sky maturing into reds and golds which stained my rearview mirrors.

After leaving the interstate, there remained a half hour or so of driving, a route possessing a deep, soft familiarity extending back into the half-remembered haze of car-seats and a two-parent household—half-remembered in point of narrative fact, yet doubly-remembered in terms of emotional weight. As stated, I'd never lived in Ohio. It was a place I would wake up to after excruciatingly many hours of cramped half-slumber in the back rows of the childhood minivan. Ohio was a place with stars in its sky; a place with a smell of grass and open space; a smell of, okay, not quite nature, but of something at least fresher than Chicago's exhaust and garbage. Ohio was a place with roads whose winding provided me with a plausible excuse to slam into my brothers in the back row of the minivan, provoking the sort of low-level half-serious fraternal strife which is so oddly magnetic to a young boy. Ohio had felt wild and limitless, a place of running streams and wildlife to be inspected. Never mind that the vast wildernesses of my remembrances had in fact mostly been, in retrospect, narrow strips of carefully curated faux-forest, cultivated to provide homeowners with the illusion of privacy and to separate the subdivision from the Walmart and the Walmart from the interstate. This Ohio was still imbued with the significance of remembered woodland wandering, a rare treat for this city kid; a paradise of muddy boots and falls through thin ice purposely tested up to and beyond its limits by the red-cheeked unsupervised boys of my extended family, one of whom had been Danny—those woods becoming, in later years, the clandestine testing ground for firecrackers and pilfered cigarettes. The roads of this particular patch of northeastern Ohio, undistinguished in themselves, represented, to me, the final stretch in a journey to a realm made mythical by the weight of memory.

It struck me, more heavily than it had when I'd first heard the news, that my Grandparents' house was now unoccupied, Grandma having died and Papa having been moved into assisted living. That destination of a lifetime of Christmas Eve treks through blizzard conditions had been rendered a lifeless ruin of brick and mortar, structurally sound yet devoid of that which had rendered it meaningful; emptied out of the hordes of relatives who would descend upon it the afternoon of the 25th, the khaki-slacked legs and middle-aged bellies encased in garish, knitted wool forming a maze through which we kids would thread ourselves until we were banished to the basement, at which point the real rough-housing would begin.

These fondnesses now resided in dead memory. When Grandma'd died, attendance of the holiday get-togethers had plummeted. I myself hadn't been back since, the obligations of grad school having been my excuse. There had long been a trickle of migration, emigration. In my earliest years, indeed, I can remember how the oldest of the cousins had begun earning their various degrees and departing for pastures greener than those of poor old Cleveland. But with Grandma's death and the coming-of-age of a number of the younger cousins, the trickle had become a hemorrhage. All my cousins had recognized the critical importance of that predominant sorting mechanism of the post-industrial USA, namely the university, as a proxy for cognitive talent. That unprecedented force had, in the course of a mere few generations, denuded the US hinterlands of their most precious and promising intellectual prospects; funneled them into elite, coastal educational institutions; and settled them in enclaves of their fellow gifted, in which enclaves had been formed a high and haughty culture, one progressive and cosmopolitan outlook uniting the New Yorker or the San Franciscan more with the Londoner, Berliner, and Singaporean than with the Akronite or the Waupatoan. For this reason, the majority of my relatives had made sure to be well prepared for the SAT, performing well enough to leave Ohio forever behind. Except for Danny.

My parents had formed the vanguard of this migration, seeking and finding their respective fortunes among the ranks of the professional class in the late eighties, before my birth. They had been the first of their siblings, my aunts and uncles, to do so. By now, even their generation had largely dissociated and dispersed. Uncle Jack had taken a job at a hospital in Philly. Aunt Jenny had found herself boxed into middle-management and escaped to a more enticing opportunity in parts Southwest—her kids were gone anyway, she'd said, implying that there was nothing in particular attaching her to the earth upon which she'd coincidentally happened to have been born. Danny's imposing mother had made a late-stage career change and was pursuing a PhD in Boston, while his father had obtained a position at a significantly larger hotel in Florida. They'd divorced, of course, Danny's parents, though they'd stuck it out until his high-school graduation. The oldest generation was extinguished but for our ailing, disoriented grandfather. As stated, Danny was the last remaining member of our clan to make his home in Ohio.

He'd come out into the driveway to greet me with a beer and a brief hug of the masculine, back-slapping variety. He resided in his childhood home, which looked rather the worse for wear as a result of Danny's stewardship. He had never been particularly concerned with outward appearances. It was a ranch house with a to-my-urban-eyes quite expansive backyard. His parents had simplified the divorce proceedings by entrusting it to him, meaning he had only to cover the property taxes with his meager pizza shop manager's wage.

The neighborhood had become dismal in the prevailing years. Boarded up houses and futureless youth. A pall of hopelessness in the very air. There was a collapsing shanty of a house right on Danny's street, where a couple of gray-skinned young people flopped lifelessly amidst a collection of empty beer bottles on the concrete slab of a porch, their cigarettes burning down to their fingers, their various piercings sparkling in the setting sun. They'd looked seventeen or eighteen. It was my inquiry as to this very house which had, in fact, occasioned Danny's retelling of his father's story, this being the aforementioned Mrs. Feretti's longtime residence. Of recent events in the life of Mrs. Feretti, Danny had had quite a lot to say.

*

By all accounts she'd borne most admirably the burden of her family's unceremonious implosion. She'd never remarried, never replaced the departed child. Instead, she seemed to have filled that void with a zeal for civic-oriented behavior. Parish fish-fries. Town council meetings. A decade of involvement with the Girl Scouts. Additionally, she had returned at long last to the relative glitz and glamour of downtown Cleveland to take a job as an administrative assistant[16] at a law firm. Somehow, due to events unbeknownst to Danny, she'd ended up at a non-profit operating out of a well-appointed office in a newly rehabilitated former factory in The Flats.

Lionel Schwarz's People to People 501(c)(3)[17] was devoted, in a phrase, to serving Cleveland's down and out. They housed the homeless, fed the hungry, and were early adopters of the harm-reduction approach to addiction outreach (needle exchanges, safe injection sites, etc.). It being the mid-nineties, the age of "superpredators"[18] and an era in which politicians of every stripe competed for the honor of being considered "tough on crime," it is no surprise that P2P ran frequently afoul of a police force that still enjoyed widespread public trust, and could not therefore be easily cowed by the demands of activists and their partners in the media. Though she'd started off on the drearily non-ideological administrative side of things, Mrs. Feretti had found herself more and more drawn to the activism that gave her a profound sense of meaning. Her regular participation in various sorts of direct action brought her into frequent and contentious conflict with agents of The Law, for whom she began to develop an unbridled contempt.

Riding around in the P2P van and devotedly ministering to the "down and out" denizens of areas of Cleveland so blasted as to seem post-apocalyptic, Mrs. Feretti had gradually earned a degree of acceptance and recognition from those very denizens. She prized this above all things. She began to neglect the suburban civic functions whose execution she'd previously seen to so assiduously. Danny had theorized that the urban denizens' dependent status had tended to a previously unnourished maternal impulse of Mrs. Feretti's, for which reason (he proposed) the acceptance and recognition of these grim specimens had been of more worth to her than the acceptance and recognition of the prosperous suburban community which had already accepted and recognized her.

With time, Mrs. Feretti assimilated to the ideological ethos of P2P, an interlocking set of seemingly divergent concerns, duties, and commitments. The sheltering of illegal immigrants (just as radical a position in the nineties as was the harm-reduction approach to addiction care pursued by P2P).

---

[16] Administrative assistant having been the preferred term in the 1990s, rendering "secretary" outmoded and even slightly offensive.

[17] Be it noted that Danny pronounced "Lionel Schwarz" with a certain nasal, East Coast, stereotypical ethnic accent.

[18] t. Hilldawg.

Anti-eviction protests. Direct actions against police brutality. All punctuated by the periodic hurling of flaming debris. Perhaps it was mysterious to her that these seemingly disconnected political positions somehow hung together, though I see no indication, at least in Danny's narrative, that Mrs. Feretti had been particularly engaged with political theory in her earlier years. Perhaps she had wondered, at first, why it was that the cheery, Catholic retirees of the Night Ministry, who spent their nights distributing foodstuffs and comfort to those who needed them, were regarded not as natural allies in the fight against poverty and deprivation, but were instead held in universal contempt by the P2P crowd. Sure, the Night Ministry folks mixed some Jesus in with their soups and sandwiches, but it couldn't be denied that the soups and sandwiches (and condoms and needles) distributed from the P2P van had their own ideological adulterants. Whether or not Mrs. Feretti initially asked such questions, however, it became evident that she had undergone an extensive ideological overhaul within the span of a few years.

In solidarity with the Occupy Movement, she and some of her new compatriots had staged an occupation of the township's meeting hall, disrupting a school board meeting and eventually being led out in handcuffs by a very confused Officer Stuart Boscovic, a former classmate of Feretti's, who'd repeatedly wondered aloud at her seeming desire to be arrested, saying "Jesus Molly, we get it, no one here's trying to, like, suppress you or nothing, but you gotta just calm it down—there's a meeting going on for Christ's sake." This had been relayed to Danny's dad by Danny's civically engaged mother at the dinner table the next day, both shaking their heads sympathetically.

She'd gone on to lobby for the construction, first, of a halfway house for juvenile offenders and later a receiving center for refugees, conducting her public advocacy in a hostile and accusatory tone which her fellow residents had found to be more baffling than offensive. Again, they shook their heads in pity, remembering the tragedy that had befallen Mrs. Feretti in her youth.

Though she was ultimately unsuccessful in her lobbying for those particular large-scale projects, she met with less resistance in other endeavors, most notably a voucher program which saw several "dis-advantaged youths" from East Cleveland granted tuition-free access to Danny's Catholic high school. And when one of the "youths" had become mired in legal troubles after a certain "sexual misunderstanding" with a cheerleader, Molly Feretti had been front and center in the ensuing controversy, wielding the word "White" with a vicious sting, in response to which the White residents of Waupatoic county, so entrenched in their normative Whiteness as never to have consciously racialized themselves,[19] were simply nonplussed, baffled, and unable to react. She'd featured prominently in the coverage of what had developed into a national news story, publishing editorials in the Cleveland Plain Dealer that got picked up by HuffPo. Some years later she'd been interviewed for a BBC retrospective documentary that had focused primarily on the social struggles of the other "disadvantaged, urban" voucher recipients in the aftermath of the rape (the documentary interspersed with black and white photos of Emmett Till, drinking fountains, firehoses, and various domestic terrorists, both bowl-cutted and khaki-shorted—"typical kike-engineered guilt propaganda," in Danny's words). When BLM had arisen in the following years, she'd been a vocal participant, though she'd taken on a supporting role, removing herself to the proper, respectful distance which Allies must assume towards POC. And of course, with the advent of Trumpism, she'd cranked up her advocacy to a keening pitch.

Of note is that Waupatoic County, historically a working-class Democrat stronghold, which went to Obama in 2008 and only narrowly to Romney in 2012, went overwhelmingly MAGA in 2016.

When the zombified-looking youths had taken up residence in the Feretti house, accompanied by rumors that Mrs. Feretti was running an informal drug rehab or perhaps even a halfway house, the residents of Waupatoic had had enough. Danny assured me that it was certainly no rehab, which I could confirm from the beer bottles I'd seen strewn about. But when the matter had been brought to discussion at the next meeting of the town council, Mrs. Feretti had surprised them all by showing up with a sheaf of documents in hand establishing the Whole Soul Youth Home as a subsidiary of Lionel Schwarz's—once again, Danny pronounces Schwarz's name in a grotesque parody of a Jewish accent—People to People 501(c)(3), as well as certifying the house as an official dispenser of addiction and homelessness alleviation services, recognized by the state of Ohio.

Mrs. Feretti had gone on to tell them all how despicable she found it all; their lily-White NIMBY-ism, their callous disregard of the most

---

[19] Indeed, the "thing to do" in Middle American polite society is to implicitly deracialize oneself—a cultural norm enforced at all levels of White society; except, of course, for those much despised, looked-down-upon, and generally lower class sorts who bore the title "Racist." Thus the bafflement.

disadvantaged and marginalized products of *their* society. As usual, the Waupatoans were more baffled than incensed by their onslaught. But as Mrs. Feretti began to really hit the stride of her rant, Linda Green, a plump older woman, mother of three grown children, and a person whom Danny had seen at every St. Matthias parish fair, every Fourth of July parade, every high school football game of his childhood, stood up and broke quietly but forcefully in.

"Molly, I just don't understand why you're doing this. We all know this isn't a rehabilitation service you're running. You can smell the marijuana on the street—on *our* street—and we all know it's coming from your house. I was out with the dog and I could smell it just yesterday, in the middle of the afternoon! I've never heard of such a thing—you call this rehabilitation! Molly you've been a neighbor for coming up on thirty years now. And you've been a part of this town for just as long. We've been watching with confusion and sadness as you've become somebody we don't recognize any longer, but we've minded our business. This is a step too far. People've had possessions go missing, which is, well, that happens from time to time— things can be replaced—but now we're hearing about our kids being offered, well, drugs. Hard drugs. In our neighborhood. You can call it a rehab if you like but I'll call it what it is—it's a flophouse. Full of junkies. On. My. Street. There's no other way of saying it. You can go on saying how it's so bad that we're White, if you want. You can talk about abandoning the 'disadvantaged' or the 'marginalized' 'til you're blue in the face—I'm a Christian and I'll happily do my part. But you have to be reasonable. You have to look at it from our side."

At this point, things had apparently taken a turn for the disorderly, Mrs. Feretti taking exception to the implication, *totally without merit, lacking any evidence*, that her kids—*"her kids"* is what she called them, Danny had emphasized—had had something to do with thieving. She'd apparently held forth at length, although my impression of this grand monologue is admittedly rather garbled, first because the environment in the town hall had been so chaotic, and second because its content had been related to me by a Danny who hadn't been able to get through his account of it without collapsing repeatedly into helpless laughter.

She had apparently launched into Linda Green for "privileging 'sober' consciousness," and imposing a false construct of normative sobriety. Danny had explained, between violent giggles, that it was basically a "copy-paste+find-replace" of the "health at any size" mantra of the Fat Acceptance Movement. Mrs. Feretti had gone on about the "oppressive essentialism inherent in the social construction of a 'natural' state of consciousness when, in fact, all consciousnesses exist at the intersection of various spectra, with the privileging of 'so-called' sober consciousness being a mere imposition of the supposedly neurotypical (who all too often happened to be heterosexual White males) upon the cognitively diverse."

Things had really spun out of control when Linda Green had stood up to interrupt the bizarre rant and had made a, to Danny's eyes, utterly innocuous move to walk towards Mrs. Feretti, which had provoked an aggressively defensive response from some of the "disadvantaged youths," because yes, by this point Mrs. Feretti had apparently begun to go about her daily business in the company of an entourage of sullen, brown-hued followers. Things had nearly become violent.

There had been calls made to the Ohio Department of Health & Human Services, requesting that the status of the Whole Soul Youth Home be revisited, which had come to nothing, Danny'd said, "Cause when your name's Schwarz, there's certain things available to you that's not for the likes of us goyim." The local police had responded to a series of calls regarding the house and had made a few arrests the first time around. The second time, however, they'd found nothing. They took to patrolling the area of their own initiative, but after some months of this behavior, Vice Media released a ten-minute documentary on a certain group of young POC attempting to fight drug addiction and various other sorts of adversity with the help of a certain White female ally, only to be targeted and harassed by the police force of a White, Midwestern township. After a national outcry and a great deal of negative media coverage, all police attention had been stopped.

Mrs. Feretti had gotten her children, some of whom were undoubtedly in their mid-twenties, enrolled in the local high school, where they proceeded to take on leading roles in such student organizations as the Gay-Straight Alliance or the Waupatoic High School Students of Color or even the various student councils. "Her army is growing," Danny had growled in some sort of Lord of the Rings voice. "But that's just Weimarica for you, I guess." He'd chuckled ruefully, stomped his empty beer can, and fiddled with the top button of his black work shirt. He had a shift upcoming, 7 to close. Finally, he sighed heavily, dropped his smoke into his nearly finished beer, and hove himself up.

"So there's sandwich shit, there's cans of soup, pasta—or if you wanna actually, like, cook something, I think there's maybe chicken. Check the vegetable drawer… I dunno what's there. Whatever. Knock yourself out.

There's beer, of course, which, help yourself. Just leave me a couple, huh?"

I'd assented and he'd ambled off to his rickety old Malibu, backing out of the driveway and gunning the engine to skid ninety degrees out into the street. It was odd to commune with Danny in an Ohio that was so changed, denuded of the dense network of associations that had been the source of its significance throughout my life. I sat for a long moment more and wondered whether I'd made a mistake in coming.

*

I could only stand a few days at Danny's. It had been with a strange and idealized feeling of homecoming that I'd gone back there to that place which was as close to an ancestral homeland as I'd ever had. I had imagined, though not quite consciously, that this return to my roots would somehow calm the inner turmoil that plagued me. Instead, I found a place that seemed divested of whatever it was I'd so loved about it. The scrubby woods that had seemed so boundless to my youthful self were choked with trash, their fragile existence besieged by the ever-present shopping centers and fast-food restaurants and featureless little clumps of housing that ever intruded on what remained of a once wild country. But is this not how it had always been, an America of waste and plastic and gasoline, charming to me, the Urbanite, in its kitschy obsolescence? The people had always been fat and the food had always been processed. I had always (unfavorably) compared the chain restaurants and cineplexes of this foreign America to the avant-garde theaters and boutique eateries of Chicago.[20]

Maybe it was just the same old Ohio. Danny being an outdoorsy type, we'd spent my second morning slogging silently along the muddy trails of the Waupatoic River Valley, which remained, so far as I could tell, the same as it ever was, down to the fresh and invigorating shit-smell of its mud. As I've repeatedly said, this land is as close to ancestral home as I have. I would cry bitterly upon leaving as a boy, not yet accustomed to that feeling of self-uprooting, the separation of oneself from the extended self of the Clan that is *of you*—or *of which* you yourself are. That was before I knew that Self-Uprooting is a feeling to which one must become inured, if one is to slough off the burdensome dead skins of ancestry, identity, The Particular, and

---

[20] Which I'd never been to, incidentally (the theaters and gourmet restaurants), neither as a child nor in my current state of semi-adulthood, and to which I had, indeed, no particularly desire to go; but in whose mere existence I, the Urbanite, took a peculiar pride.

slither rejuvenated into the ranks of that elite for whom Place is but a coincidence and for whom Attachment is but a pesky and troublesome myth (an "imagined community," if you will).

Most likely, my newfound feeling of alienation in this land that I had once imagined to be somehow mine stemmed from the erosion of the top soil in which I'd always imagined myself to be firmly rooted, the decay of the Clan itself. Perhaps the overwhelming feeling of dread and hopelessness in the air stemmed from the fact that this erosion of topsoil was by no means an isolated phenomenon of my particular clan, but was instead the story of a region, of a folk.

It's sort of a tragedy of the commons, the death of the ancestral clan, if envisioned through a certain lens. There's a good, namely the extended family, which produces positive utility for its members *vis-a-vis* a sense of belonging or that half-eerie sense of familiarity when a close relative explains his thinking on a given subject and you recognize it to be somehow kindred to your own; or that sort of "falling-away" of certain masks in the family's presence (and, yes, those masks' replacement by certain other family-specific masks); or the odd sense of a shared idiolect. Imagine being able to partake in this good without having to participate in all the irritating and possibility-limiting maintenance work required for that good—the clan—to continue to exist. Imagine, for example, being able to go off into the comparatively limitless outer world to seek one's individual fortune, while also knowing that the public good, the cherished topsoil which nourishes your roots, will forever await your return, the work to maintain it being done by less fortunate or less talented relatives who keep everything in working order while we, the Urbanites, flit periodically in and out, drawing off the accumulated stock of the common resource at our pleasure.

The problem: if all the plants uproot themselves, the topsoil will be irretrievably blown away by the remorseless wind. Erosion. For my parents, the only members of their generation to pursue this strategy, the public good of the extended family had remained largely intact. It was my generation that scattered to the winds. Except for Danny.

Whatever the effect of my family's dissolution, there was no doubt that this new Danny had helped to foster my sense of alienation as well. He was as clever as ever, and his worldview had broadened and deepened in the years since we'd seen each other. He'd been doing serious reading, pursuing knowledge in directions I never would have predicted. And yet his divestment from the society of which he was a part was total. I think this divestment and hopelessness may have accounted for his enamorment with the symbols and ideology of what can only be described as the Great Satan of our otherwise languid political culture, our Emmanuel Goldstein, the Big Kahuna himself: namely Adolf Hitler, Führer und Reichskanzler des Großdeutschen Reiches.

The morning after my arrival at Danny's house, after we'd both availed ourselves of hefty portions of eggs, bacon, and black coffee, we'd spent some silent time together in the living room, each attending to his own personal reading material. Danny turned to a thick hardcover volume that had been sitting on his coffee table. I fished a crumpled sheaf of printed paper from my backpack—some turgid, theoretical journal article devoted ostensibly to applying a critical and clarifying lens to "The Post-National Constellation," but which seemed instead to be chiefly concerned with coining and manipulating opaque terminology to formulate cryptic symbolic strings which I suspected to amount to an elaborate structure of triviality and tautology. Having tired of closing one eye and scrunching up the other while plowing uncomprehending through the same sentence for the fifth time, I turned to Danny and asked what he was reading about.

"The ethnic cleansing, enslavement in concentration camps, and mass murder of ethnic German civilians post-WWII." There'd been something in his tone. The choked sound of words through clenched jaws. "And not just by the Soviets, Matt. They kept them as slaves in jolly ol' Britain as well." Something unnerving about it, the sense that this wasn't just an idle research interest for Danny. He'd looked at me pointedly, remarking "you don't hear too much about *that* ethnic cleansing, huh?" I'd half-shrugged. I knew vaguely about the population transfers. I'd stumbled upon the existence of the work camps on a late night Wikipedia trawl. And it was true that I'd not heard about any of this during my state-curated course of education. But something felt eerie and taboo about Danny bringing it up. He'd let the subject lapse and we'd turned back to our respective tasks.

"Fuck!" he'd burst out eventually. "I can't focus for shit when I know I have to work a shift. You ever get that? You try to read something—or even just watch TV or whatever—but you just can't do it, even though it's still hours until you have shit to do? I can just feel it there, looming. The shift." He slammed the book down on the table and lit a cigarette.

"You've been making pizza too long, my dude. You spend too long rolling out dough and bossing shithead teenagers around and it'll wear on you."

"Doesn't matter the job, man. Doesn't matter what shift. If I work nights then the shift just looms over the whole day. Drink coffee until it's time to switch to beer. And if I work days I come home dead."

"You ever think of going back to school?"

He snorted. "The fuck for?"

"Well, with a degree you could get out of... *here.*"

"Right. Cause you know you've made it in the world once you find yourself in a $2000-a-month studio apartment surrounded by faggots, shitskins, and guilt-ridden race traitors." He'd taken the edge out of his voice halfway through, squinting mischievously to indicate a less than serious attitude. But I knew he was dead serious.

When he'd gone, I'd poked around the stacks of books which littered the dark house. It became progressively clearer that what I'd tried to dismiss as cynical shock humor—the racial epithets and Jew-baiting—stemmed from something deeply held and chillingly sincere. It was when I uncovered a particular flag under a stack of books whose authors included David Irving, David Duke, and George Lincoln Rockwell that I could not deny any longer what I'd already known. My cousin was in the grips of something. I stayed another night, and then another, always thinking I'd find the moment to bring it up, but in the end I left Danny a brief note and sped back West, across the featureless eternities of agribusiness that line I-80.

*

As I drove, I surfed the radio waves, alternating between the sounds of this foreign country, Middle America, and the more familiar cosmopolitan sounds which the cities beamed out into the hinterlands. The evangelicals rambled on about what they rambled about. I grew irritated with them after a time and switched to NPR, where the New York cabal was running a piece on systemic racism. *"Wonder how many of them wear small hats,"* whispered Danny's voice in my ear, and I shook my head to dislodge the distasteful thought, turning the radio knob to what turned out to be a country music station, utterly foreign to me. Mass-produced prole-feed no doubt. Danny-thoughts aside, I freely admit that I couldn't and can't help but consider the whole anti-racism shtick to be slimily disingenuous. But the country music was unendurable as well and after some minutes I switched again and on the next station the music was pop, mass-produced and negrified,[21] shallow to the point of unbearability (*"You ever wonder who is*

---

[21] In retrospect, this is another Danny word, I must admit it slipped into my thoughts without my noticing.

financing the production of this trash," another unwelcome Danny-thought intruded). After some fifty miles on the road, I turned off the radio to drive in the non-silence of rushing air, whirring engine, and trundling tires against the concrete of the Ohio Turnpike.

I drove on in near mental silence for some time, but around the Indiana border, I suddenly started to think about Mrs. Feretti once again. No doubt the story Danny had told me had reflected his personal biases, and I found myself looking with skepticism on certain aspects of the entire narrative. Had Molly Feretti in fact been so thoroughly average in her youth as Danny's story had had it? Or had there been, even then, a lurking radical streak that had been submerged by the dominant cultural consensus of Boomerica? Was it, as Danny would have it, a consequence of the untimely deaths of baby and husband that Mrs. Feretti took the path she had taken, becoming the local avatar of that ancient archetype of the village witch? Could it really be as simple as Danny'd had me believe—the junkies and illegals and Blacks as her ersatz-children? Or was there something more. I'd read Ehrenreich on witches (and no, she doesn't echo, for any anti-Semites in the audience[22]) at some point during my ill-fated graduate studies (trying to impress some feministic romantic quarry, if I remember correctly), but I hadn't found her thesis all that convincing.[23] But now, hurtling through the cornfields of the flyover hinterlands, I could not help but wonder whether there existed, in fact, some secret knowledge to which the likes of me were not privy. How else could someone like Mrs. Feretti have veered so sharply and confidently away from the cultural consensus of Waupatoic County?

Perhaps it was all as Danny had described it. Perhaps Molly Feretti, that excruciatingly average product of Midwestern femininity, had been warped and twisted almost beyond recognition by a chance occurrence that stripped her of her natural role as wife and mother. Perhaps she had been propelled by utter happenstance into the clutches of the Eternal Jew, Lionel Schwarz, whose poisonous ideology had been pumped into her virgin veins with the aid of an echoey, Levantine media establishment which relentlessly enforced and reinforced a particular type of false consciousness, presumably out of an atavistic race-hatred or a fear of repeating what Danny, on the night before I'd left, had termed the Holohoax (which he'd

---

[22] But why had I thought to google "is Barbara Ehrenreich jewish?"

[23] That witch-burning represented a patriarchal appropriation of secret folk-knowledge, particularly medical knowledge, as part of a broader initiative of wresting away from women the control of their bodies.

tried to play off as a joke when I'd displayed visible signs of distaste). Perhaps this was the series of events that had produced the Witch of Laura Lane. And yet I felt that something must be missing.

As I drove, my mind wandered further, namely to the end of Danny's father's story—*or rather, the lack thereof.* It seems somehow evocative of a broader trend of our disintegrating social world: the father who fails to impart his lessons, the son therefore left unable to reproduce the civilization he'd inherited. But what could the lesson have been? Why, lest we've forgotten, had Danny's father seen fit to tell him such a story? Remember that what originally inspired the story was Danny's father's description of his own perceived inadequacy as an emotional support to his wife. It was of this inadequacy that this unfinished story was intended to be illustrative. Uncle Jay[24] might have told it something like this:

"Listen Dan, didja ever hear about what happened to Mr. Feretti? Mrs. Feretti's husband? They had a kid you know. He woulda been three, four years older than [Danny's oldest brother] Lewis. Frank Feretti was doing real well for himself—some sort of, what the hell was it, driveway repaving or something. I think he was in sales, working on commission, definitely making more than the rest of us who graduated with him. He didn't have anything more than his diploma, but that's all you really needed back then. You could do okay.

"And so they had a kid, which was pretty normal then, young as they were, a little boy, and there probably woulda been more on the way too. But so one day Frank's in the car on 271, driving into the city for whatever reason, and he's got the kid with him. And things weren't like now, with everybody strapping their kid into a car seat until they're sixteen years old and child-proof locks on everything and nobody plays outside cause you might get dirt under your fingernails. My point being that safety measures were less… modern. So Frank's driving and the little kid's on his own in the back seat, crawling around. To give you an idea, seatbelts weren't even, like, obligatory back then, which I'm telling to say that Frank Feretti wasn't being negligent or anything. By the standards of the times. So long story short, the kid gets his hands on the handle of the car door, pulls it, and just—*goosh*—all over 271. Just… splattered.

"So what Frank did, which is the point of what I'm telling you, is, when they brought him down to the police station—they've gotta bring you to

---

[24] Whom I hadn't seen since his divorce from Aunt Kath and his subsequent uprooting to Florida, where he'd found a new job and a Cuban immigrant to shack up with.

the police station after something like that, even if everybody knows it was just a terrible accident—but yeah, when they get down to the station, first chance Frank gets, he slips off, I guess they weren't keeping too close an eye cause everybody knew Frank Feretti was a good guy who'd just had an unbelievable, terrible bad break, not some sort of monster, criminal… but so off Frank slips, first chance he gets, into a closet. And he takes off his belt and *gak.*" He mimes a hanging. At exactly this moment, Danny's father is distracted from his story by the sound of the horn which signals the end of the hockey game.

If this had all take place a mere five years later, in the age of TiVo, might things have been different? Had my uncle been able to rewind, at his leisure, to the third period highlights he'd missed in real-time, rather than cutting his story short to watch the postgame coverage, then might the Danny I'd encountered in late autumn of 2017 have been somewhat less resentful, harsh, bitter and vengeful?

Short answer? Probability negligible. A longer answer? The missed opportunity described in this story is but a singular instance in a lifetime of missed opportunities, lost forever to a world in which Danny's father'd had to look over his shoulder and mumble that Danny ought not to tell his mother before relating the sort of lesson that I believe he'd been trying to relate. And even had Danny's dad taken a significant number more of those opportunities, his counsel would likely have had little effect, drowned out by the perpetual chorus of remonstrations against so-called gender essentialism, all but circumambient in these troubled times (*"And who is it that is lodging these complaints,"* whispers the unwelcome Danny-voice in my mind).

This all depends, to be sure, on the veracity of my interpretation of the lesson Danny's dad had tried to teach him all those years ago. Sitting at a rest stop in Elkhart, Indiana, I scribbled intermittently in a notebook between bites of a Hardee's cheeseburger, trying my best to puzzle it all out:

Something about the fear inherent in love—a man's love in particular. We'd rather die than face the betrayed and broken face of the Beloved whom we've failed. Something about the burning sense of inadequacy and undeserving we men try, futilely, to quell by feats of strength. So different from the woman, whose worth is inherent to her, carried within her. The eternal angst of male replaceability—YOU WILL NOT REPLACE US (no coincidence, the gender ratio at that particular shitshow). The peril of being forced to demonstrate your worth, again and again, in a chaotic universe that will inevitably thwart you, thwart you not out of pique but blank indifference, shattering you, the you you've built in the eyes of your Beloved. It's this same fear that drove Uncle Jay into an overwhelming fog of confusion and self-doubt when faced with the prospect of comforting his wife in times of emotional distress.

Sometimes I believe that there once existed an Old Wisdom. I believe that this wisdom was lost when men were no longer permitted to communicate it to their boys. I believe that the enforcement of a new, nominally egalitarian orthodoxy has resulted in the pathologization of the Old Wisdom. I believe that this pathologization has crippled men's ability to see real women. I believe that what we see is a clutter of primordial archetypes, Witches and Mothers, Angels and Whores. Sometimes I don't believe in the Old Wisdom. Sometimes I believe all that's ever existed is Witches, Mothers, Angels, Whores. But I don't know. My father taught me even less than Danny's did.

"And who pathologized the Old Male Wisdom," whispers Danny's unwelcome voice.

My cheeseburger has gone cold. The sun will be directly in my face, to the west, when I start again. I close my little notebook, dissatisfied with my unfocused scrawlings. It'll be another four hours until I'm back in Chicago. The wind is bitter when I walk out to the car. It's starting to feel like real winter. I start the car and gun it to 80.

Danny would say it's the Jews. Everything I'm wondering about—the Jews. Jewish feminism pathologizing the Old Male Wisdom. Jewish academics blasting the new narrative on repeat from the ivory towers. Jewish media controlling the information choke-points of the broader society to throttle unapproved worldviews. I knew the script already. I'd seen it pop up in just about every public, unmoderated online comment section or forum I'd ever entered.

I didn't buy it. I couldn't accept it, but for the life of me I couldn't begin to imagine what had gone wrong... the death of religion, perhaps... *"...and who led the charge against public displays of religion in American civil society, Matt? Who promoted the twin towers of soulless materialistic political economy: neoliberalism and communism?"*

"Danny, atheism is an Enlightenment value! Or at least a consequence of deism! Materialism is already implicit in European scientific thought—hell, you find it going all the way back to the Greeks!"

Had we done it to ourselves? Was it the Devil's Bargain of materialism? Enlightenment hubris? Or had this Old Wisdom I'd imagined never in fact existed? Could it be that this Old Wisdom, had it in fact existed, was a mere relic of a patriarchal social structure not worth saving?

Suffice it to say that upon arriving home from Danny's, I found myself in a state of great uncertainty. I fought my way through the brutal traffic on the Skyway and on Lake Shore Drive, scrounged up a handful of cash, and bought eggs and beer. I ate four eggs and drank six beers and turned in for a night of restless sleep.

All I knew in my sea of uncertainty was this: if I were to cross Laura Lane and walk to the house three doors north of Danny's, if I were to knock on that door and request admission, if that door were opened by the small, energetic, slightly disheveled older woman I'd seen on the front porch, joking around with a small crowd of smiling young people my second morning at Danny's, if I were invited to tell my story, if I were offered a cup of tea, a bowl of soup, a bed, or a helping hand, I would not have said no. I know that I'd be just as utterly unable as the other men of my generation to distinguish between the milk of mother's kindness and the sweets that fatten naughty boys for eating.

- *Poverty and Plenty* -

None of the jobs that Grace had had over the years had quite metastasized into a career as such—certainly not in the way that the high-strung wives of Colin's finance colleagues all seemed to have careers. Between the years she'd taken off when Elijah was young, the additional years she'd had to devote to him when he'd had his various learning and behavioral difficulties—which seemed, finally, thank God, to have been overcome—and the highly inopportune manner in which the financial crisis had lined up with the downtown PA position she'd gotten and promptly been laid off from, it eventually became an unfortunate fact of her life that she was one of those people who could not identify herself with some sort of workplace vocation. This wasn't something that she would necessarily have minded all that much, were it not for the fact that two-career households were the norm in the sort of upper-crust, urban-progressive social circle which she and Colin inhabited—she resented the impression she sometimes got that she was looked upon as being a simple housewife, and thus a discredit to her sex. Even the non-high-earning wives among their Lincoln Park friends had passions, vocations, and involvement with the arts or with charity—a purpose in life which they could point to, a word with which they could label themselves.

Though her work history couldn't be summed up in some high prestige title—lawyer, psychologist, teacher—and even though her income would never have been sufficient to handle the mortgage on their townhouse, the two car payments, and the tuition for the private school Elijah had had to attend; the string of jobs she'd held over the years had still provided her with something meaningful. She'd walked dogs, managed a cafe in Lakeview, worked summers at a gardening supply store—the sorts of jobs where the majority of her coworkers were either overeducated hipsters or burnt-out stoner layabouts, most of them about two decades her junior. Despite the lack of prestige, the jobs had provided her with dignity, with stories to tell, and with a sense of her place in the world, especially as Elijah grew older and started finding his way, and being "mommy" became less and less of a viable source of identity.

Still, these jobs had, on some level, seemed like hobbies; if she got fed up with them (which she repeatedly had), they could be dropped at will, as Colin's salary could carry the three of them if need be. It wasn't until his stroke, when he was forty-eight and she was forty-seven, that she finally felt the full weight of financial responsibility. That summer, when he'd finally been discharged from the hospital, they'd relocated to the lake house in Wauconda so he could recover somewhere more peaceful, and she'd gotten herself a job at the public library a few towns over, just south of the Wisconsin state line. They'd stayed there for the next year or so. Because her circumstances required her to do so, she had been forced to settle into her role as breadwinner, caretaker, setter, and keeper of Colin's physical, occupational, and psycho- therapy appointments, and had found that that responsibility suited her very much indeed.

When Julie had come to visit her, she'd marveled at the change that had come over her friend, though marveling at the dramatic transformations Grace seemed effortlessly and periodically to undergo was nothing new from Julie, who was such a creature of habit that leaving the five block radius of Hyde Park where she lived and lectured had become a nigh horrific ordeal of formless anxiety and dread, endurable only for such worthy purposes as visiting her oldest friend. To Julie—the only daughter of Brooklyn academics, who had grown up to be a respected professor of literature at the University of Chicago—the outer fringes of the suburbs, where people owned jet-skis and listened to country music, were like a separate country entirely, and she had spent the afternoon of her arrival walking around with Grace, owlishly peering, marveling at and drawing back in horror from this land that she mostly knew by way of fiction. When Colin had arrived back from his therapy later that evening, Julie had divined from the few moments they'd spoken that Grace had had another motive in being so insistent that she come visit; as upbeat as she had made sure to be with respect to her husband's recovery, it was immediately clear to Julie, who had known Colin as long as Grace had, that something was not right with him.

The next morning, the air remained uncleared. The two friends had swam before breakfast, read on the porch, and later driven the boat across the lake for a hamburger, just for the novelty of arriving by boat at the little beach-bar. Finally, in the afternoon, they had allowed the little pontoon to drift on the little lake as they finally talked about the subject that needed discussing.

The thing was, that after six months in the hospital and over a year of intensive therapy, Colin's speech was no longer slurred. His movements were nearly restored to their previous ease, though there was a bit of a hitch in his walk. Perhaps he seemed to forget things a little more than he had, but all in all he'd seemed to have recovered remarkably well in most respects, even losing thirty pounds to get back to a trim 185. Still, he seemed drained and listless, as if the trauma of the stroke had aged him much more than the time that had elapsed since the day Colin's assistant had called Grace, informing her through tears that her husband had collapsed at his desk, and had been carted off to St. Joseph's in an insensible state.

Grace had never before needed to nag and badger her husband about anything; theirs had always been the sort of relationship in which the nagging had gone in the other direction. She'd started dropping hints and later outright suggestions that he call up Peter and set a date to return to work, seeing as the bank had been generous enough to grant him an open-ended leave of absence with pay. Being back in Chicago would probably perk him right up, and he'd always loved his work, lived for his work, she thought; but when she'd bring it up, he'd just look at her dolefully until she stopped talking, before making some vague excuse. He'd spend days vegetating, and without a direct command, was loathe to change his clothes or leave the house at all.

There hadn't been much more for Julie to do but listen as her friend expounded. What else could anyone do?

*

It wasn't until some months later, when Grace arrived home from her shift to find him slurring, stumbling, and incoherent, that the pieces had clicked into place. Sure that this was the second stroke, she'd called in the paramedics, but after they'd restrained and sedated him, they'd quietly informed her that what she'd taken for a stroke bore all the signs of acute intoxication. When one of the paramedics asked her whether she had ever known her husband to use drugs, she had almost burst out laughing. Colin, perhaps the most cautious and anal-retentive person she'd ever encountered, on drugs?! Laughable as it had seemed though, the suggestion had been enough to convince her to reconsider a few previous unexplained events in her and her husband's life together, and when she found the orange translucent pill bottle in his jacket pocket while snooping around later that night, the prescription made out to someone unfamiliar, she'd googled "benzodiazepine" with a sinking heart. As she'd read through the search results, she'd had to admit to herself that the unthinkable might in fact be true.

The ensuing months were perhaps more wrenching than those that had followed the stroke, which she'd since learned to have occurred as a result of a days-long Adderall bender, simply because of the lies and betrayals that had been revealed. When he'd woken up in the hospital bed, his blood having already tested positive for a cocktail of benzos and prescription amphetamines, he'd tearfully admitted as much as he absolutely had to: that he'd initially been prescribed the drugs for legitimate, work-related purposes, and that they'd just taken hold of him. He falsely swore that it hadn't been going on for any more than a few months before the stroke, and truthfully confessed that the reason he'd been in such a state the night of the second episode was that, when he had relapsed, he had foolishly taken the same dose as he had been taking before the stroke, at which point he had had a high tolerance.

More lies came out, as they always do, but for the months of Colin's in-patient rehab, her own sense of betrayal took a back seat to her husband's health. Her job at the library had been her sole refuge from it all. At the time, Grace had thought that she was living through the peak of the crisis, but it was only upon Colin's release from the recovery center that the true awfulness, the cycle of lies and relapses and betrayal, would begin.

*

Grace had jumped at the chance when Maggie had asked for a volunteer to come in early to let the electricians in. The loss of two hours of sleep had been a less than attractive prospect for the rest of the librarians, but Grace had reached that age where sleep becomes sparse and restless. Leaving the cabin that morning, with the sun peaking over the horizon, she took a few moments to proudly survey the riches that were growing in the garden that grew wilder and more ambitious with every season. Those years at the gardening center had served her well.

It crossed her mind that Julie had stopped sending her pictures of cheap Uptown condos back in the city; it was as if they'd both realized, though only as the ten year mark approached, that Grace had left the city for good. When the terms of the divorce had left her in possession of the lake house, but without a place to stay in Chicago, she and Julie had bemoaned her fate, but the fact was that she would have ended up having to sell the townhouse in any case, if only to pay Elijah's college tuition, to which Colin certainly wasn't in any state to contribute. She and Julie had adapted, and weekly coffee had been replaced with weekend visits in the summer and the occasional long-form telephone call. She'd realized with time that she loved living out in the not-quite-country.

One of the things Grace loved most was the way that the roads began to wind. Too far inland to have been touched by the erstwhile development of the now-decaying lakeshore port cities (e.g. Waukegan, Zion, Kenosha) and too much of an economic backwater for there to be an interstate nearby, Grace's neck of the woods was characterized by two-lane roads through nothing-towns and the occasional lakeside resort that saw its heyday in the mid-twentieth century, when Chicago's laboring classes would pack the kids into their American-made cars for a weekend at the Chain O'Lakes. She snaked along that morning, between the lakes and rivers and farms and forest preserves which checker that particular region of northern Illinois, a tiny corner of that dead-flat Midwestern cornfield of a state where the land, as a result of long-retreated glaciers, rolls in a subtle and pleasing way, feeling very much at peace with her lot in life.

She pulled into the parking lot ten or so minutes early, and the contractor van was already parked outside, a few passenger sedans pulled up beside it, the electricians leaning on the various vehicles smoking cigarettes and muttering sleepily to each other. When the senior-most member of the crew walked up to introduce himself, she'd shaken his hand and told him her name was Grace, in response to which he'd peered at her for a long moment, before breathing, "Well how about that." He'd had to tell her his name for her to recognize him, but the name had set free an avalanche of remembrances.

Eight hours later, when he and the rough-looking young men he'd introduced as apprentices had finished climbing around in the ceiling and revealed the newly-retrofitted, exceptionally efficient LED lights they'd been contracted to install in the atrium, she'd been getting off shift as well. Seeing as they'd only had a brief couple of minutes to exchange pleasantries that morning, she'd suggested the two of them drive into Antioch to catch up over coffee and pie, her treat, but he'd excused himself, saying vaguely that he had a lot of work to do back at the company warehouse in poor old shabby Waukegan. Something about the way he'd said it had made her suspect that he would have preferred that their paths not have crossed at all.

*

Steven had indeed had mixed feelings about encountering Grace again, but it was also not untrue that there was a good deal that had to be done at the warehouse. Despite the fact that he'd taken what Johnny had described as a part time hobby job as a favor, just to keep himself busy in his retirement, maintaining the warehouse had somehow fallen to him. Johnny, to his credit, had suggested hiring a part-time worker to keep track of inventory, receive shipments, and maintain order and cleanliness, but to Steven, the idea of having some stranger unsupervised in the warehouse had seemed like more of a liability than anything. Seeing as the only sort of employee you'd be likely to find to do that sort of unskilled wage work in Waukegan would either be young and inexperienced or older and somehow damaged, and seeing as their warehouse contained spools upon spools of copper wire, pallets of transformers, bundles of conduit, as well as various company-owned tools, it seemed to Steven as though the constant temptation to pilfer would end in ruin, or at least in the unpleasant circumstance of having to snoop around to collect concrete evidence and then fire a person. He told Johnny that between him-self and the apprentices who made up the rest of the crew, they'd be able to handle it themselves.

Steven hadn't figured on the odd attitude endemic to "this new generation." He always made sure to ask the young bucks if they wanted to earn some overtime pay helping him clean up in the warehouse, but for whatever unfathomable reason, the prospect of making time and a half didn't have the allure it had once had. Steven could remember having witnessed fairly serious altercations, back in the day, when guys had felt they weren't getting their fair share of overtime hours. Whatever the reason for this behavior, none of the apprentices had been interested in picking up some hours on the day he snubbed Grace's invitation. As such, Steven had found himself back at the warehouse by 3:30PM, sighing as he hand-counted step-down transformers, noting down his tallies on a yellow legal-pad to make a list which he'd type up and email to Johnny, who handled the ordering, making sure they were well stocked for their upcoming jobs. It wasn't any sort of air-tight inventory system, but it at least gave them a rough idea of what was going on.

The warehouse was a rented space in the corner of a pallet recycling factory on Green Bay Road, on the very western edge of town, where three shifts of Mexicans and ex-cons worked twenty-four hours a day identifying the broken deckboards on the wooden skids, wrenching them off with crowbars, and attaching fresh boards with nailguns chained to the floor. The assembly line whirred, the nailguns popped, the forklifts honked, the reggaeton thumped, the men shouted to be heard, and Steven counted inventory all the while. When he emerged from his tedious hours amid the din, the rush of traffic along Green Bay was as a soothing lullaby. He rolled a cigarette in the darkening evening, before heading home to the relative pastoral calm of his little property in Arcadia Hills. He planned to end his day as he always did with a few beers and a few hours of reruns on broadcast TV. Then he would sleep, wake up, and do it again, wondering why in the world he didn't retire for good.

That night he couldn't quite manage to get into his routine though. Seeing Grace after all those years had shaken him more than he'd ever have thought. It wasn't as though it was the only time he'd been unsuccessful in love, but none of the subsequent failures had been quite so crushing and shameful. What's more, seeing her had recalled to his mind the memory of a time when life had been rich with potentialities, when he was all but certain that he'd make something more colorful of his life than his dad, from whom he'd picked up the electrical trade working summers as a teenager. Looking back at the years of gray and thankless toil that had taken place in the interim, he wondered how he had let it all slip past. As he always ended up doing when he felt this way (which was often), he found himself leafing through the contents of a shoebox he kept on a closet shelf, in search of a photograph of a country that no longer existed, where a younger Steve and a younger Johnny stood in the shadow of a tower that had since fallen in a hail of American bombs, and between them, a dark-eyed woman relegated to the same past tense as the country she'd lived in. For a brief time at least, as the photo confirmed to him, Steven had indeed lived.

*

Though Steven's wasn't a name that had crossed her mind in decades, Grace was still bothered by the idea of his bearing ill will toward her for the way things had turned out, all those many lives ago, especially seeing as her memory of him was unreservedly warm. Maybe his feelings towards her had been stronger than she'd accounted for.

The last time they'd seen each other had been across a crowded room in the apartment of someone whose name she didn't know, through a haze of beer and youthful exuberance, after they'd snuck into the Dead that time. She'd been nominated to approach some miserable delivery guy humping kegs of beer into the stadium, employing her most sultry feminine wiles to inquire as to whether she and her friends might be permitted to make an unauthorized entry. The delivery guy had bashfully assented, so she'd beckoned to the troop of teenage longhairs, Steven among them, and they'd made a successful dash for it, darting through various storerooms and out into the roiling crowd. The jams had undulated in a most mellow and groovy fashion, the crowd like some great beast rippling along with it, all the old heads doing that wavy-armed hippie dance that's almost pre-sexual, dating to an era where White body movements were not yet so pervasively negrified. A smoldering roach had come her way, and just as the high kicked in, right in that particular spot behind her eyes, the jam had coalesced into "Scarlet Begonias" and she'd swayed through the rest of the show like some ecstatic dream. Even though it was off-peak Dead, when hard drugs had entered the picture and Jerry wasn't looking too great, this particular show was one of the transcendent ones, a show that would be remembered by the real Heads, the tape-traders who could recall set lists from memory— though this would be lost on Grace, who was a casual fan at best. She'd been high, eighteen, and newly graduated, with just a few months of summer separating her from college and then adulthood. With her relationship with Ronnie finally ended, she had felt gloriously hopeful and free.

When, after the show, Theo had started chatting with some older hula-hoop chick who was throwing an after party at her place, the whole crew had been invited over, Steve included, and they'd found themselves at a genuine adult house party, with no worries about if the place would still smell like weed in the morning or if the neighbors would call their pa-rents. There was weed and beer and later a little coke and the people, being hippies, were quite the friendly and mellow bunch. She remembered being chatted up by some brown-eyed twenty-five-year-old with a warm voice and a full beard, and suddenly seeing Steve there, up against the wall, despondently and unconvincingly pretending not to be looking at her. Everyone else had more or less found someone to pair off with but him, even though Theo had tried to give him a little pep talk and get him to approach the hula-chick's roommate. Grace had been annoyed, and had consciously ignored him, and eventually he'd slipped out into the night.

He couldn't be holding a grudge over that, more than forty years later, could he? Well, that and the way things had unfolded when he'd told her how he felt, a few months before the Dead concert, when they'd been very close? She supposed that perhaps he could be—maybe she'd misjudged or forgotten how much it had meant to him. After she'd told him it was not to be, things had most definitely changed between them. No more late night phone calls or Sunday afternoon walks through the neighborhood, which she hadn't realized at the time had started up just as things with Ronnie were going bad, and had given her an emotional outlet. It wasn't something she'd consciously planned, but looking back she could see how this could be considered bad form.

In any case, by the time they found themselves at that house party, her feelings towards Steven had become characterized chiefly by pity for his evident heartbreak, sadness at the loss of his friendship, guilt over having led him on, and contempt for the abject way in which he mooned about, avoiding her eyes and hamfistedly pretending not to be following her every move. She had been frustrated that he couldn't just take a hint and move on—it had already been three or four months since he'd laid it on the line— not realizing that he'd spent the previous three years aflame with secret, hopeless desire, before finally working up the courage.

It's funny how we conspire to forget those memories which show us in an unflattering light, she'd thought to herself back at the reception desk, as for the first time in decades she remembered how, in the months before The Dead, she'd fanned the flames of a false indignation to absolve herself of that lingering guilt, complaining to Meg about how boys will deceive you with their friendship when really they want something else, and then they'll try to leverage the friendship as if now you owe them something when you'd thought their friendship had been freely given, which was true enough as a description of a not-uncommon pattern of behavior, but which she knew in her heart didn't quite fit Steve, who'd been quite decent and understanding about the rejection, if somewhat pathetic. Thinking back at the library reception desk those forty years later, she seemed to vaguely remember calling him a creep in that conversation with Meg, implying that he'd schemed to scoop her up as soon as she and Ronnie had broken up, which really hadn't been at all fair of her. She hoped it hadn't gotten back to him that she'd said that, though it would certainly explain why he hadn't wished to renew their acquaintance, those many decades later.

In any case, she'd been relieved that night at the house party when Theo had looked around the room and wondered aloud where Steve had gotten to, and they'd all looked at each other and figured that Mr. Dolan had pulled a classic Irish goodbye, which he was wont to do. And then, semi-seriously at first, they'd all started talking about the possibility of spending some time following their favorite bands around on tour that summer. And because Theo had a car, and she'd had a couple hundred dollars of lifeguarding money, and because they were all newly minted adults, they'd actually ended up hitting the road, the sort of thing they'd been idly imagining all throughout high school, Grace promising her parents she'd be back when the pool opened—she'd signed up to work that one last summer. Then, once she'd missed the start of lifeguarding season, she'd promised them at least to arrive back home in time to pack her things for the drive down to Normal, Illinois, for her college orientation. But that promise was not to be kept, for as it turned out, without knowing it, Grace had already set out on a journey that would see her travel from coast to coast, picking berries on organic farms and trimming pot plants for cash under the table, working festivals in season and tending bar in the winters, basically living a life of rootless, restless, careless ease all the way into her mid-twenties, until Julie, whom she'd met picking apples in the remotest corners of British Columbia, had invited her to a party with her grad school friends, where she'd met a strait-laced future-banker with a finance degree, whose earnest fussiness she'd found so arrestingly different from the attitudes of the flaky, easy-going granola-dudes she'd had in her early twenties. It was at this point she'd turned an unexpected corner into conventional adulthood. Life had been so absorbing that it had never entered her mind to wonder what had ever happened to good old Steve Dolan.

Grace was distracted from her remembering by the ringing of the library phone, and an accented voice which had introduced itself with an improbably American name had explained that it was his company's policy to conduct a post-installation customer satisfaction survey for quality control. It had taken her a moment to work out that he worked for the electrical contracting company that had sent out Steven's installation crew (in point of fact, he was the company's owner), but when she'd sorted out what precisely was going on, she'd been happy to participate. The guy was chatty, and some little comment she'd made had initiated a history of how he'd founded the company. To reciprocate his friendliness, and to pass the slow hours of a weekday morning spent behind the reception desk, she'd mentioned having known Stevie Dolan way back in high school, and what a pleasant coincidence it had been to see him again—who would have thought he'd end up an electrician, just like his dad, when back in high school he'd fancied himself something of a poet.

There was an intake of breath on the other side of the phone, and the guy had become effusive—though, to be fair, his resting state was near-effusive to begin with—telling her all about how he and Steve went way back, back to the time of Yugoslavia if you can believe it, how Steve had got him his first job in America, at Mr. Dolan's contracting company no less (such a shame he'd died so young—hard work will do that to you), how Steve was godfather to his children, and how Johnny'd had to drag him out of retirement to serve as a mentor to the apprentices when all Steve really wanted to do these days was to putter around his cabin and work in his vegetable garden (in which, Johnny'd added, Steve used "traditional Serbian village method," which he'd learned from Johnny's own grandfather). Then he'd transitioned into a well-worn rant, triggered by Steve's mentorship to the younger guys, about what is the problem, Grace, with young American kids, cannot arrive on time to work, cannot work extra hours to get ahead in life, always excuses, even my sons become this way to certain extent, in spite of growing up in immigrant household, what is happen to—he'd paused to search for the exact phrase—American ingenuity? He'd made oblique reference to the insidious communism that he, as an ex-Yugoslav, could not help seeing everywhere he looked, though this particular brand of myopia made his Bernie-bro son sigh and roll his eyes. They'd chatted for a few more minutes, but Grace was no longer fully engaged. Steven in a garden, and so nearby, somewhere over the Wisconsin border, where it wasn't quite suburbs anymore—how funny that things had turned out so similarly for them. And yet how differently. Imagine, Steve Dolan in Yugoslavia, of all places. She couldn't remember the last time she'd even heard the word.

*

What led Steven Dolan to Yugoslavia was simple, if absurd—he'd seen a pamphlet down at Halsted and 18th while heading down to the apartment of a college buddy of his. The pamphlet advertised a volunteer exchange program funded by some private foundation in partnership with the US and Yugoslav governments. He'd taken down the information and applied on an absolute lark—he probably couldn't even have found the country on a map at that point. When his application had been accepted, he'd almost forgotten that he'd applied, but once again, on an absolute lark, he'd left his job writing copy at some downtown marketing agency and started preparing to spend six months in a country he knew nothing about.

He'd retrospectively justified his decision by claiming to have been terribly unhappy at the job, but the truth was that he'd found it tolerable enough, just like everything else in his life so far, with the exception of the years of unrequited love. But tolerable enough wasn't enough, suddenly, and he found himself explaining to his irate parents that he was throwing away the first white-collar career anyone in the family had ever had for something he'd never given a second thought to: namely, adventure.

It really was quite a behavioral aberration. Steven had always been, above all else, subject to social pressures, and with the loss of the impractical and dreamy influences of his burnout high school friends, who'd all left the city, the chief social pressures that influenced him after graduating high school had been familial. Thus it was that he had found himself slogging through a completely uninspiring business degree[25] at affordable, no-frills University of Illinois at Chicago while living at home and spending his every free moment pulling wire and bending conduit with his dad's team of commercial electricians. And it had worked out well enough for him, for in those days the cost of attending a humble, local school was not exorbitant, and a bachelor's degree still provided a reasonable degree of utility *vis-a-vis* future job prospects. The Dolan parents, who had watched Steven's older brothers gravitate toward the same destiny of rough hands and tired backs that had been their family's wont for generations, had thought that they were home free with Stevie, their last hope. They looked at him with both relief and great expectation now that he'd escaped that rough patch in high school when he'd fallen in with those useless dopers and had become seemingly prosperity-bound. Now, to be informed at Sunday dinner that their last hope was giving up the suit and briefcase life for... Yugoslavia? To voluntarily decamp for the Evil Empire?[26] In Reagan's America? It was incomprehensible. His brothers

---

[25] He'd much rather have studied literature, but, characteristically, hadn't had the spine to stand up to his parents, who would have deplored such an impractical choice.

[26] Mr. Dolan was unaware of the Soviet-Yugoslav split. He was similarly ignorant of Yugoslavia's seminal role in founding the Nonaligned Movement, and would not have cared

piled on, doubting his patriotism, while his mother fretted about his safety and the possible consequences of leaving his job. For the first time in his life, however, Steven was resolute. In any case, he'd already bought his ticket, for fear that he'd be unable to stand up to their onslaught.

Thus it was that a thoroughly dumbfounded Steven found himself in 1980s Belgrade, which seemed to him for lack of worldliness to be simultaneously the embodiment of all things Soviet, all things European, all things ancient and historical and foreign, but which really was nothing more or less than its gritty, wonderful self. He drank too much beer in a dingy pub, made a little conversation with an older guy who'd spent some years working in London, and prepared himself for the marathon train journey which would bring him to his destination, a place called Knin, Croatia, which, in the antebellum era, was of no particular significance.

*

Julie had found Grace captivating from the moment she'd spotted her on the train platform in Bear's Blood, B.C., a picture of ease with her flowing garments and impossibly tiny frame-pack, even as Julie wrestled two suitcases down the narrow stairs. She'd known immediately that such a creature was not a native of rural Canada, and Grace would later say the same about Julie, owlish and pale, the ideal type of a scholarly East Coast Jew. Grace being Grace and Julie being Julie, it had of course been Grace who had initiated contact there on the train platform. They gravitated to one another right away, establishing a comfortable rapport even before old Harold McClintock had pulled up his rattly old Ford pick-up truck to take them out to the orchard where they'd be working as hired hands for the summer.

Grace had hopped into the front seat of the truck and within a few minutes was bantering comfortably away about vegetable crops before the War and the many ways in which the youth had gone astray. The old man had told them that he only hired girls these days on account of he'd be failing in his duties as a Christian were he to tempt fate by placing young men and women in an unsupervised situation, his falling-down farmhouse lacking the entertainment options then-prevalent among city-folks. "The

---

to inform himself, even if someone had corrected him on this distinction. To him, Yugoslavia was a commie country and thus Soviet, with any further distinction amounting to pedantic hair-splitting, if not ideologically suspicious apologia.

road to perdition!" he'd abruptly proclaimed, "is the, well, the thing which when men and ladies, young ones especially—and no supervision or oversight these days and none of the elders seem to have the gumption to act as guides or authorities! Perdition! So either all boys or all girls it would have to be, I reckoned. Now then I says to myself, I says, boys, strong as they are, have all the more ability to clobber an old chunk of coal like myself about the head with a butter churn and make off with the horse and buggy, which is what my Uncle Remy—a Frenchman!—would always say about hired men." And then he grinned, chiefly at the fact of the two of them being rather taken aback at his unusual mode of address. "You like Scrabble?" he'd inquired with sudden seriousness in his eyes, turning first to Grace, and then over his shoulder to Julie, the truck leaving the ruts of the road entirely and a tree looming in the windshield before Grace wrenched the steering wheel in the right direction. "Yar," he'd grumbled, followed by a string of muttered invective which seemed to be more than a little misogynistic in content, although the nigh-impenetrable rural Canadian argot in which it was rendered made it difficult to tell for sure.

Grace's light packing had wowed Julie all the more once the former had explained a little about her lifestyle as they settled into the room they'd be sharing: she'd spent the last five years on the road, with no more than three months in any one location, living all the while out of the little frame-pack. She'd been almost nonplussed by Julie's questioning, simply responding, "Well, you just wash your clothes more and don't buy anything new." Then she'd turned the tables, asking what on earth Julie had needed two suitcases to bring, in response to which Julie had, with no little embarrassment, shown her the stacks of books, the toiletries, and the East Coast snacks she hadn't been sure of finding here, "abroad" in the Great White North. Though she'd felt foolish, Grace's jibes did not give the impression of having been mean-spirited in the least, a good sign given the close quarters.

Anyway, it wasn't that Julie was some spoiled, materialistic girl who couldn't get by without a blow dryer—it was just that the only time she'd spent outside of the direct control of her fastidious, cosmopolitan parents, Brooklyn academics both, had been the four years of undergraduate study she'd undertaken in the rarefied environs of Princeton University. In other words, Julie's six week adventure to the rural interior of the continent to engage in physical labor had been a true step into the unknown for her, a rejuvenating touch of novelty before plunging full-bore into the demanding environment of the University of Chicago's literature department. Meanwhile, this sort of adventure was nothing out of the ordinary for

Grace. When she told Julie about the various short-term jobs, festivals, meditation retreats, hitchhiking adventures, perilous mishaps, chance acquaintances, and love affairs that had made up her twenty-four years of life thus far, Julie felt as though this golden-haired hippie-fairy had lived a whole lot more than she had, despite their similar years.

Those six weeks at the farm sealed a friendship that would last in one form or another to the bitter end. The two young women had perfected the Harold McClintock impressions they'd still occasionally perform as sixty-year-olds on the pontoon boat in Wauconda. They'd pelted each other with fallen apples, lounged in the summer shade, and wondered at the old man's Scrabble prowess—they'd team up two on one and still be defeated handily. The old man would be rattling on with nonsense stories all the while about, say, the Depression-era hobo adventures of his Great-Uncle Freddy, who'd come over from County Killarney, and had once heard from a drunken Swede as they both waited on the boarding call from their respective captains, who'd put in at Hermitage Bay there, which in those days was a whaling port though you'd never know it now—the young folks have packed and made for better opportunities and seems they've taken the town with them, not to mention the effect of the ever-tightening regulations on the fishing industry, not that I can begrudge the young fellers their chance, can I, seeing as I did the same when I was a boy and the wages in Calgary were tempting...

Julie would sit there rapt as he talked, scribbling bits down with a surreptitious pen to immortalize the old fossil for the folks at home, who must have thought it a caricature, as Grace interjected the occasional question to keep him talking. Grace too was an object of Julie's chronicling. It fascinated her to no end that this girl with a promising future had leapt out over the abyss to spin hula hoops and sway to the carefree strains of the groovy music, trusting that the next apple-picking or bar-tending gig would "manifest" when she required it to. What really made the friendship stick, though, was the fact that the fascination was mutual, for Grace admired and even envied Julie her diligence and calm, the capacity for humble toil which would allow her to establish a respected niche for herself in certain highfalutin circles as an eccentric but estimable structuralist holdout against the deconstructionist mania that had swept through the world of literary theory.

When they'd hugged farewell at the train station in Vancouver, they'd promised to meet up in Chicago whenever Grace's wandering path happened next to take her there. And indeed they had done so, catching up at a Hyde Park party thrown by some of Julie's U of C colleagues (one of whose roommates, incidentally, was Colin), an event where Grace's vaguely oriental-patterned harem pants and jangling bracelets and flyaway hair had singled her out in that crowd of sweater-vested and pants-suited dowds who'd been gathered together to study at the nation's most suicidal university, all of them taking themselves very seriously indeed.

*

Incredibly, there had only been one time through all those years that any real discomfort had entered into her friendship with Julie; it had been the time that Grace had called to talk about an ongoing fight she'd been having with Colin.

The whole ordeal had started at one of Colin's company's interminable holiday parties, a black-tie event in a ballroom on the twentieth floor of one of the skyscrapers overlooking Grant Park—the sort of thing which could accurately be termed a soiree. The only remaining hint of her hippie youth had been the pewter Grateful Dead earrings that were subtle enough to wear with her evening gown.

It being the nature of conversations to tend toward whatever topic is held in common, holiday parties full of bankers are bound to foster a great deal of talk about markets and equities and whatever other deadly dull nonsense she'd eventually had to gently tell Colin she simply wasn't interested in learning the first thing about, and thus Grace had bounced from group to group, counterfeiting nonchalance with admirable success, her discomfort evident only in the prodigious number of martinis she was slugging down. One group composed exclusively of wives had seemed promising, as far as non-financial conversation went, but then the conversation had foundered upon that other seemingly unavoidable common topic—one's children—and she'd felt the need to bow out. It wasn't that she was embarrassed by Elijah. It was the looks of sympathy she couldn't stand. But how else were they supposed to respond when each of the other moms had sung her child's praises in her turn. "Isn't it terrible how much pressure they put on kids these days? And so early! Billy's already thinking about the ACT, and he's in seventh grade!" "Oh yes, I totally agree, Madisyn is already into AP classes, and it's only her sophomore year." What was she supposed to say when the conversation came around to her, and all she had to talk about was dyslexia and speech therapy and the fight to keep him in as many standard classes as possible and all the ways that the "special needs" label complicated his social life and led to behavioral problems. It wasn't that she was embarrassed. It just wasn't a conversation she felt the need to have, again.

And of course Colin had been nowhere to be found, though seeing as he was all but certain that they'd be naming him partner later that very evening, she couldn't blame him for having other things on his mind. In any case, she'd always prided herself on not being the sort of wife who dragged down every social occasion by needing looking-after—and there were certainly some of those, even at that very party. Thus, she had headed back to the bar, which at least gave her something to do, when someone noticed the earrings. An affinity for the Dead had always been a venerable quality in her book, and as they'd stood in line she'd found herself in an easy, pleasant conversation with a tall, scruffily-bearded man with a ponytail and a slightly rumpled suit, which he somehow wore more elegantly than the buttoned down fuddy-duddies with their neatly pressed creases. When they'd gotten their drinks, they'd retired to a corner to wait out the party, relieved at having found a momentary respite from the circumambient uptightness.

He was a dependent spouse as well, a jazz musician whose gigs and private lessons afforded him enough income to scrape together rent for a shoebox apartment in some skeezy part of town, but who freely copped to the fact that his current lifestyle was possible only as a result of living on what jazz guys apparently called "wife support." Maybe his air of unconcerned cool was a veneer to cover an underlying discomfort with this situation, but it genuinely seemed not to bother him, which allowed Grace, herself usually quite defensive in this sea of two-profession couples, to let her guard down. This, plus the alcohol, had her telling this stranger within five minutes of meeting him about the horrible feeling of inferiority she had suffered during her years as a "housewife," and how her current job at a coffee shop didn't confer all that much more prestige on her than being a "stay-at-home" either.

He got her to open up about the coffee shop. The shithead college kid employees who thought they were better than the job. The shithead burnout employees, restaurant industry lifers, who had less in the way of ego problems, but tended to be an absolute mess in one way or another. The shithead yuppie customers, who seemed to think that people who worked behind counters were deserving of whatever passive-aggressive nastiness they could think of to throw at them. The wacky band of misfit regulars to whom the cafe was a second home. The drama and exhaustion of running a place with shoestring margins. The fact that her twenty-five-hour work week, weekdays 6AM-11AM, left her with just four precious afternoon hours to rest her head or run an errand before the human tornado—whose love and joy left just as much of a trail of mud and broken vases as his periodic tantrums—reentered her home.

It had been quite a while since she felt like she had anything interesting to say about life, but the saxophonist assured her that he could see where she was coming from, that the day-to-day life of a working musician involved many of the same tribulations and class-struggles as the less-heralded parts of the service industry. They too entered buildings through the service entrance in the back (which he said should be called the "servant's" entrance). They too were fed their hurried shift meal in the kitchen, out of the view of their lords, the paying customers. They too dealt with an unending stream of bullshit from entitled assholes. At a jazz club, you might be treated like an artist—though that milieu brought with it its own particular brand of bullshit—but on the jobbing gigs that got you through the month, playing background music for weddings and Italian restaurants and corporate receptions like this very event (there were indeed a couple college kids listlessly playing through standards in the corner of the room, which Grace had almost entirely failed to register, which the saxophonist said proved his point), you were just another low-wage chump to be kicked around.

Giggling in the corner of the sumptuous downtown ballroom, with the tuxedoed waiters scurrying to and fro and the chandeliers twinkling above them, they'd lampooned the pretensions of the elite to whose party they'd been invited as guests, whose cups ran over into theirs but to whose number they decidedly did not belong. It was fun like she hadn't had in years. They'd even snuck out onto a balcony to take a couple hits of California medical. For a moment, she remembered what it had felt like to be the kind of person to dance in fields and roam the country, and as Colin had driven them home that night, she found herself wondering how things had gotten so off track. She'd reached into her purse to feel the crisp outline of the business card the saxophonist had given her, ostensibly to discuss the possibility of having his trio come play at the cafe some time. She'd known that she would make the call.

Apparently, she'd already set off alarm bells that first night after the party, when she'd gushed to her husband, whom they had indeed made partner that night, about how funny and just, like, cool Chris was, but it wasn't until the saxophonist had been playing her cafe on Thursdays for three or so months that Colin had finally snapped and aired his grievances. It had been a dumb little blow-up, precipitated by a dumb little event. She'd forgotten to put her phone on silent and when it had "dinged" late at night, Colin had wanted to know who it was. Things had kicked off from there. He didn't like them texting, particularly not late at night, didn't like them "hanging out" at the cafe after the Thursday gig, and sure as hell didn't like hearing all the time about what fucking funny thing had happened to fucking Chris this time.

Though she'd expected commiseration regarding Colin's overbearing and controlling behavior from Julie of all people, who was a fairly strident feminist (or would have been, had her personality allowed her to act in a way that anyone could reasonably describe as strident), she was surprised when instead Julie had just sighed and said, "Grace, you just don't see how much you have." When Grace had objected, Julie had cut her abruptly off. "Look, I have to go. But just know that there are a lot of us out here who would give a whole hell of a lot to have someone be possessive of us. I get that you haven't technically done anything wrong, but I don't think it's unreasonable for Colin to be a bit uncomfortable with you making friends with some man. Especially since it is pretty obvious that you like him." Things had gone cold between them for a long few weeks after that, but eventually Grace would thank her friend, telling her that she had broken off her acquaintance with the saxophonist, whom she had eventually concluded was indeed a smooth operator trying to get into her pants, and they'd never mentioned it again.

*

Steven had never had sufficient exposure to children to get over his awkwardness around them. He wouldn't make funny noises or toss them in the air or fool around until they got the giggles, but he *had* figured out that they appreciated being taken seriously just as much as grown-ups do— and perhaps even more so, seeing as such treatment can be some-what rare in a child's life. So what he would do, in lieu of goofiness, was let them be the boss for a while. He'd get down on the carpet and listen carefully as they explained the different toys and the role each played in the game-world they'd created. And then he'd pick up a lego spaceman and play the game according to the parameters the child had defined.

Goran and Nikola, having known "Uncle Steve" since birth, were well accustomed to his somewhat awkward demeanor. When he came over, as he often did for Sunday dinner, they'd immerse him in whatever game-world they had constructed, at least until Liljana called them in to eat. Sometimes a parent will tell their kids to quit bothering whatever adult they've invited over to the house, but Johnny could tell Steven came to see the kids almost as much as he came to visit him. As he entered the game-world, Johnny could see his friend progressively shed his awkward demeanor, and by the end of it, he'd have the kids climbing all over him, chasing him around the room.

There was a comforting sameness to the Sunday dinners at the Dragaš home. If it was a winter Sunday, there would be football on the television, as Ivan, whom everyone including his wife called Johnny, considered it to be a central aspect of his assimilation to make sense of this enigmatic game. If it was basketball season, he'd diverge slightly from his rigorous program of Americanization, for he was an admitted partisan when it came to the league's few Serbs, though none of them had yet matched up to the legendary Vlade Divacc, who was entering his career's twilight.

Meanwhile, Liljana would be in the kitchen making something hearty and delicious—their division of household labor was quite traditional in a lot of ways, though Johnny also took pride in their having shuffled around responsibilities so his wife would have time for the night classes that would lead, eventually, to a nursing career. Steven, who had no particular interest in sports, would stand in the kitchen while she cooked, chopping vegetables or wrapping meat in grape leaves. He'd learned to make a passable prebranac just from watching her. She'd used to joke about finding him a nice Serbian girl, but had stopped when it became clear that it just made him reflect sadly on his terminal bachelorhood.

They'd eat, the kids would be wrangled off to bed, and then Liljana would leave the two of them alone to sip at little glasses of that plum brandy that Balkanites are absolutely mad about. Liljana had once told Steven that he was the only person Johnny would talk about the war with, but the truth was that they'd exhausted that subject long ago. Even then, he'd had remarkably little to say about it. In Vukovar, he'd seen and done some terrible things. In Pakračka Poljana, he'd had some terrible things done to him. And then, when the Croats let him go in a prisoner exchange, his parents had pulled some strings to get him out of the country, and that was the war. As for Milena, well, all Steven knew was that in '93 when he'd asked a newly arrived Johnny how she was, he'd looked away.

Those nights on the porch, they'd mostly sit quietly, with some occasional shop-talk sprinkled in—the latest dumbass thing some apprentice had done, an accident on a site one of them had heard about, or whatever new wrinkles the bureaucrats had introduced into the permit system. They'd talk about the kids or Steven's garden, which was beginning to exceed the limitations of the narrow lot in Chicago where he was living at that point. The closest they'd come to the war was the occasional reference to that halcyon antebellum summer they'd spent in Golubić, before Knin was synonymous with the Krajina Republic.

They remembered the ill-fated visit to the anything-goes grog shop which was really just the porch of some elderly peasant's shack, where Steven and Johnny had drank themselves sick on bootleg šljivovica—and the way Mr. Dragaš, head engineer at the local hydroelectric plant, had winked merrily as his wife mercilessly dragged the two of them out of bed and sent them to pull weeds the next morning, only relenting after Steven had twice vomited under the beating sun and tutting mildly as she'd sent him back to bed (she'd shown no such mercy to her son). The camping trip up into the rugged foothills of the Bosnian Alps, where Mr. Dragaš had told them (over brandy) about life before the war, and about hiding in those very hills when the Ustaše had come to Knin.[27] The way Johnny's ancient grandfather had persisted in speaking broken French to Steven, as it was the only foreign language he knew, despite the fact that neither Steven nor any of the other members of the Dragaš family had the faintest idea of what he was talking about. The Dragaš parents were still hale and hearty in their mid-eighties, though now located in Belgrade; there were no more Serbs in Golubić. Every now and then Johnny would call them up after Sunday dinner so they could say hi to Steve.

Only rarely would Johnny mention the 1990s. And only on a single occasion, when he'd had more than usual to drink, had he broached the unmentionable topic, laughing himself hoarse over the night Milena had reluctantly taken the two of them out to one of the dirty rock clubs she'd frequented. How he'd immediately failed to live up to her injunction not to embarrass her and drunkenly gotten on the wrong side of some Novi Belgrade mobster. How it had been Steven who'd saved him from a beating, simply by being an American, which was quite the curiosity in those days.

---

[27] Though the engineer, a mild-mannered, cultured man, as well as a true-believing Yugoslav, had intended this as a lesson on the folly of nationalism, for Johnny, the popular narrative of the Second World War had had quite the opposite effect, inculcating a pro-Serbian sentiment which had impelled him to join the war effort, though now, as an Americanized and settled family man, he could look back more clearly on the cynical manner in which romantic nationalism had been used as a smokescreen for criminal gangs to profit.

Johnny sighed. "The gangsters were more gentle before the war. They were still mafia, you know, but not so crazy. They had rules." They'd lapsed into silence before he suddenly spoke up again: "That's what happened to Milena, you know. Wasn't some war thing. Some mafia guy just start shooting in the club and hit her by mistake. Assholes. Man, but that night she took us out in Belgrade… good times…"

Another pause.

"You know, she'd ask about you sometimes, after you left. She really did like you very much, Steve. My sister could be sort of harsh person. Bit of a bitch really. But this was just her way of joking."

"I know, buddy."

Johnny had taken a deep, rattly breath and Steven had ventured a tentative squeeze of his friend's shoulder, and the subject had dropped. On the walk home, cloudy-headed and nostalgic, Steven would think back, for the first time in quite a while, to the thing with Milena, back to the second time he found himself on the very cusp, unable, once again, to cross the threshold.

*

Johnny couldn't have known that Steven and his older sister had become rather friendly towards the end of his stay in Yugoslavia. Indeed, to all outward appearances, Milena had regarded Steven with a haughty disengagement at best. Her return to the Dragaš family home during the summer of Steven's exchange had upset the tranquility that had established itself during the first three months of his stay, though this had less to do with Steven than with the fact that economic circumstances had sentenced her to yet another blistering Krajina summer in a town she was looking forward to leaving behind forever.

Unlike her younger brother, Milena had been a near-adolescent when the family had moved back to the home-village from Belgrade, and the formative influence of those years in the capital had made her into a cultural outsider from the moment of her arrival in Golubić. Being a very proud and stubborn girl, she had spent her adolescence marinating in contempt for the village children who had ostracized her, as well as for the backwardness of the village itself. Having finally left for the university, she had hoped to find some sort of summer job in the city, but the economic situation at the time had been such that she'd been unable to do so. Envious of her Belgrade friends who were no doubt drinking beers in Tašmajdan Park or swimming in the Danube at that very moment, she'd been moody and standoffish from the start.

To make matters worse, her parents had set her and Steven even more at odds by insisting that she share Johnny's (then known as Ivan) room to make space for their guest. Steven had offered to give Milena her room back, but Mrs. Dragaš wouldn't hear of it, and thus it was that their first meeting had been characterized by awkward, one-sided chit-chat as the glowering young woman transferred her possessions out of her childhood bedroom.

They hadn't had much to do with each other for a while after that. Johnny, who unlike his sister had fully assimilated to the provincial lifestyle (indeed, he'd done so to such an extent that his parents, educated people who thought of themselves as cosmopolitan Belgrade Yugoslavs despite their village roots, worried about his provincialization), had been enthusiastic about showing Steven all the wonders of Croatian summer, as well as showing off his prestigious new friend, older and an American to boot, to his schoolmates. They'd fished and swam and hiked and, when Mrs. Dragaš could track them down, were put to work, giving Steven the first taste of the gardening hobby that would be his source of inner tranquility in later life. Meanwhile, Milena had barricaded herself in the house with her books. For the first month of summer, they'd scarcely seen each other at all.

He couldn't remember why it was that the rest of the family had been out of the house, but for whatever reason there came an afternoon when she, thinking she had the house to herself, had slipped down to the living room to spend the afternoon reading. He'd peeked at the spine of the book and seen an old favorite and, before he'd even considered how rude it would be to interrupt her, had blurted out that he absolutely loved that one. She'd looked up slowly, her eyes narrowed to convey her irritation, but then explained that she'd read it once in translation and, having come into an English copy, had decided that a second read-through would simultaneously serve her literary and language-learning goals.

"I'm surprised Americans have such high respect for socialist literature."

"Well, I dunno about it being socialist—but socialist or not, the point is if it's a good book."

"Of course it's socialist. This is book about capitalist exploitation. The banker evicts the farmers. The police stop them to organize themselves when they become laborers. The other workers are tricked not to have class solidarity, but instead to hate 'Okies.' Socialist themes."

"Well I guess I hear 'socialist' and have a certain reaction."

"Yes. You are an American, after all."

"But to me, saying a book, or whatever art, is socialist, capitalist, whatever, that just makes it into propaganda. Like the art is subordinated to the ideology."

"Ah, I see. You are a romantic. Art for art's sake."

"And what's wrong with that?"

"It's naive."

"Maybe so, but seeing everything through ideology is just cynical. It diminishes the beauty of the work."

"Beauty, he says. The beauty of the laborers beaten by capitalist police force to extract surplus value."

"The beauty of the heroic spirit of man. The beauty of the journey to the frontier, over the mountains to the promised land. That's a whole lot deeper than some sort of debate about economics."

He'd surprised himself with these positions he didn't know he held. She'd come at him so aggressively that he hadn't had time to fall into his usual cycle of self-doubt. They went on for hours that way, Milena pressing him on everything, and Steven, for once, standing up for himself, simply because she didn't give him the option of playing the limp push-over he'd grown accustomed to playing. Having becoming acclimated to her causticity, it didn't even really bother him when his boneheaded reference to "communist" Yugoslavia as being part of the "Eastern Bloc" stoked her ire, or when his vague assertions about American liberty had occasioned a furious arm-flailing rant about Vietnam and the Greek Junta, or even when he'd crossed the line entirely by daring to mention that US had in fact fought on the same side of WWII as the Partisans ("ah, yes, this is such similar thing to drop nuclear weapons on civilian population in defense of colonial empire—just like the anti-fascists who died at Jasenovac after fighting the Ustaše" [not incidentally, she'd gestured broadly to the west as she pronounced the word "Ustaše," though consciously she certainly thought of herself as being far above any sort of ethno-religious factionalism]). Knowing that nothing he said would spare him her contempt, he became inured to it, and in turn gradually comfortable dishing out some scorn of his own, as a result of which she'd warmed up to him somewhat, though for her, warmth took the form of a barrage of yet more withering sarcasm and fiery criticism. The two of them developed the routine of sitting, reading, with their backs against a certain cherry tree as the sun set. Did he remember correctly, all those many years later, that one of those afternoons she had looked at him, black eyes through a curtain of black hair that had fallen in her face, with something like an invitation in her eyes?

When the six-month exchange had come to an end, Steven had said his goodbyes to the elder Dragašes, all set to make the long trek back to the capital, spending a final weekend there before his flight. Johnny had been plotting for weeks, first begging his parents to let him tag along to Belgrade to see his friend off, and then—the more daunting of the two tasks—pleading with his sister to let him cram into her student apartment for the weekend and maybe, just maybe, to consider compromising her street cred by taking her kid brother and a dopey foreigner out to the hippest joints of the Belgrade underground. Johnny's persistence had paid off on all accounts, and it had, indeed, been a night to remember.

What Johnny, whose leglessly drunken teenage body they'd had to haul from the tram up to Milena's fifth floor walk-up, didn't know, couldn't know, was that something had occurred at the end of that night, from which Steven had surmised that his unfortunate fate was sealed.

With Johnny snoring on the couch, he and Milena had stood at her door with something in the air between them. He'd cleared his throat and said he'd better be on his way. They'd shared one of those sterile hugs where neither party wishes to take on the vulnerability of demonstrating the warmth they feel, for fear of it being a one-sided display. Then he'd started down the stairs. Turning around to look back up at her, with the thought of maybe saying something, he realized that he'd been here before, a few steps down, looking up at a woman who stood at the threshold that he would not, could not cross. And he knew that this would be the cycle he'd repeat.

He had thought he'd forgotten about Grace, but as he'd trudged, cursing himself for his inaction, down Bulevar Zorana Đinđića toward the Old City as Belgrade slept, he knew that the nightmare was still with him, that in a way it was occurring still. He could still feel the torture of the long moment that elapsed after he told her how he felt, him standing a few steps down from the threshold, she under the transom, staring past him, collecting her thoughts. It was the culmination of years of longing, years of friendship, years of long meandering walks around the neighborhood, of late-night telephone conversations where they talked of their hopes and dreams. And then Grace had settled on a response, two words that would serve a certain purpose, to keep him on the hook for a little while longer, or perhaps to let him down more gently over the weeks and months that it took for him to realize that his time would never come.

"Not now," she'd said.

It wasn't as though he'd never had a woman. As a result of his loneliness and desperation, Steven had continued to frequent singles' nights and speed-dating events long after such things had become relics of the past. Furthermore, he had been quite early to the online-dating game, having registered for various services long before doing so was normalized. There'd been a few faltering starts that went nowhere, but as he, and they, aged, the feelings had become less compelling. The thing is that once you get to your thirties, and everyone but you has been through it all, love assumes a pallor. These single moms and post-wall whores couldn't ever understand the fluttering unease that Steven still exuded, and he couldn't help but feel contempt for the way in which they were so evidently depleted. For him there would never be a bloom to look back on that would justify the prolonged wilting that inevitably follows.

*

Here are Grace and Steven, working in their respective gardens on a steamy summer Saturday, three days after their chance meeting at the library. They're closer together in space than anything but fate's serendipity or an amateur writer's hacky plot devices could explain or justify—maybe fifteen minutes along the winding country roads of north-ern Illinois—but they'll more than likely never meet again, for it is here that the hack writer's contrivances will reach their endpoint, leaving them to live out their remaining years in peace. Remembering how Ivan Dragaš had described Steven's green thumb during their phone call that Thursday, Grace shakes her head in mild appreciation of the twists and turns of life; there's certainly a kind of poetry to them, whether they are possessed of any deeper significance or not. How funny it was that she and Steven had ended up in such similar circumstances by such different routes, alone in their respective gardens, among the crops their labors have grown.

Then she shrinks Steven down and puts him on a pantry shelf suitable for memories of charming insignificance. Perhaps he'll gather dust up there, or perhaps in an idle moment, she'll take him down to look at him, Stevie Dolan, that nice boy she'd known in high school, who once had been to Yugoslavia.

As for Steven, he has looked away, once again and hopefully permanently, from the memory of Grace Carter, and as he averts his eyes, the memory resumes its usual monstrous proportions. He'll go back to living his life as he has since that evening on her porch—free from the oppressive memory, provided that he is fanatically careful never to so much as glance in the particular direction in which it looms. Even though he never, never thinks about her, there's a sense in which his life since he knew her has been devoted to the cause of avoiding the accumulation of similar monsters, that eternally lurk but do not pounce, provided you keep your gaze properly averted, and provided you ignore the sibilant whisper, "not now," knowing in your heart that those words, in truth, mean "never."

~ Rescuing Nadezhda ~

The old man must have picked his name out of a hat or something, Radner figured. After all, a finance reporter at an outfit like the *New York Times*, hoary and once-prestigious but relegated since the Reconquest to regional status, had no business writing up the long-form authorized biography of a reclusive but much-heralded Galician author for the paper's weekend magazine. But for whatever reason, the letter, written in imperfect English, had demanded in no uncertain terms that it be Radner and no one else who would conduct the interview and write the corresponding piece. The author could easily have made his triumphant return to public life in the Tribune if he wanted (or *Die Presse*, for that matter—who knows what he was thinking picking an English-language outlet at all). The boys in Chicago would have had one of their foremost cultural commentators pull out all the stops to make the piece a memorable one. Instead he had demanded Radner who, when some sadistic professor had assigned the old Galician's most famous novel back in college, had found his prose to be irritatingly pompous and self-indulgent, to the extent that he'd read it at all.

Radner was already accustomed to presenting himself as something of a philistine, a baseball-cap-wearing finance bro in a world of effete literati. Being the sort of person to derive great pleasure from motiveless needling, he had heightened these efforts to the maximum degree in the weeks after his flummoxed superiors had thrown up their hands and assented to the author's demand, entrusting a potentially epochal artistic event to Aaron

Radner of all people. He had amusing himself by deliberately mispronouncing the world-famous novelist's name and "confusing" him with various other Ruthenian and Malorussian authors just to up the ire of the many colleagues who would gladly have paid a steep price for such a pearl of an opportunity as that which Fate had seen fit to cast before this self-declared swine.

Must have picked his name out of the staff directory at random, Radner figured once again, the cirrus wisps affording him an occasional view of the distant waves below. Something to do with that tendency of artists to become supremely self-important, setting out unusual demands so as to confirm their bigshot statuses. In any case, a free trip was a free trip and New York was no place for a human to be in the summer. Thus, silly as the whole project seemed, Radner was determined that it should go forward, simply for the opportunity to spend a few days pleasantly drunk on the Krakiv Market Square. He had put on his most reverent mask in the meeting his superiors had called, which had really been more of a condescending talking-to, where they had cajoled him to please, for the love of God, not to make a mockery out of this assignment. He'd even concocted a little anecdote about how one of the old man's torturous, prolix stories had "really gotten him through some hard times back in college." His air of gravitas had reassured them and, perhaps because they'd expected more of a conflict, he'd found them an unusually soft touch when it came to expenses. Starting with a survey of the various significant landmarks of the author's Lemberger childhood, Radner would go on to Krakiv (which, upon independence, had ended up being named the Galician capital over Lemberg, as a sop to the unfortunate Poles), where the author had risen to literary stardom. Finally, he would make the trip out to the remote Carpathian village where the author had apparently been living in anonymity for many years, continuing to pump out ever more esoteric and impenetrable material, which had continued to find a considerable readership among the world's benighted poseurs, who were, in Radner's opinion, simply unwilling to admit that the emperor had no clothes. The article would, of course, culminate in the proffered interview. Radner's superiors had given him two weeks, with a *per diem* that was beyond what he would even have been comfortable asking for and sent him on his merry way.

In point of fact, all the research Radner was planning to do had occurred the very night that the trip had been confirmed with his superiors. He'd gone home and, with a level of motivation which typically eluded him in his regular work, cobbled together a few thousand words of high-flown fluff from some online reference books on the history and geography of the region and the biography section of the author's Wikipedia page. He'd written in the memoir-adjacent post-gonzo style then popular among the middle-brow commentariat, casting himself as a character in the story— making much of the "breath of cool Carpathian air" that had rushed into his train compartment informing him that he was "on the cusp of arrival," and inventing a stereotypical old babka on the train who'd offered him smoked plums and dusted off her long-abandoned schoolgirl Viennese to chat with him a bit. Fluff—just what the weekend magazine specialized in. Per Radner's calculations, a couple quotations from the old man himself would round out the piece nicely, the accumulation of which would take one afternoon, maximum. Taking drive-time into account, he had every reason to think that twelve and a half days of his fourteen day trip could be spent sampling fine cognac and nibbling pastries in one of the sunny, cobblestone plazas of the old town.

As it turned out, he didn't even make it down to the Carpathians for a full week after his arrival in Krakiv. The Galician capital was both cheaper and more amenable to his taste for decadence and dissipation than he remembered. It wasn't until late morning on the eighth day that he'd finally figured that he might as well get the interview over with; he'd already peremptorily rescheduled with the old man on two separate occasions, and it wasn't as though the Krakiv restaurants would be getting any less alluring in the days that were to follow. And so he'd stumbled through the blinding sun, much the worse for wear that hungover morning, to rent a car and set off, far later than he would have liked, on a seemingly interminable journey across the plains, and then up into the mountains on cracked and pitted roads, checking into a rural hotel as the northern summer sky took on the fitful glow of not-quite-night.

The next morning's short journey from the rural hotel up into the mountain villages seemed to take just as long as the trek from Krakiv. The roads were gravel at best and mud at worst, and between the several times his little coupe had gotten stuck, the fact that the anonymous backroads didn't seem to properly correspond to any map he'd been able to download, and the maddening fact that every few meters he had to stop the car to open the ramshackle gates that the peasants had put up in an attempt to corral their wandering cows, he didn't arrive at the location the author had given until the late afternoon.

And then there was the matter of the old man himself who, despite having been the one to set up the interview, didn't give any indication of being willing to sit down and answer questions anytime soon. Some amount of this sort of thing was, of course, fully justified by Radner's earlier cancellations, but as the hours mounted, and Radner followed along as the old man puttered around, seemingly aimlessly, in the weed-choked fields of his property, his frustration mounted, heightened all the more by the unstemmable flow of irrelevances the author emitted in a quite fluent Viennese, his Ruthenian accent just thick enough to strain the ears. They stopped to slurp down cups of vinegary homemade wine (which explained the purple stains on the novelist's ratty white t-shirt), and Radner listened half-attentively to the half-baked theories of the half-crazy man, who haphazardly mixed profoundly unfashionable, decades-old philosophical and aesthetic theories with an idiosyncratic theory of magic, which included vague allusions to Hutsul shamanism. It was with great relief that Radner finally entered the rotted out hull of a once-grand country house in which the Author of Halych apparently made his abode.

A faded middle-aged woman whose face seemed at once forlorn and hostile had bustled into the sitting room to set out a pot of tea. Only nodding briefly in response to Radner's words of thanks and introduction, she had stalked out of the room, the author responding to this with an irritated exhalation and dismissive hand gesture, looking apologetically in Radner's direction to indicate his embarrassment. "My daughter, Nadezhda," he said, by way of explanation.

Finally, after the seemingly interminable journey, the two of them looked at each other, seemingly on the verge of sitting down in the once-fine armchairs to begin, at long last, the interview. Radner had to admit that the house's interior outperformed its exterior. The furniture seemed to match in vintage the oil-painted portraits of various Austrian heads of state from back in the days of the Empire, a period which large portions of the population of the Federation of Central European States—even the non-Austrian majority—looked back on with much fondness. The carpet was thick and seemingly handwoven, and the lighting was warm and soft. As Radner stood marveling, the author looking on with no little pride at the impression his decor had made, the woman emerged from what seemed to be a kitchen, slamming down platters with evident ill-temper (again, the same apologetic expression from the author toward Radner). Radner had, once again, attempted to address her, complimenting the aromas with a smile, and once again she had only responded with a brief and expressionless nod.

"It's not as though I force her to cook, God forbid," the author muttered, embarrassed. "I suggest, perhaps, once or twice, would be nice to have something to do. Maybe saying cooking as example… and since then she act like… well…" And as if to distract himself, he had proceeded to give Radner an in-depth tour of the feast at hand, which was indeed decadently varied, with zrazy and deruny and soljanka and Apfelrotkohl and various pickled vegetables and roasted meats and Senfeier and plentiful smetana and of course the freely flowing Grüner Veltliner and walnut-stuffed prunes and sirniki with cherries for dessert. In the course of the feasting, the interview had left Radner's mind entirely and, as much as he had enjoyed the fine cuisine of the capital, none of it came anywhere close in quality to the magnificent offering he tucked into in this most unlikely of locations. The more he ate, the more he seemed to enter a sort of trance and as the author talked at length, no doubt spilling his proverbial guts in a manner which, had Radner been in a state to properly listen, would have provided ample material for the piece he was supposed to be writing. He was saying something about magic again… always magic with this guy… magic as a matter of concentration, of will… the unique power of the writer, who can become, very nearly, a sorcerer… who directs the will of thousands, millions of readers… who, if he is truly a master of his craft, can work miracles….

Radner heard and didn't hear. He ate as if he'd never eaten before (and, being a man of decadent tastes, be it known that he had indeed lustily eaten on many a previous occasion). Finally, when the author had offered him a thick, hand-rolled cigarette of Zacarpathian tobacco (a picture of good old Joseph II on the package), he had taken a long draw and, as the Author of Halych bade him look long and deep into the glowing coals in the wood-fired furnace, felt the smoke's effects drifting out from his chest and into every limb, every muscle, soothing every ache and setting his ever-whirring mind at ease, at which point he had dropped promptly off to sleep, the old man looking on with an air of great satisfaction on his face as the journalist snored in his chair.

*

Radner awoke in mid-shiver, his every muscle clenched against the bracing mountain chill, and rose to his feet, stiff and cursing, in what appeared to be a decaying ruin having nothing in common with the wonderful manor where he'd spent the previous night. Morning dew was in evidence. The structure he found himself in was roughly constructed, and a splintered edge of the floorboards he'd slept upon had snagged on his shirt as he'd awoken. Outside the house, the previous day's ramshackle but charming hobby-farm had been reduced to tangles of unkempt and thorny undergrowth—which was, of course, impossible, but Aaron Radner had no interest in such topics at that moment. While on the one hand he really had to hand it to the crazy bastard—hauling out all that furniture for reasons unknown must have been no small task—the journalist was finished being toyed with. He would fabricate quotes, or maybe call the author up if he needed some supplementary material to get the piece written. Frankly, the paper could fire him if they felt like it. What Radner was absolutely not willing to do was to spend one moment more in this land of absurdity, listening to mad old geezers drone on about magic, being lulled and, frankly, most likely drugged to sleep, and then left to freeze in some wreck. Cursing, he hobbled stiffly across the property and started up his car with the heat cranked (thank the Lord that whatever madness had inspired the Author of Halych to empty out his house of all its furniture and decor, all the kitchen appliances, and the furnace, as well as to lay waste to his own fields, hadn't also inspired him to drive Radner's rental car off a cliff or God knows what).

Even to think too much about the previous night was to wonder if he'd gone somehow insane, so Radner decided to stop thinking entirely, at least until he'd reached the bottom of several pints of Czech beer back in Krakiv. The return journey went more smoothly than the trip there, and Radner made good time, though it seemed to him that the roads had somehow gotten worse overnight. If not for the fact that he had resolved not to think, the usually journalistically perspicacious Radner would no doubt have become curious about the change in road conditions, as well as about the sudden and inexplicable proliferation of the Cyrillic alphabet, which had been very much out of fashion in Galicia since the Liberation of the European USSR in 1953. But things being as they were, Radner didn't register the strangeness of his surroundings until a good many hours into the trip, when the unaccountable appearance of what seemed unmistakably to be a border crossing right in the middle of the great highway connecting Krakiv and Lemberg impeded his further progress.

There was no explaining it. Furthermore, there was no explaining the two very odd flags which adorned the crossing's respective sides: blue and yellow, red and white—or rather, the explanation that suggested itself as he drew closer to the "crossing" was a wholly impossible one. "You are now leaving Ukraine" was written both in what seemed to be an old Ruthenian dialect (Radner had a vague familiarity with Galician Slavic via his grandfather, though as we've mentioned, he used his more fluent [and more prestigious] Viennese to get by when traveling in the Federation) and in English below (English!?), and in the distance, Radner could see that the opposite station's inscription read "Welcome to Poland," both in the Latin-scripted Polish dialect of Galician and, once again, in English. The only explanation that occurred to Radner was that he was looking at an impossibly detailed pop-up demonstration of some kind, organized, perhaps by... Polish nationalists? It didn't seem all that likely, the com-mon wisdom being that since the intervention and consequent establishment of the autonomous province in 1923, the Poles had become more German than the Germans, serving over-proportionally in the Wehrmacht which protected their last remnants of territory, perched perilously on the very cusp of the all-devouring Soviet behemoth... and as for partisans of the Ukrainian SSR making territorial claims in Central Galicia, well, that upped the ante in terms of sheer, half-baked chutzpah, as far as Radner was concerned... not to mention the logistical impossibility of setting up such a permanent-seeming installation as this "border crossing" in the two days since Radner had sped past this very location... and the lack of police presence didn't seem characteristic of the usually assiduous Galician authorities... not to mention the guns and uniforms that the demonstrators were wearing, which seemed to place them more in the category of militant insurrectionists than that of activists. And yet the rest of the cars on the highway slowed meekly and patiently waited for the militants to check their documents. It was yet another absurdity in the series of mounting absurdities that had engulfed the journalist in the previous few days.

The only reason Radner was even aware that the Poles had once been predominant this far south was that, growing up, he had heard the endless tales of his Polonized (or better, Galicianized) great-grandfather, who had made his way to what was then the United States after the fall of Krakiv and the consequent Soviet occupation. The trauma of the invasion, as well as the subsequent intervention of Hindenburg's reconstituted Reich, had made Great-Grandpa Radner so fanatically pro-German that he and his oldest son, Radner's grandfather, had ended up joining the partisans of the Midwest Alliance, whereas the other side of the family, Trotskyists to a man, had all hailed the landing at San Francisco as their deliverance from yet another pogrom, yet another utterly unjustified attack, inexplicable but for the fanatical, pathological hatred of the Goyim.

Family history aside, Radner had no patience for the absurd theatrics of militant irredentists. Skipping over the line of patiently waiting, thoroughly compliant cars, he rolled straight up to the illegal barricade and began furiously honking his horn, only drawing back from his attitude of pugnacity (and stopping with the aggressive honking) when a number of furious militants had come out wielding their very genuine-appearing weapons. Radner had had to snap abruptly into a highly conciliatory mood, rolling down his window and inquiring in his most diffident Viennese as to the meaning of all this, which had been greeted with an expression of evident puzzlement.

"English?" the militant had inquired, lowering his weapon.

"English? I mean, yeah sure. I was just wondering what is going on, sir, frankly. Why the road is blocked. I have business in Krakiv and I just drove through here two days ago with no problems…"

"Go line. You go line for border. Understand?" said the militant in a harsh and authoritative tone. Radner saw that a further ten or so militia men had emerged from their installation, weapons in hand.

"I understand. I suppose I just wanted to know—"

"Go line!" the militiaman boomed, the ten men behind him raising their weapons in a show of force. Really shocking stuff. Beyond the pale that Galicia would allow such lawlessness. But, men with guns being men with guns, Radner had meekly done as they had demanded, pulling to the back of the line, where he readied his camera on the off chance that he was bearing witness to world-historical events. Could there have been some sort of coup attempt? A secret Polish militia kicking into action and seizing territory? Could he, perhaps, have a journalistic scoop on his hands? For the first time since he'd compromised on his principles, taking the cushy desk job at the *Times* and giving up on the image of himself as an intrepid globe-trotting journalist communicating in clipped, hard-boiled diction and squinting undeterred in the face of danger, he felt the stirring of that old feeling of purpose. When he arrived at the front of the line, his camera was poised inconspicuously on the passenger seat, rolling as the terrorists demanded his passport. They examined it, seemingly puzzled, and finally ordered him out of the car, whereupon he brought the camera with him to continue document this shocking breach of law and order. It continued to role as the terrorists shouted out, "Not filming! Not filming!" up until the moment that the camera was slapped out of his hands and onto to the ground.

They kept him there for quite a while, repeating that his Arcadian passport was invalid, pretending not to understand German, and generally alternating between authoritarian wrath and a surprisingly convincing simulacrum of confusion over the simplest things. It was a maddening experience, and the sun had begun to redden in the sky by the time the militants, seemingly as frustrated as Radner himself, had finally released him, warning him that attempting to cross borders without proper documentation was a punishable offense, especially considering his behavior in so doing.

The only thing keeping Radner from boiling over with rage was his hope that the footage he'd captured might be salvageable from the damaged camera. He sped back east, into Lemberg, luckily without en-countering further obstacles, where he planned to check into the first decent hotel he saw before proceeding to the nearest electronics repair shop.

His troubles, however, were not at their end. In the hotel lobby he had once again become embroiled in yet another absurd dispute. The slender, oddly androgynous receptionist (with a shocking number of tattoos protruding out from under his unbuttoned shirt-cuffs) had, like the militants, refused to speak German and, even more infuriatingly, refused to accept either koronki or schillings. Without guns in his face, Radner had felt less compulsion to be even minimally polite, and the entire situation had almost escalated to a physical confrontation before his better judgment had interceded. This general pattern had recurred at each of the next two hotels Radner visited, which finally gave him cause to consider that whatever it was that was occurring was deeper and more worrisome than a mere political crisis. He wondered whether it was he who was in fact losing his grip on reality. Finding himself with nowhere to go, he settled on the only destination he could think of. Turning his car southward, he wound his way back up into the foothills of the Carpathians, the only break in the silence and the perfect starry darkness being the gentle rumble and glow of his little rental car as it made its way along the winding dirt paths.

Though he arrived in the dead of night, Radner could see as he pulled up to the broken-down old house that a light shone in the window, and as he climbed the steps, the front door opened to him from the inside. The old man, in the silk pajamas and floppy nightcap of an earlier era, had waited up for him, knowing somehow that in the end, Radner would be back where he'd set off from that morning.

"What the hell is happening," Radner asked brusquely, too disturbed to allow himself to be derailed by the author's tactics.

"So I finally have your attention?" the Author of Halych rejoined with a twinkle in his eye, pouring out rich, silky coffee and proffering a pouch of tobacco.

"I don't know what is going on in the world, but I am sure it has something to do with you. With whatever... I mean, there are Polish militants setting up checkpoints and no one takes koronki or speaks German... it's like some kind of absurd dream, which is a thought that keeps crossing my mind—that I'll wake up back in your living room... or maybe I'm even back in New York. But I keep trying, and I can't wake up..."

The author looked at him with a knowing, withholding expression. "This is what it takes to get attention of a man like you. Who will not listen to what I have already told. Magic, Mr. Radner. Magic is causing these things."

"Magic."

"Magic."

A pause. "Goddamnit, I don't have time for this..."

With an insolent little grin, the author replied, "If you need go to some important appointment, I will not say to stop." He gestured to the door, in response to which Radner deflated. He sat meekly down on the floor, his back to the bare wall, and sipped at his coffee as the impossible truth was explained to him.

At great length, the old man explained once again, the magic of attention. That things like visualization or the repetition of mantras have an effect over and above the mere psychological effect which dictates that a redirection of one's focus leads one to notice what was already there. That the little serendipities that accompany these redirections of focus are not coincidences—or not *solely* coincidences. That there are certain shamanic ritual practices, certain energies which can be drawn upon, as intensifiers of the magic of one's innate focus, and that certain of these pre-Christian practices have survived in a particularly continuous form among the Hutsuls of the Carpathians. That far more powerful than such traditional sources of energy as the moon, the sun, or the tall oak tree is the power of a cunningly crafted incantation channeled via the written word into the consciousnesses of the unwitting masses. That by harnessing this power, even history, the immutable past, becomes much more fluid than the uninitiated could imagine. That the past is not a stone but a flow that can be redirected, though the current can damn well pull you under, dash you on the rocks, if you don't know what you're doing.

That the principle of history's mutability, if applied, for example, to the doomed (or perhaps not so doomed) war that old Pilsudski fought against

Uncle Joe, might have profound consequences for the here and now, so many decades down the line. That Pilsudski's unlikely victory would render unnecessary the intervention of the reconstituted Reich and the liberation of Warsaw which gave the Western Slavs such an overwhelmingly positive opinion the Germans. That instead of the resurrection of the Empire, the Weimar Republic would remain intact throughout the twenties. That the reaction to the Weimar Malaise would give rise to a Reich of an entirely different character... and the Author of Halych proceeded to explain to Radner, in great detail, what you, the ever so sophisticated and educated reader no doubt know already.

Radner was tired. Rather than answering with the usual snark and attitude that was his wont, he just sighed, deflated, "Can you please just tell me in plain German what is going on? No more riddles."

And so, the Author of Halych explained to him that he had unwittingly attempted to cross the border between the independent republics of Poland and Ukraine, between which dear old Galicia had been divided (and indeed, in favor of whom, the very name of Galicia had been all but forgotten). Radner's passport, which proclaimed his citizenship of one of the post-American states, had no validity in a world in which the Second Civil War and the Midwestern Resistance had not occurred, in which the United States of America had not merely survived but prospered, ascending to a position of world hegemony. Not being in possession of any Ukrainian hryvnias, he had been unsuccessful in carrying out the various transactions he'd attempted in the city that was now called Lviv. He was lucky, the old man concluded, that nothing worse had happened: that the authorities hadn't seen fit to indefinitely detain this raving madman traveling on false documents, that he'd had sufficient benzene to make the journey back, etc.

Radner looked as though he were trying to shake himself into wakefulness. It had to be a dream. There's only so much mismatch between one's expectations and one's absurd reality which can be under-gone before one collapses entirely.

"Yes. Lot of information. I think better if you go to sleep, and in the morning we can discuss more the meaning of all what is happening."

Obediently, meekly, Radner obeyed him, and as the old man tucked him into the warm though slightly dusty bed with the tenderness of a grandfather, the journalist fell once again into a deep and enchanted sleep.

The next morning, when Radner had awoken to find the rental car packed to the brim and the author poised to take him on yet another impossible journey, he had snapped into his usual contemptuous skepticism, bellowing that going to Kiev would be impossible, that without a visa citizens of the Reconquered Territories could not hope to cross the Soviet border, that they would waste yet another day, and that, in any case, he had a deadline, as well as a flight out of Krakiv. But as the old man allowed him to air his grievances, feeding him whopping portions of smoky grits with mushrooms, Radner felt his resistance gradually, inexplicably decreasing. With his belly full, he had compliantly loaded up into the passenger seat of the car and allowed the old man to pilot them down from the hills and out into the steppe, across which they sped the whole day through in a state of silence. Radner's attempts at inquiry (as a part of his newfound meek compliance, he found himself acceding ever more to the author's insane and impossible beliefs about reality—to a degree which, in moments of clarity, he found to be quite concerning) were met by a preoccupied laconicity from the previously voluble old man. The journey was a smooth one, the border crossing at Brody having vanished just as mysteriously as the one at Krakovets had appeared. The plains had streamed by, and it had been all silence but for the engine's roar. It was in a similar silence that they found themselves nursing brandies at nightfall in Kiev (Kyiv?), whereupon it occurred to Radner that he didn't have the slightest notion of what it was that the Author of Halych had in mind for this trip to Kyiv. It occurred to him to worry about the ease with which he had gone along with this nonsense. It was as he was preparing to demand an explanation, steeling himself to accept no diversions, that she stopped at the crosswalk in front of the window of the cafe that the author had picked out for them to sit in, heavily made up and scandalously attired, undoubtedly a streetwalker, but unmistakably Nadezhda nonetheless. They watched for a long moment as she waited for the light to change. Then she continued on her way.

Radner turned to the author, and watched as an entire complex of dark emotions played across his face. Though pain and anger could be distinguished it seemed to him, the journalist observed that surprise was not among them. In a clenched voice, the author began to speak, and the purpose of their journey became slightly clearer. "Fifteen, twenty realities, each with deeper divergence than last one, I conjure to existence. With my writing, you understand. Magic. All of it for her. Each time, she become more miserable than before. I am too old now to improve my writing. Every year, fewer readers. The magic of the Pilsudski event is now beyond my powers. But I had hoped…"

Radner waited, in suspense, for the old man to finish his sentence, but no further words came. "Why have you brought me here, Artem? Why do you want me to see this?"

Another long moment. "I want you to document, like I say in letter to your newspaper. There is no purpose but this. I bring you to write my story. Like I just say to you, I have come to realize, rescuing Nadezhda, this is something I cannot do. All my efforts for nothing. But the efforts themselves were worth doing, and I am happy for trying. I make something interesting, even if it was not successful."

"But why me? Of all the people in the world? I fill up the finance section of a mid-market paper with bullshit articles I copy from the wire service."

The old man grinned. He rustled through his leather satchel and produced a copy of the *New York Times Book Review*, explaining that Radner's own *NYT* was as close as there was to a global paper of record in this bizarre world of American Hegemony. The cover story was a rave review of one Aaron Radner's memoirs of his time spent covering the ongoing proxy warfare in eastern Ukraine. As Radner scanned the reporter's biography, confirming it to mirror his own in many particulars, he felt a pang of jealousy as he beheld the intrepid, publicly heralded explorer who bore his name. Who bore more than his name, in fact, for as Radner flipped through the article, the accompanying pictures showed a face that was indubitably his.

Everything about the Alt-Radner seemed as though it had had its colors somehow intensified. Like his counterpart, the Alt-Radner's face bore signs of prolonged dissipation, but on him the premature begrizzlement seemed like an added touch of ruggedness, whereas Radner had only tended to become more chinless with time. The Alt-Radner wore his shirt untucked and rumpled in a manner that would only have looked sloppy on Radner himself, as he knew from years of experimentation, and the evident ease and confidence of the Alt-Radner's body language in the various pictures, many of them candid photos from the various warzones where he had worked, seemed like that of an entirely different man than Radner, who became sweaty and panicked under the slightest pressure.

"I know you can write, Mr. Radner. That's why I picked you." But Radner didn't hear him, so entranced was he by this vision of himself, which was everything he had once wanted to be. "We leave tomorrow morning, okay?" the old man said. "I will bring you back to Galicia, and you can write this story. Change what you need change—I know story about magic will not be published, so maybe treat this as metaphor. 'Author creates alternate realities to assuage the regrets of life.' Something like this. But you do this according to your inclination. I have faith you will do great job."

They retired for the night, but Radner's mind would not cease churning. Nadezhda. Nadezhda. The author's phrase, "rescuing Nadezhda," had some unaccountable familiarity to him, and even as the author snored in the next room, Radner puzzled as to its meaning, continuing doing so until finally realizing that this was the title of that self-indulgent and unbearably avant-garde story of the author's which he had passed off to his superiors at the newspaper as having been a great source of inspiration to him when he'd read it back in college. Feeling that the night would be a sleepless one, he located a PDF in the wilds of the internet and reread the piece in the context of what he'd learned from spending several days in the presence of its creator.

The author wrote of the Whatness of All-Nadezhda, that fond old saw of long-dead Modernity, an abstract and likely hypothetical entity including and indeed superseding the particular divergent strands of Nadezhdaness made manifest in the many realities conjured by the Author of Halych. For the unmanifest, the infinitely many latent but unconjured Nadezhdas, partake in All-Nadezhdaness just the same. Piecing together, from the Shadow-Nadezhdas made manifest, the Whatness of the All-Nadezhda, the Author of Halych is led to at least one concrete conclusion: that Nadezhda does not want to be rescued, and indeed requires no rescuing.

"Why so?" he muses, our author-narrator, as he follows Kyiv-Nadezhda, Whore-Nadezhda, along a bustling thoroughfare, watches her enter the grim Brezhnevka in which tricks are known to be turned. "Why so?" as Drug-Nadezhda shivers under a bridge, as Slave-Nadezhda sobs in a Tel Aviv warehouse, as Dead-Nadezhda (Na-dead-da) rots under Galician, Ruthenian, Ukrainian, Polish, German clay. Though these Nadezhdas are but flickering shadows projected onto stony walls, this magical ingress to multi-Nadezhdiality affords us greater insight than allotted to most.

Nadezhda, after all, means hope, he informs his non-Slavic readers, and perhaps it follows therefrom that Nadezhda must be a creature who seeks out misery. That hope dies in prosperity, and is best nurtured into a state of gigantism by a very particular degree of deprivation. That the true pathology in many cases of abject misery is not hopelessness, but a glut of unjustified, and excess hope. Is it any surprise that she goes in for whorehouses and heavy-handed no-goodnik husbands and Alt-Mirandan solitude in the Carpathian foothills?

Or perhaps, wonders the Author of Halych, in a moment of

uncharacteristic self-reflection, Nadezhda is not Hope; not a signifier to be moved about on a page; but a flesh and blood girl who is disappointed, repeatedly, by a father who cannot see the person behind the numinous abstractions he has piled atop her from birth, who is steered ineluctably into misery by the puppeteering tendencies of the old man who only wanted to save her, and was never interested in ascertaining who or what she was in the first place.

*

The old man hadn't been overly surprised by the note he'd found on the journalist's door the next morning when he'd gone to rouse him for the journey back to the mountain homestead and thereby, to the reality he'd built as a monument to himself, where his name would be chiseled into stone. The interview with the journalist (which would enter the hearts and minds and wills of the *NYT*-reading public and thus provide a magic boost) was but the first step in this comprehensive plan, a vanity project for his old age. But when the note had appeared, derailing his designs, the Author of Halych was already wise to the twists and turns of magic; the more you attempt to control it, the more it slips through your fingers. So when Radner, in the loose, unfiltered prose of a man attempting to write in a style not merely functional for the first time since the forgettable poetic efforts of his adolescence, wrote at length of the reawakening of his journalistic vocation in light of the unaccountable events of the past days (leaving unspoken the effect that the sight of the Alt-Radner had no doubt had), it had struck him as just the sort of hiccup that the magic would throw his way. Perhaps his story would go unheard after all… unless the journalist's disappearance in the Carpathians resulted in a police inquiry, and then, inevitably, a media kerfuffle with him at the center of it. It might even work better than the original idea.

So Radner was gone, then? Off into the Ukraine without a hrynia in his pocket, no doubt with vague hopes of unlocking his own elusive whatness, using this alternate self to light the shadowed contours of his inner self. The author knew that the journalist would be hoping to undo the damage done to him by time, to become the fuller self he so envied (the author had seen this in Radner's eyes). Yes, Radner was bound for New York, that Titan of Atlanticism. He would learn the symbols and shibboleths of the American Century, decipher the riddles of contingent events. And with time, as his explorations failed to lead him to the deliverance he sought, even as such explorations of reality's inner nature had failed to satisfy the author's quest, he too would turn to the dark path of sorcery, which never quite leads one where one wants to be led. Yes, Radner would do all these things, but what the author didn't know was the first destination on the journey. What he didn't know was that Radner had read his old story with new eyes— "Rescuing Nadezhda," the story that had put him on the literary map—and that Radner had become curious about its central, nagging riddle. At that very moment, the author was engaged in the process of tracking down Nadezhda, not—or so he told himself—in the hopes of rescuing her, but simply, for once, to listen to Hope (or a woman) and hear what she had to say.

~ When the Normies
Began to Hate ~

It was not preached to the crowd
It was not taught by the state
No man spoke it aloud
When the Normies began to hate

Days and weeks had become years and decades, and all the while Phil Bauer had toiled, Sisyphean, maintaining a certain minor skyscraper in the center of the Midwestern city of his birth. Though he was an electrician by trade, his superiors had quickly learned that whatever Phil Bauer tried his hand at generally turned out just fine, be it patching drywall, basic plumbing repairs, or anything in between. Possessing that particular blend of traits that make a born tradesman—perfectionism balanced by practicality, attention to detail offset by a willingness to experiment with different solutions—Phil had become an indispensable man to the property managers. By dint of the proceeds of his labor, Phil had paid off a house and, together with his wife of nearly thirty years, raised two children to adulthood. What's more, he found his work to be engaging and worthwhile. Petty and inevitable tribulations aside, he was as satisfied with his station in life as one could reasonably expect to be.

One momentous weekday morning, Phil Bauer awoke at the crack of dawn. He caught his usual train downtown and, not having checked the news, sipped from his thermos of coffee expecting this day to be like any other. The spectacle which greeted him upon his arrival in the center of the city, however, could only be described as dystopian. The broad and usually teeming streets were abandoned but for a veritable army of police, all in riot gear, some of them toting rifles. The evidence of the previous night's events was plainly manifest—shards of glass from the windows of the looted shops; the packaging of the stolen products fluttering in the wind; the smoldering of a burnt-out hulk which just yesterday had been an office building whose head engineer was a professional acquaintance of Phil's, a guy with whom he'd talk shop with over beers, whom he could call for the loan of a box of lightbulbs or cleaning supplies when his own crew ran unexpectedly short.

Phil walked aghast through the wreckage, swiveling his head with mouth agape, his gait slow and unsteady. He felt a nameless dread. Being acquainted with a number of city cops (two of his brothers had served on the force for decades), it had been without a second thought that he'd approached and greeted one of the many officers swarming the streets, inquiring as to what had happened. The masked officer did not return his friendliness in kind and instead peremptorily barking at him, masked and expressionless, to move along.

He'd spent his day replacing tiles in the drop ceiling. Most of the offices were empty, as the well-heeled salaried employees of the various firms had been advised to stay home for the day. There was a tension in the air, perhaps resulting from the fact that the subject of the previous night's events was studiously avoided. Phil knew, without having to be told, what had happened. They'd burned dozens of cities in recent weeks. His own hometown was simply the latest target of the racial terrorism that was regularly unleashed, at the slightest pretext, with the tacit approval of all the people whose opinions actually mattered. While no one needed to be told what had happened, there were those who did need to be informed by the information-elites that what had happened had not, in fact, happened.

After work he had, of course, had to walk through the wreckage of the city once again, the board-up crews working overtime to slap plywood over any holes in the glass. Phil Bauer's internal turmoil had ratcheted up to a deeply uncomfortable level. To make matters worse, his wife was out at the monthly meeting of their Catholic parish council, after which she customarily went to the corner bar with some lady friends. Alone for the night with a twist in his heart and a knot in his stomach, Phil Bauer did as Americans do, and began to drink.

He poured himself a whiskey, and then another. He turned on the ballgame to distract himself, but even there it encroached, The Narrative: with players and coaches voicing their Solidarity with The Movement in interviews; with repeated adulatory mentions from the play-by-play announcers; with kneeling and upraised fists and sappily heart-tugging commercials with echoey piano music whereby the multinational corporations voiced their support as well. And so he turned it off. He went to sit on the porch, but his neighbors' ubiquitous lawn signs, which expressed a self-abnegation of the most abject kind, had become like poison to him. He felt that there was nowhere for him to escape to.

Phil Bauer had always been a fundamentally apolitical person. He'd left it to the university-educated yuppies who were his friends and neighbors to fight the political and rhetorical battles of the day. When such issues came up, he'd nod along and do his best to keep the conversation short, always looking for an opening to steer the conversation back to baseball or his brother's latest comedic misadventure. At some level, he felt that the serious and sober discussion of "the issues" was not for the likes of him, though he certainly had his own private way of looking at things—which, incidentally, was not infrequently at odds with the perspectives of those around him. If you'd really pressed him, you might have cajoled Phil Bauer into admitting that his political reticence was in no small wise a function of his sense of class inferiority.

You see, the people who'd surged into this once undistinguished urban neighborhood and transformed it into an aspirational destination complete with organic farmers' markets, a walkable public square with cute boutiques and street musicians, and an active, engaged citizenry, were people of a very different social stratum than he. These people had moved here from various elsewheres, but they shared in common that their elsewheres were prosperous and sheltered. They were the children of families already at least a generation or two removed from the working class, the sort whose parents had been in such a financial position as to have been able to make the move to the then-fashionable suburbs during the White Exodus from the race riots and Negro criminality of the sixties and seventies. They were university educated and outspokenly progressive to a man. Their lawns were festooned with the iconography of the various causes in vogue, from The Gay to climate justice to diversity. Of course, were they to be faced with a level of diversity beyond a certain threshold, they would run for the hills with the rest of the Deplorables, though even this would not have dulled the shrill tenor of their advocacy.

It was only because they'd chanced to purchase their home shortly before the yuppie influx and resulting spike in housing prices that the Bauers had been able to afford to live in such an area at all. On the whole they'd immensely enjoyed their time there. Sometimes it seemed as though the yuppies of their very same age group were a generation apart from them, not to mention from the Miller Lite drinking, NASCAR watching, blue-dog union Democrats (or defected Democrats) their friends from childhood had grown into. If Phil had lived in the exurban sprawl to which most of the city-born working folks the Bauers had grown up with had decamped, there's little doubt that he'd never have learned to like craft IPAs. He'd never have gotten in the habit of checking out local indie rock bands with some of the other neighborhood dads. Perhaps most important was that his kids had would never have had the chance to breathe the rarified and upwardly mobile air of this little yuppie paradise, of which opportunity both had taken full advantage, having finished their tertiary degrees and entered the professional class.

Sitting at his computer and scrolling Facebook while nursing his fifth whiskey, Phil was not aware that he was about to shatter his tranquil relationship to the community around him. He saw profile after profile of raised fists and black squares. All the phraseology that had irked him from the beginning, though he'd never put into words precisely what it was that needled him so. For years, he'd listened in silence, denying, even to himself, the welling tide of—what was this emotion?—that the narrative-web spun by the Brahmins of the white-collar, urban elite occasioned in him. Now, some threshold had been crossed. He could no longer look away from the insipid buzzwords on the tongues of his friends. "People of color" (which was somehow distinct from the antiquated and indeed evil term, "colored people," which Phil's pop had used all the up to the day he'd died, though he'd always, as far as Phil knew, avoided that other word). "White allies" and "Black bodies." Silence had become violence and arson had become "mostly peaceful." As Phil Bauer scrolled, his blood boiling and teeth clenched, the booze he'd imbibed had pushed him to take a step he'd never before taken.

He would speak his mind.

In the rough diction of a high school graduate who hadn't written more than the occasional invoice in the previous decades, he rampaged through the comment sections. It was the quintessence of boomer-posting. Unconventional capitalizations abounded. Nary a mark of punctuation was in evidence. Even as he typed, he knew how his comments would come off in comparison to the exquisitely crafted, painstakingly revised multiparagraph essays of Solidarity that people like his next-door neighbor Toby, a high school teacher, or Andrew, the banker father of his son's childhood best friend, had published. But he simply couldn't stop himself, so righteous and volcanic was his wrath. And when the responses had begun to roll in, he'd only become more incensed.

Some of the responses, particularly those of his immediate social circle, were measured and calm, written in good faith. Others, particularly those from the young people in his life, were absolutely vicious. Jake Schwarz, Andrew's son, whom Phil had known as a five-year-old; whom he'd taken on family trips and fed pizza to at sleepovers; whom he'd had on the baseball team that he and Andrew had coached one year; had responded simply, "you are the problem" before blocking him. His daughter had DM'd him begging him to stop. He'd swigged more whiskey and posted even more vituperatively. Only when his wife had arrived home had he been able to tear himself away, launching instead into a bellowing rant.

She'd listened patiently, her eyes wide with concern, until he'd spoken his piece. Finally, deflated, he'd asked in a broken voice, "What the hell is wrong with these people? Is it me that's lost my mind? Didn't they see what those thugs did downtown last night? Don't they know how hard people worked to build those businesses? I just don't get it."

She'd responded, tentatively. "Well… Mrs. O'Malley was talking at the meeting about all the Black Lives Matter and what have you—you remember her? Her oldest girl was a year behind Vicky, the really fast one that played point guard—but anyways what she was saying was that," she squinches up her forehead to get the terminology right, "that if we're not, um, 'actively deconstructing' the 'systems of oppression' then it's like we're supporting those things cause of the White privilege and what have you. And that the, um, African-American men get thrown in prison more than Whites and how that's not fair. And how all the poverty comes from the discrimination they had to deal with so we've just got to be patient and help them recover to a better level. Equity, she said a lot, which I'm not totally sure what the difference is from equality there, but, you know, I'm trying to learn. Listen to the experiences of people of color and so on. I mean, that video was… awful. Those poor kids."

"Goddamnit Ginny you saw how that bastard walked back around the car! He was fighting, waving a knife around, the taser didn't work, and he goes into the car! You remember Davie Peters that worked with Pete down at that real bad precinct on the south side—took a bullet to the shoulder cause he let some little punk reach into the car. Act of God that he survived it, but his arm's all jacked up, even still. You know how many cops have died like that? Poor kids my ass… that punk shoulda thought about his kids before he resisted arrest! That's on him, not the cop that took him out!"

Ginny sighed. "I just don't know Phil. It's crazy times. But it'll blow over soon. You'll feel better in the morning."

But he didn't feel better. Nor did it blow over. When he disembarked from the train the next morning, his head still throbbing from the previous night's bender, the boarded-up windows imposed themselves upon his vision. When he returned home in the evening, the sanctimonious signs in his neighbors' yards had made his jaw clench. How could they believe what they said they believed? Once again, it was only Ginny's patient intervention that pulled him away from the computer that night, where Phil Bauer's war of words raged on. And in this manner, things continued for some time.

His stomach churned constantly with mingled rage and anxiety; he hated the conflict with the whole of his being, but he could no longer bear to keep silent. He still saw his closest neighborhood friends regularly—none of the real friends had excommunicated him, though some had muted his Facebook posts. When they were together, the matter of Phil's war was studiously avoided, and sometimes it felt as though things were as they had always been. They'd drink some beers, take in a ballgame, swap news of their kids or the goings-on around the parish. But sometimes a tension interceded, if only in Phil's heart; he felt as though he wasn't quite sure where he stood with them, these guys he'd known for years. Sometimes, he even felt a contempt for them, as friendly as they were to him—what was a man to feel toward a well-heeled pontificator happy to parrot the hegemonic beliefs of a decadent and rapidly collapsing society so long as it wasn't his business burning to the ground?

And over time, it seemed that some of the anxiety and dread had begun to abate, particularly after Phil caught a permanent Facebook ban for a post in support of a young militiaman who'd fired on rioters in Wisconsin. It was for the best, Ginny had said, and patted his arm.

Then came the next month's meeting of the parish council, from which Ginny had returned early, puffy-eyed and not wanting to talk about it. He wondered whether he was crazy to think that there was something accusatory in her expression when she looked at him. It had taken some probing, but he'd pressed the issue until he'd ascertained what needed ascertaining: his wife had been the recipient of public blowback as a result of his outspoken and newfound political beliefs. Launching into yet another tirade, he marched purposefully toward the computer—the arena of conflict—but this time instead of her usual forbearance, Ginny had cut him abruptly off: "I don't know why you couldn't just keep your big mouth shut!"

"Shut!" he exploded. "I've had my mouth shut since we moved to this yuppie shithole! It's about damn time these assholes heard what I've got to say!"

"Phil," she urged, "I'm asking you, as your wife, to let this go, okay? Can you please just do that?"

He could do that, at least on the one occasion. But the political coming-of-age of Phil Bauer, long overdue, was a force of nature that could not be suppressed, though it could, as is the case with all political impulses, be channeled and contained. You see, Phil Bauer was no connoisseur of alternative media; for him, patriotic conservatism was a Fox News product. And as he consumed this product, he was astonished to realize that he had a number of opinions he'd never before articulated.

For one thing, it made perfect sense that taxing corporations would result in more of them leaving American factories behind for that hated foe, communist China, the scourge of the democracy-loving Hong-kongese. If anything, corporate tax rates ought to be lower! And taxing capital gains not only disincentivized investment—it was also immoral! After all, those hard-working, job-creating, entrepreneurial-spirited investors had already paid taxes on their investment principal, so taxing the returns on investments would be like a double taxation! Socialism, that was the real threat; if those Marxist snowflakes ever got power, it would be goodbye private enterprise and hello gulags. At least there was at least one country left that still had balls, even in this world of libtard pansies and lazy millennials (hello, avocado toast anybody?); Hannity had run a real hard-hitting segment on the Israelis, who were giving hell to those #RadicalIslamicTerrorists, who were unceasingly targeting Jewish families just like in the Holocaust.

How easy it is for a Gorgias to make use of unphilosophical men. Like plastic bags upon the wind, they go where they are blown—but who controls the weather? Phil Bauer didn't know anything except that it had made him angry to watch hordes of Blacks (though he'd call them "radical socialists," or, if he'd been watching too much Dinesh D'Souza, "nazis") burning his city. He didn't know anything but that all his buddies in the local PD were good cops who'd stood up in the face of a degree of Evil these soft, over-educated LIBTARDS AND DEMONRATS couldn't even imagine. He didn't know about IQ-differences between continental populations or the significance and intractability of in-group preference. Indeed, he had only the fuzziest awareness of the existence of the so-called nature-nurture debate. He hadn't properly hashed out the priors of the constitutional liberalism into which he, and all other American graduates of public schools, had been indoctrinated by rote. Much less had he properly considered how alterations to these priors—for example, a thorough refutation of Locke's tabula rasa—might have salient implications for one's practical politics—for example with respect to the legitimacy of universal suffrage democracy. He knew nothing about the national debt, except that it was big and frightening. He'd certainly never conceived of debt as a commodity to be bundled and traded. His views on foreign policy owed more than a little to the romantic portrayal of war-time heroics in corporate Hollywood pap.

And yet none of Phil Bauer's bourgeois acquaintances had done any of this sort of fundamental philosophical work either. Their rhetorical flourishes were lifted whole-cloth from the pages of *The Atlantic* or the broadcasts of NPR. It was the purest of social signaling that these midwits were engaged in, with a thin veneer of verbal sophistication shellacked over the top, which almost always sufficed to imbue their received opinions with a measure of prestige relative to the opinions of Phil Bauer's Vaisya ilk. And when some Latinx affirmative action hire on NPR decided to invite a transsexual Jew onto her show to deliver a "defense of looting," these denizens of the Outer Party had assimilated the arguments into their lexicons, though they all thought that such radicalism "went a little too far."

Phil Bauer knew was that something was horribly wrong, but with his anger smoothly and efficiently channeled away into an artificial reservoir of non-threatening proletarian dissatisfaction, the levels of which could be managed by benevolent overseers in high towers, he was utterly incapable of taking any sort of effective action. As the cities burned and the economic base of the country continued to crumble beneath their feet, the Bauers mulled over buying a place in Florida. If they got their current house sold before the bottom fell out of their local real estate market, they would be able to live out their final decades in a state of tranquil plenty. This sort of option, of course, would be available neither to their young adult children, nor to the opiate-deadened, un- or underemployed Flyover-nonentities who'd been less fortunate than they.

CPSIA information can be obtained
at www.ICGtesting.com
Printed in the USA
LVHW100010090822
725438LV00004B/403